SHOFAR, SO GOOD

A CAFE ARCANA MYSTERY
BOOK 2

ALIZA LEVINE

First printing, 2025

Print paperback ISBN 979-8-9902394-3-2

Cover design by Mariah Sinclair

1

———

A bite hung in the late September afternoon air as Ava Goldberg came striding out the front door of her coffee shop and made her way down the street toward her parked car. Her parents were landing at Eppley Airfield in an hour, and her sole employee, Riley Novak, had come straight from school to hold down the fort while Ava went to meet them.

In one hand, Ava held a cup of strong, black coffee—still too hot to drink—and in the other, she clutched a small pastry bag that held one of the apple cider donuts Owen O'Kelly had brought by her shop earlier that day. Owen had suggested he come with her to the airport, but she'd squirmed her way out of the offer. Her mother, Sara Goldberg, was always a handful, and Ava knew that showing up with a tall, handsome blond man in tow would cause her mother's eyes to narrow.

Ava didn't know *what* she and Owen were. Sure, after the dramatics of the summer, they'd been on a couple of dates, been seen around town together on several occasions. But the reality remained that whatever they were, Ava's mother would never accept it—not when Owen wasn't Jewish—and starting the new year off with a fight wasn't Ava's idea of a good time. No, Ava wanted this Rosh Hashanah—her first time hosting her parents for a holiday since she filed for divorce two years ago—to go off without a hitch. It was for this reason she'd told Owen it wouldn't be a great idea for him to join them for the holiday dinner, which was still a bit of a sore spot between them.

As she drove, Ava rolled down the windows, feeling the cool September air drift through the front seat of her car and tousle her hair. The day had turned out to be warm, but the promise of fall filled the air—and less than a week until October, the most glorious month in the Midwest. Just the thought of crisp, dark nights and crackling bonfires surrounded by glowing pumpkins brought a chill of excitement to Ava's skin. Those days were coming. But she'd have to get through the holidays—and her parents' visit—first.

Once at Eppley Airport, Ava whipped her little car into a space in the parking garage and headed to the airport's sole arrivals hall. As she leaned near the wall of a lonely gift shop, the clatter of dishes and the hiss of a steam wand from the nearby Scooters Coffee drifted toward her. She pushed away the temptation. What her jittery nerves needed was calm. She had to be relaxed if she was going to field the barbed questions her parents would almost certainly have come armed with. Besides, they could stop at Arcana on the way back—her father had yet to see her shop in person.

A steady flow of passengers began to trickle through the terminal exit, their luggage trailing along behind them. Tired dads with toddlers on their shoulders and Huskers caps pulled down low on their brows strode down the hall, accompanied by somehow still chipper moms who cooed and tugged at their babies' feet. The occasional fresh-looking older women, who must have primped in the airplane lavatory before exiting the plane, strode by as well. Sara Goldberg would be one of these.

And there she was. There *they* were, Mike and Sara Goldberg, coming down the hallway toward her, each with a carry-on bag trailing on the carpet behind them. Sara saw Ava first. Her darkly fringed eyes lit up as she waved a hand in the air. Ava almost smirked as she caught sight of her mother, noting how put together Sara Goldberg looked. *As expected.*

"Ava!" Sara called, elbowing her husband in the ribs. "Honey! Over here."

Ava grimaced and gestured to her mother to keep her voice down. They were in public, after all. As the pair neared her in the hallway, Mike cast one last look at his iPhone, then tucked it into the holster he wore at his belt. *Ever the dad.*

"How was the flight?" Ava asked, throwing an arm around her mother's waist and standing on tiptoe to give her dad a peck on the cheek.

"Not as bad as the last time I flew to see you, aside from the food—which, I can assure you, has gone downhill." Sara Goldberg searched for a cleansing wipe in her handbag. She ripped off the top of the package with perfectly manicured acrylic nails and set to work wiping the last of the plane germs from her fingers. She stretched a hand out in front of her for a final inspection, bejeweled rings glistening in the fluorescent lights of the terminal.

"Can you believe it's only an hour to get here?" Ava's father's eyes grew wide. Clearly, he could not.

Sara swatted her husband's arm. "Oh, Michael, really. You act like this is the first time you've ever flown into Omaha."

"Well, it's been a while!" Mike Goldberg ran long fingers

through his wiry hair, repositioned the arms of his glasses atop his ears. "It was a pleasant surprise, that quick trip."

"Yeah? Must be nice," Ava put in, casting a teasing glance at her father. It had only been four months since she'd moved to Shiloh, and only her mother had visited her once since then. Her grandparents had lived here for many years, so the family used to gather in Shiloh for holidays. Ava lived in their old house now after her grandfather bequeathed it to her. "It took me nine hours to make it here with my U-Haul."

Barreling ahead down the hall as always, Mrs. Goldberg glanced back at her daughter. "Are you parked out front?"

"No, they don't allow waiting in the terminal loop. I'm afraid you'll have to rough it in your heels, Mom." Ava flashed her mother a wicked grin but took the handle of the rolling suitcase from her grasp.

Mrs. Goldberg sighed. "I was afraid that's what you were going to say." She tugged the handle of her suitcase back from Ava and began plodding delicately down the carpeted hallway toward the escalator.

Mr. Goldberg followed his wife onto the escalator, leaning backward against the railing. His salt and pepper hair was thick, precisely—yet effortlessly—parted and pomaded to one side. He looked every bit the professor he was in reality, which his father before him had been as well. Suddenly, his face lit up.

"Ava!" Mr. Goldberg hissed, jerking upwards off the escalator railing. Frantically, he dug through the front zipper pocket of his carry-on case. "I've got to show you something."

Mrs. Goldberg's eyes followed her husband warily. He stepped off the escalator at the bottom and pulled his luggage to the side, this time opening it up completely to rifle through the pile of crisply folded button-down shirts and chinos layered inside. At this, his wife jumped forward.

"Not in the airport, Michael," Mrs. Goldberg barked. "No one wants to hear that."

"It'll only take a second," Mr. Goldberg said, dismissing her with a wave of his free hand. "Ava needs to hear it."

Hear it? As curious as she was, Ava had to admit she shared in her mother's wariness. There was no telling what kind of bee Michael Goldberg might get into his bonnet next, and she wasn't sure she wanted the whole of Eppley Airport witnessing whatever it was. Hearing whatever it was.

"Aha!" Mr. Goldberg said in triumph, extracting a small plastic sack from beneath his socks and underwear. "Behold."

"Oy vey," Mrs. Goldberg muttered under her breath, taking a few steps away from her husband. She turned her back.

As soon as she saw the outline of the sack's contents, Ava rushed forward to snatch the package from her father's hands. She knew what was inside. It was bad enough that she'd no doubt have to listen to it for three days straight, but there was no *way* she would let him blow that thing—

A piercing wail, something like a dying elephant, shattered through the bustling sounds of the airport. Ava's hands shot to her ears, her face stricken with horror. But no sooner had her palms covered her ears than the dying elephant sound sputtered out, leaving her father with cheeks puffed out and blue in the face, gasping for air. He lowered the ram's horn from his lips and beamed at Ava, his eyes gleeful.

"Did you hear? I got it there—for a split second, I had it!" Mike Goldberg announced, pumping his fist in triumph.

"Uh," Ava said. From where her mother still stood at a distance, Ava could see Sara Goldberg scanning the perimeter, as though to check if the coast was clear. Her shoulders were hunched. "Yeah. You're really on your way, Dad."

Thank the *lord* Owen hadn't come along. Ava was sure she would've died of embarrassment.

"I'm saving my chops for the ride home," Mr. Goldberg said, sliding the ram's horn back in the plastic sack.

Mrs. Goldberg approached her daughter and husband, catching wind of what Mr. Goldberg had just said. "If you try that in the car, Michael, I swear on all that is holy—"

"Jeez Louise, honey," Mr. Goldberg said, pushing his glasses up on the bridge of his nose and striding toward the exit. "I'm kidding! But really, I need to be practicing. I've only got two days to get my blasts down."

Ava pretended she didn't hear him. She still couldn't believe he'd actually pulled out a shofar inside the airport. Honestly, it was a wonder that security hadn't come rushing over to see what had happened. The sounding of the ceremonial ram's horn was a central part of the Rosh Hashanah synagogue service, and becoming truly skilled at blowing the horn was a notoriously difficult feat to achieve. Her dad was not there yet.

"Wait," Ava said, surveying the suitcases her parents wheeled behind them. "You guys didn't check any bags? And by that, I mean *Mom* managed to fit all her shoes in *that*?" She gestured to one of the small carry-on hard-shells.

"Don't be ridiculous, Ava," Mrs. Goldberg laughed. "We're going to be in *Shiloh*. I'm not going to risk getting a Louboutin run over by a tractor."

Ava barely managed not to roll her eyes. Instead, she led her parents out to the parking garage and settled into the driver's seat as her dad loaded their luggage into the trunk. As she wound her way out of the airport lot and headed toward the interstate, Ava listened to her parents chatter: about the ever-dwindling amount of legroom on planes, how United's frequent flyer program wasn't all it was cracked up to be, and which neighbor's relatives were in town for the holiday. So far, the idle talk was harmless—pleasant even. She just hoped to god it'd stay that way.

2

———

"Downtown Shiloh hasn't changed a bit," Mr. Goldberg remarked as Ava turned onto Main Street. The cool late afternoon breeze drifted through his open window as he gazed at the storefronts lining either side of the street.

"Oh, I don't know," Mrs. Goldberg said from the back seat, clacking her nails together in thought. "It looks to me like it's had quite a glow-up since the early 2000s—must be those lake people I read about in the Facebook groups. If you ask me, they've done the place a favor."

Ava grit her teeth. Shiloh offered the charm and quiet that Ava loved. Although she was sure the fancy lake community just outside of town was wonderful in itself—and no doubt had contributed to the number of out-of-towners frequenting her cafe—she took issue with her mother's implication that Shiloh had somehow been previously lacking. She swung the car into a parking spot outside of Cafe Arcana and killed the engine. "Well, here we are."

Unbuckling his seatbelt, Mr. Goldberg craned his neck out the open window to take in the cafe. His gaze moved over the huge bay window, now decorated from the inside with dainty garlands of autumn leaves. "It looks lovely already!"

Climbing out of the car, the three of them stood for a moment on the sidewalk, peering up at the rustic, cozy front of Cafe Arcana. The sign that Ava so loved swung gently in the autumn air. The sign offered patrons both the best coffee in town (especially considering it was the first and only coffee shop in Shiloh) as well as tarot readings. That later footnote was, no doubt, why her mother looked at the window display instead of acknowledging the sign of her daughter's pastime. Her mother had been here before—during Shiloh Days a few months ago—but her father hadn't yet visited Cafe Arcana. Although she was sure he would love the place, her heart still beat a little faster as they moved toward the front door.

"We're technically closed now," Ava said, glancing through the window at the clock inside. "But Riley's still here, and we can put on a pot of fresh coffee."

As they filed in through the front door, Sara followed Ava, sliding her sleek black sunglasses back on her head. She held the door for her husband, who followed her inside and then stood, lanky as ever, hands on hips, gazing around Cafe Arcana in pride.

"Ava, this is magnificent," her father said as he took in the cafe, its rustic tables and chairs, the exposed brick and polished hardwood flooring she'd opted to keep, and the bookshelves along the back wall. He offered her a slow, ceremonious clap of his hands. "Really, really well done. *Kol ha kavod.*"

Surprising even herself, Ava felt herself blush. Her father didn't offer praise easily, and, given that just a few months ago she hadn't even been sure Arcana would survive this long, the compliment hit hard.

"Hi," Riley piped in from behind the counter. She offered a sheepish wave to Ava's father and a shy smile to Mrs. Goldberg, whom she'd met on the woman's previous visit to Shiloh.

"Ah!" Mr. Goldberg exclaimed, striding across the room to offer Riley his hand. "This must be the notorious Riley."

"Uh... I guess so," Riley said, the tops of her ears turning pink. She cleared her throat and let her hand dart up to shake Mr. Goldberg's. "I mean—I'm Riley. But I don't know if I'm notorious."

Mr. Goldberg chuckled. "Ha! I like this one. We're going to get along, kid."

Riley, unsure what in her reply had earned such instant approval, managed a weak smile and cast a wide-eyed glance at Ava, who shrugged. Riley had suffered a difficult home life, and Ava had opened her home to her while she finished high school. Ava had never related the private details of the reason for that invitation, and Riley knew that. But Mike Goldberg, like most dads, was forever doing his best to remain "cool," starkly oblivious to the fact that he never had been.

"Here," Ava said, slipping behind the counter and nudging Riley out of the way with a playful hip check. "I'll get some coffee going for us. Dad, Mom, you guys look around."

Grateful to be out of the spotlight once again, Riley grabbed a bag of beans from a cupboard and began grinding. Over the din of the grinder, Ava barely heard the clang of the doorbell, but her gaze snapped up when Riley waved a quick hand toward the door.

"Hey," Owen said as he strode through the door, his arms full of yet more paper sacks. Without a glance around, he made his way behind the counter and slid open the pastry case. "You kept mentioning pumpkin spice earlier, so I went home and whipped up a few scones. They're an experiment."

Ava's eyebrows rose. She looked to her parents, who were examining the titles on the bookshelves, and didn't seem to have noticed that anyone else had entered the shop. Owen's gaze followed Ava's as he drummed his fingers casually on the countertop.

"I also thought I could say 'hey' to your parents," Owen said, shooting Ava a small smile. "You know, welcome them into town."

His green eyes were expectant—god, maybe even hopeful—and it just about broke Ava's heart, not knowing what to say. This wasn't how she'd wanted the three of them to meet—she'd been banking on more time to mentally prepare herself, to figure out how she'd position things. Maybe figure how to avoid the meeting altogether.

"Oh," Ava said, avoiding both Owen's fervent gaze and Riley's curious glance as she moved to set the coffee brewing. She smiled weakly, hoping her voice sounded more convincing than it felt. "Yeah, that's a good idea. Good timing."

"I smell coffee!" A cheery voice boomed, and Ava looked up to see her father coming toward them. When he saw Owen, he stopped short, a smile breaking out across his face, and stuck out a hand in greeting. "Mike Goldberg. Pleasure to meet you."

Owen shook Mr. Goldberg's hand, giving a brief nod of his tousled head. "Owen O'Kelly. Welcome to Shiloh!"

"Dad," Ava said, trying to act as natural as possible. "Owen's a good friend of mine. Owns the hardware store down the street. He's the one who makes all our baked goods."

She gestured to the spread of open pastry boxes lining the counter behind them, hoping the smile she flashed looked more real than it felt. *Get it together, Ava. It isn't like Owen and I are engaged. It isn't like I need approval of a 'friend who makes my baked goods' or of a fellow shop owner who helped me out this summer.*

"No kidding!" Mr. Goldberg tilted his head to the side and gave Owen an impressed nod. "Well, I hear you've really been a life saver around here, then. All that vandalism this summer and such."

Owen smiled, gave a slight shrug of his broad shoulders. "I've no doubt she'd have made it on her own."

Ava swallowed back that Owen had done more than just clean up the vandalism. Last summer, together, they'd worked to clear the name of the husband of her childhood friend Rose, accused of murdering a prominent Shiloh community member. And, in the end, it was Owen who arrived in time to stop Ava from ending up dead herself. Suddenly, a guilt trip edged into her mind; Owen wasn't just a friend who baked the shop's goodies. Most parents would be pleased to meet this man. Most women would be pleased to introduce him as their...

Mrs. Goldberg cleared her throat from across the room. Nearing the group, she sat down at the table nearest the bay window overlooking the street and began rubbing lotion into her perfectly manicured hands. "Ava. Could a person get some coffee?"

Ava shot her mother a stiff glance. Mrs. Goldberg had met Owen when she visited Ava during the summer, and, although they hadn't discussed it, Ava suspected her mother had picked up on the nature of Ava and Owen's relationship. Not surprisingly, since Owen wasn't Jewish, it seemed Mrs. Goldberg was less than thrilled. But seriously? Her mom wasn't even going to say *hello*—even when Owen was standing right there? And to think Mrs. Goldberg had always harped on Ava about the importance of politeness...

Ava was about to issue a sharp reply when Owen's eyes flashed to hers. Although the shake of his head was almost imperceptible, it was undeniably there. Biting back her reply, Ava drew a deep breath, willing herself to let it go. Now wasn't the time for a squabble. Her parents had only just gotten here, and if Owen was okay with the way things were unfolding, then she would be as well.

"Yeah, it's almost done." Although she directed the words at her parents, she kept her gaze on Owen a second longer, letting him know they were on the same page. "Sit down, and I'll bring it over."

With her parents seated by the window, Ava turned to pour two cups of brewed coffee. She turned to Owen, who was still lingering by the counter, his huge hands tracing circles in the wood grain. "You want coffee?"

"That'd be great."

They were silent a moment, the soft drone of Ava's parents as they discussed the hue of crown molding along the ceilings humming in the background. Riley had wandered to the back room to finish the dishes. Ava shot Owen a half smile as she set his coffee on the counter.

"So," Owen said, taking a sip of his coffee. "We're still on for the game tomorrow night, yeah?"

Crap. She forgot she'd promised to go to the homecoming football game with him. Afraid the realization that she'd forgotten their plans would register on her face, Ava turned quickly to survey her parents. They were still chatting about the architecture of Shiloh's downtown buildings. "We are—but I won't have a clue what's going on."

Owen laughed. "Don't worry. We'll make a Shark out of you in no time."

Ava had a sudden vision of herself on the Shiloh football field, dancing around in the Shiloh Shark costume. *Hmm. Possible idea for a career change if Cafe Arcana ever goes south.* Smirking, she grinned at Owen, picked up her parents' coffees —and stopped.

Someone stood outside, their back to her shop's window, apparently finishing up a phone call. Ava's entire body went cold. All other thoughts gone, Ava set the coffees down on the counter. She watched her mom wave through the glass, beckon to the man standing outside. And then, as he ended his phone call and slid his phone into his pocket, Ava watched as her ex-husband smiled, shook a wisp of dark, glossy hair off his forehead, and stepped in off the street.

3

"Hey."

At first, Ava couldn't respond to Noah's greeting as she hadn't even fully grasped that he was *inside her shop*.

Inside her shop.

Somehow, her ex-husband—this man she'd loved, who'd cheated on her with *her friend*, and whom she'd spent the past two years trying to forget—was standing inside Cafe Arcana. There was no way. It had to be a fever dream.

"But—you're in Chicago," Ava managed to croak out. She stared at Noah, her spine rigid. He only smiled at her in return.

"Noah, honey," Mrs. Goldberg gushed, heels clomping across the hardwood floor as she went to her former son-in-law, arms outstretched. Her mother had been thrilled at her daughter's marriage to a Jew, a doctor no less. And upset when Ava wouldn't forgive his "little indiscretion" of sleeping with Ava's friend and appalled when she actually divorced him. She greeted him now like a long-lost son—which, in essence, he was to her. Or at least a lost son-in-law and doctor-in-the-

15

family. "I forgot you said you had that conference at UNMC! How *are* you?"

Beside her, Ava saw Owen jerk with a start. He knew that name. Even if he'd never met Noah, never even seen a picture of the guy, Owen recognized that name. *No, no, no, no, no.* This was not good. This was not good at *all.* More than anything, Ava wanted to shoot a reassuring glance at Owen, let him know she was *not* in on this, that she'd had no idea Noah Shapiro would be in Omaha, would show up at her door—but she couldn't bring herself to look at him. She was sure her cheeks were burning.

"I'm great. A little burned out on presentations, but hanging in there." Noah wrapped a solid arm around Sara Goldberg's shoulders, then turned to his ex-wife. "Ava, your mom told me this place was amazing, but wow—this is phenomenal! I want the tour!"

Ava cleared her throat, finally chancing a glance at Owen, who'd moved back a couple of steps and now stood surveying the group from a distance. Their eyes met, but she couldn't read his expression. Setting her jaw, she turned her attention to Noah. "Not to be rude, but—why are you here?"

Mrs. Goldberg clucked her tongue, but Noah only chuckled. He shoved his hands in the pockets of his crisp, ironed pants, cast a glance around the cafe, and smiled. His teeth were impossibly white and straight. "I've been in Omaha for a conference this week, and Sara mentioned she and Mike would be in town for Rosh Hashanah. I've got a buddy out here in Shiloh, so I figured I'd come say hi to you all, too."

"But—but *why*?" Ava sputtered. "Why would you *do* that?"

Unperturbed, Noah shrugged. He had, Ava thought grimly, been married to her for four years. He knew her inside and out

—her bluntness didn't faze him. "I thought we were in a good place. I wanted to come to support you."

Ava gave a sharp laugh. "It's a little late for that."

"Oh, Ava," Mrs. Goldberg chided, frowning at the coffees on the counter. She picked one up, sniffed it, then took a sip. "He was in town anyway—and it's the holidays. You don't want to head into the new year on a sour note."

"Exactly," Ava snapped. "I don't. Which is why I'm asking him to leave."

Mr. Goldberg raised his hands, gesturing at all of them to calm down. "Now, now. Let's all just take a deep breath—"

The clang of the doorbell made them all look up. Ava's heart sank at the sight of Owen's broad back retreating from the shop. From the sidewalk, he gave her a sharp wave through the window, one corner of his mouth pulled up in an uneasy smile, then continued on his way.

"Freaking *great*," Ava breathed.

She pushed past Noah and her mother, all but jogging out into the street. Owen was already halfway up the block. At the sound of her thundering footsteps on the sidewalk, he glanced behind him. As Ava jogged the rest of the way to meet him, he watched her with one eyebrow raised.

She slowed to a stop, aware that her parents and ex-husband were probably watching her from the window. She had no idea what she'd had in mind when she ran out here. She only knew she had to do something. *Say* something. Her ex-husband had shown up, for god's sake! She could only imagine what was going through his mind.

"That was *not* planned," she blurted out.

Owen nodded, his gaze flicking to the window. Ava didn't dare let herself do the same. She kept her eyes on Owen, and when his gaze moved back to her, she wore a pleading expression. She had the sudden urge to throw her arms around him, bury her head in his broad chest, interlace her fingers between his, and squeeze. But she couldn't—not with her parents standing there watching like that.

Owen tilted his head back toward the window without breaking eye contact. "You'd better get back to your family. Let me know how the donuts and scones sell."

With that, he cracked a small smile, a dimple flashing in each cheek, and walked away. As his figure moved further down the sidewalk, he raised a hand in farewell. The farmer wave. As if she needed another reminder that Owen was a native Shiloh-an and, as such, would keep his emotions under control.

After another few seconds watching him disappear down the block, Ava drew a deep breath, straightened her shoulders, and pretended to scroll through her phone. There would be questions when she got inside, so she may as well *try* to have an excuse ready. She knew she wasn't ready to face them with the truth—what Owen meant to her. She hadn't come to terms with that even to herself. So, she fingered the phone. What *would* she say? *Rose had called? Owen forgot to leave a pastry we ordered?*

When Ava entered the cafe, her parents and Noah were milling around the place, studying the artwork hanging on the walls and attempting to seem uninterested in her abrupt departure.

"I love this one," Mrs. Goldberg remarked, tipping her head toward a muted watercolor on the back wall. "It's that lake, isn't it? The one near the school?"

"Larkspur Lake." Ava poured herself a cup of coffee. She

wasn't sure where to go from here, but she'd sure as heck need another dose of caffeine to handle it.

As Mr. Goldberg joined his wife to admire the painting, Noah drifted toward the counter. He leaned an elbow on top of the pastry case, a wisp of hair falling across his forehead. Ava could feel his gaze on her. She ignored him. This was *her* turf. He had no right to show up out of nowhere and taint this sacred place with his dirty, cheating—

"I'm sorry."

Well. Those were the last words she'd expected to hear. Throughout their divorce, she'd grown quite used to Noah's chocolate eyes that would stare into her in that pleading expression. But his apologies had only smacked of him being sorry he got caught. Now, an apology had come unprompted.

She looked up at him, set down the espresso shot she was tamping for no good reason. The chocolate eyes were there, of course, but they were gazing at her in earnest. Something in her chest began to loosen—but *no*. She steeled herself. They'd been around this block before, plenty of times.

Her reply was cool, her voice low, as she tried not to draw her parents' attention. Her mother, no doubt, listened in regardless. "Sorry for what?"

Noah spread his hands. "Barging in like this. Bothering you on your turf. Running that guy out."

"Huh. Glad to see you managed to learn right from wrong over the past couple years." Although the brewed coffee urns were fresh and full, Ava dumped a bag of beans into the grinder. She would ignore the part about running Owen out. Noah didn't need to be privy to any information regarding Owen.

Noah had to speak over the noise, but if her remark bothered him, he didn't show it. *Too bad.* "Okay, not uncalled for. I deserved that. Anyway, I just wanted to say I'm sorry. I really mean it."

Ava suppressed an eye roll. He seemed sincere, but then again, he'd also seemed sincere under the *chuppah*—and look where that had gotten them. She finished her grinding, slid the filter full of ground coffee into the brewing basket. "Apology accepted."

"Happy to see you two getting along," Mr. Goldberg remarked, having tired of the art and making his way to the front of the shop. "Now, how about those scones?"

Ava had half a mind to protest. They *weren't* getting along— she was just refusing to let Noah's presence bother her, a skill she'd been forced to hone since the divorce. Still, she wouldn't say anything. Maybe if she kept a stony exterior, not hostile, but also not warm, everyone would get the picture, and Noah would head back to Omaha. So she used a pair of tongs to place three scones on a plate, sliding it toward her guests. "They're pumpkin spice, apparently. I haven't tried them yet, but every-thing Owen makes is fabulous, so I'm sure these are, too."

Mr. Goldberg bit into a scone and his eyes lit up. Ava was surprised his glasses didn't fog over, given the utter glee that emanated from his eyes. Her father jerked a thumb at the front window, in the direction Owen had disappeared. "*That* guy? He made these?"

"Sure did," Ava said, crossing her arms over her chest in pride. Owen's baked goods had all but saved her shop; she had no qualms about bragging up the chef. "I take it these are good?"

"Good? They're *amazing!*" Mr. Goldberg was already

halfway done with his scone, and a fine dust of cinnamon sugar glistened off his sweater.

"Really good," Noah agreed. He nodded at Ava, like they'd just discovered some sort of secret she needed to capitalize on.

Mrs. Goldberg munched politely on a piece of scone she'd broken off, sliding the rest of it toward her husband's side of the plate. "I'll just have a bit."

Ava knew better than to protest. Her mother was always watching her waistline. She turned to her dad instead. "Perfect. I'll ask Owen to make some extras for us to have on Rosh Hashanah. They'll be good for breakfast."

"Speaking of Rosh Hashanah," Mrs. Goldberg cut in, wiping her fingers daintily on a napkin. She inspected her nails, avoiding Ava's gaze. "We're having dinner Saturday night. If Noah's already in the area, away from family and all, I thought it might be nice—"

"Nope. Don't finish that." Ava rapped her knuckles on the counter to get her mother's attention. Sara Goldberg finally looked up, her eyes wide and feigning innocence. "I am *not* going to spend a freaking holiday with my *ex-husband*, Mom. Get a grip!"

Mike Goldberg cleared his throat. Ava knew there was no way this thought had only just occurred to her mom, and her father had clearly known about it. "Ava, your mother has a point. It's Rosh Hashanah. Noah's alone. You *were* married to the man—would it kill you to let him eat a meal with us on the holiday?"

Ava shot a furious glance at Noah. His dark eyes looked guilty. "Did *you* know about this?" she demanded.

Noah grimaced, glancing at Sara and back to Ava. He

shrugged his lean, muscular shoulders. "Sara may have mentioned it. I wasn't expecting you to go for it, though."

"Are you people for *real*?" Ava was livid. Not only had they all been talking behind her back, but they'd also been scheming, *plotting*. It was a takedown. And here she'd thought her parents just wanted to be with their daughter for Rosh Hashanah. Of all the scummy, conniving—

"Good evening!" A cheery voice cut into Ava's rage, dissipating it into unsatisfying little shreds. One of her best customers and a town matriarch, Juanita Martinez, had just come through the door, looking as cheery and full of life as always. "I hope it's okay I'm dropping by to say hello. I saw you were all still here."

"No problem at all," Ava said, forcing herself to smile. The last thing she wanted to do was introduce her parents —and *ugh,* Noah—but she wouldn't allow her own feelings to make her customers uncomfortable. Although she was also a friend, Juanita was still a regular patron. Ava would just have to turn on the Shiloh charm. "How's everything going? You met my mom a few months ago, right?"

"A pleasure to see you again," Sara Goldberg said to Juanita, clasping the woman's hand with a smile that didn't at all suggest she'd just invited her former son-in-law to a holiday dinner against her daughter's wishes. She gestured toward Mr. Goldberg, who also stuck out his hand in greeting. "My husband—Michael."

"Nice to see you both," Juanita said, beaming. Her sparkling eyes all but disappeared in her cheeks when she smiled. She turned to Noah then, casting an inquisitive eye at Ava as she did so. "And this must be the brother…?"

"Ah, no." Noah cleared his throat, embarrassed, but it was Ava who jumped in to correct the woman.

"My ex-husband, actually. Noah Shapiro. Noah, Juanita Martinez." Ava waved a hand, glad that Noah was finally starting to look uncomfortable.

Although Ava was rather tight-lipped around Shiloh about her past, Juanita had heard the gist of what had caused her divorce. But if she thought of it now—or wondered just what the heck Ava's ex was doing inside her coffee shop—she didn't show it, just kept the same glowing smile as she shook Noah's hand and nodded. "I knew Ava's parents were coming, but I didn't realize I'd get to meet you, too."

Noah, ever the diplomat, fielded the remark. He laughed, his velvety voice ringing out in a way that made Ava strangely wistful. "I'm in town for a conference on Monday—UNMC— and came a bit early to see a buddy of mine from med school. It's so close, I figured I'd stop by and see the place. I kept hearing what an amazing job Ava's done out here."

"We love it in here," Juanita said, winking at Ava. "I've lived in Shiloh for sixty years now, and we've never had a coffee shop. This place is just going to keep picking up speed. Plus, we all knew and loved Ava's grandfather, so it's wonderful to have a Goldberg back in town."

"You don't say," Mr. Goldberg said, his eyes lighting up behind his glasses. "You knew Melvin? He was my dad."

"Did I *know* him?" Juanita gushed. "He was my tarot reader for *years*. Ava knows all about that." She cast a knowing glance at Ava, which Ava returned.

"Melvin was everyone's favorite, wasn't he? We miss him dearly," Mrs. Goldberg interjected, attempting to nip the tarot conversation in the bud. It was no secret that she wasn't a fan of her daughter's side hustle and preferred to ignore the tarot sign that hung in the window of Cafe Arcana.

"Yes, we certainly do. Which reminds me…" Juanita said, turning to Ava. "Will you be reading tarot at the fall festival next week? Your grandfather did most years—I know I always looked forward to it—and I wondered if you might be there to promote the shop."

Ava shook her head. A couple city council members who were also regulars at Cafe Arcana had broached the subject to her, and although Ava agreed it would be a wonderful promotion for the shop, it was also smack in the middle of the High Holidays. In the end, she'd decided it was just too much for this year, what with her parents coming from out of town.

"Not this year," she said. "I felt it was too close to Rosh Hashanah. I'd like to drop by, though, to get a feel for next year."

"Very understandable," Juanita agreed. Then, as though remembering something, she held up the brown paper gift bag that hung from her arm. "And speaking of which—I come bearing gifts. Or, *a* gift, rather. *Shana tova!*"

Ava was surprised. All week, she'd been fielding complaints about Cafe Arcana being closed on Monday, as the people of Shiloh were not Jewish and had no clue what Rosh Hashanah was, other than perhaps having noticed it stamped on their calendars. And here was Juanita, showing up with a gift bag and practicing her Hebrew. *Go figure.*

Juanita pushed the gift bag toward Ava, flicking her hand in feigned impatience. "That's for you. Open it!"

Ava untied the bright red and gold ribbons that held the handles together. Then, lifting out the tissue paper, she found the gift nestled inside: a heavy, ceramic mug covered in what looked to be hand-painted pomegranates. Next to it was a Mason jar of local honey.

"Juanita, this is beautiful! Did you make this?" Ava examined the mug, delighting over the smoothness of the handle and the daintiness of the brushstrokes.

"I did," Juanita admitted, her round cheeks growing pink. She rocked back and forth on her heels, stuck her hands into the pockets of her leather jacket. "And Google told me that pomegranates, apples, and honey are all symbols of Rosh Hashanah. Since apples are a dime a dozen around here this time of year, I figured you'd already be having plenty of those. But that honey is from Eunice Caldwell's bees, over there on County Road B."

"Thank you so much! I'm sure it'll be delicious, and the mug will be perfect for my morning coffee." Ava had the unexpected urge to crush Juanita in a grateful hug, but she held back. She was getting better at letting people in town get to know her, but—*baby steps.* Yet the woman's kindness and thoughtfulness deeply touched Ava.

"Sure!" Juanita smiled, beaming at the group. "Well, I'd best get out of your hair. You've all got some family time to catch up on!"

"It was a pleasure to meet you," Mr. Goldberg said, with the others echoing his farewell.

As Juanita disappeared out the door, wiry salt and pepper curls bouncing, Mrs. Goldberg examined the jar of honey and nodded her approval. "How thoughtful of her."

"She's the best," Ava said, watching Juanita disappear down the sidewalk.

The creak of a door in the back of the shop made all four turn to see Riley traipsing down the hallway, wiping her wet hands on her apron. The girl seemed lost in thought, but as she entered the room and her gaze fell on Noah, she stopped. A hint of curiosity flickered across her face. Although Ava nearly groaned at the thought of having to introduce Noah to yet another person, she had to admit she was glad for the girl's presence as it meant she wouldn't have to be alone with her ex and her parents, the traitors.

Ava gestured toward Riley, wanting to get the introduction over with. "Noah, Riley. Riley, Noah."

Riley frowned, her eyes darting to Ava's. "That... Noah...?"

"Yes, *that* Noah," Ava sighed.

"I can't imagine you've heard anything good," Noah remarked with a grimace, turning to Riley as he offered her a sympathetic smile. "Regardless, nice to meet you."

Riley looked nervous, unsure of how to respond. She nodded. "Yeah. Same."

"Well, I guess I'd better hit the road," Noah said, brushing the same wisp of hair from his eyes. He glanced around the cafe, smoothing the top of the polished wood counter with an absent palm. He brought his eyes to Ava, and they were surprisingly soft. "It was nice seeing you, Ava. Your cafe is beautiful."

Again, something loosened inside her chest. Noah would get in his rented Corvette, bump down the cobblestones, and make his way down I-80 into Omaha where he'd sit in his hotel room for the weekend—alone. Sure, he'd probably attend a local synagogue service to hear the shofar, maybe even let the Omaha Chabad center rustle up some dinner for him, but it wouldn't be much of a holiday. Not that he deserved better. Then, Ava's eyes darted to the cup that Juanita, not even Jewish, had given her as a sign of genuine caring beyond religious bounds or past disagreements. She swallowed. She hated the thought of being an uncaring, unsympathetic hardhead even more than she hated Noah. She sighed, hardly believing she was about to say it, but...

"Fine. You can come to dinner." Her face was stiff, with no trace of a smile, but she met Noah's eyes across the counter. Across the room, she could've sworn she saw Riley's head tilt questioningly.

"Oh, I couldn't impose like that," he said, lifting his hands as if in surrender. "I was never expecting that from you. That's—I'm not—you're—"

Ava cut in, her voice stronger this time. "I mean it. This isn't, like, an invitation for us to be *friends*, but you shouldn't have to spend the holiday alone. We're adults. We can act like it."

Noah raised an eyebrow. "You're sure?"

"Don't make me second guess myself," Ava warned.

Noah broke out in a grin, and something ached inside her chest. His five o'clock shadow was dark, and she remembered with a pang the way he'd meticulously wiped away all trace of stubble from the bathroom sink when he shaved. "Thank you. That's a good deed you're doing before Yom Kippur, you know. A mitzvah."

Ava snorted. She cast an expectant look at her mother, who'd been watching the conversation unfold from her seat near the window. "You happy?"

Mrs. Goldberg sipped her now lukewarm coffee, leaving a smear of lipstick on the rim of the mug. "Happy? I'm delighted! It'll practically be a reunion."

"That's exactly what I'm afraid of," Ava said, sighing. Spending the Jewish New Year with just her parents, Riley, and Noah seemed too intimate for her liking. She'd have to call Juanita later that afternoon and ask if she and her husband,

David, would like to join them for dinner—just to keep things fun. Juanita was usually down for socializing, and she seemed open to learning about the Jewish holiday.

Noah headed back to his conference and Ava's parents left to browse the shops along Shiloh's main street. Once Ava and Riley were alone in the shop, Riley turned to Ava, her eyes wide with horrified amusement.

"Now *that* throws a wrench in things," Riley said.

"You're telling me."

"I almost wish I was going to be there to see this go down..."

Ava's gaze snapped to Riley's. "What do you mean? You're not?"

"Yeah, so..." Riley shifted from foot to foot, her cheeks flushing. "I decided to go to the homecoming dance Saturday night. Do you have any, like, nice dresses that might fit me?"

Ava wasn't sure what reason she'd expected Riley to give, but it certainly hadn't been that. Riley had been anti-social when she'd started working for Ava, and only after resolving some past difficulties had the girl broken out of her shell at all. Now she was going to homecoming? That was more progress than Ava expected. Still, she tried to keep her face smooth, unperturbed. It wouldn't do to have Riley see her shock. The girl seemed embarrassed enough as it was.

"Well, I don't go a lot of places requiring nice dresses..." Ava said. "But I can definitely look through my closet. Don't you want to buy something, though?"

Riley gave a short, clipped shrug of her shoulders. "I could do that. But maybe you'll still look through yours for me? When we get home?" She finally brought her gaze up to meet Ava's, and her eyes were hopeful. Pleading, almost.

"You bet I will."

As they made their way out to the sidewalk, Ava locking the front door behind them, Riley turned to Ava again, her voice still sounding timid. "Also... I'm sure you've thought of this, but..."

"Thought of what?" Ava asked.

"Well, Rosh Hashanah dinner. I mean, you told Owen he couldn't come..." Riley said, her voice trailing off.

But Riley didn't need to finish the sentence for its meaning to sink in.

Riley was right—and Ava could've kicked herself for being stupid enough to not take it into account. Noah—her ex? Coming to Rosh Hashanah dinner? But not *Owen*?

This was not going to go over well at *all*.

4

———

The next afternoon at two-thirty, Ava was wiping down counters in Cafe Arcana when she noticed a dull drumming sound that seemed to reverberate through the room. *What the...?*

As if on cue, the front door swung open halfway, and Owen poked his tousled head inside. His green eyes sparkled as he grinned at her, dimples winking. "Ready for the pep rally?"

Ava glanced out the window. "Oh, I forgot about that."

Riley had told her, of course. The entire student body would congregate downtown that afternoon for a final pep rally before the football game later that evening. Homecoming was a big thing in Shiloh, Ava was learning. According to Riley, the marching band would lead the way, followed by the cheerleaders, dance team, and any other students who wanted to add their voices to the boisterous cheers. Each of the classes had put together a special float to represent their school spirit, and once the lineup came to a stop downtown, all the students and teachers would vote on their favorite. However, the parade would come to a stop in front of the plaza fountain, only a block away from her shop. Which meant lots of people, sure, but none of them looking for coffee and no parking for anyone who might want some. Ava glanced across the street. All the other businesses were closing up. She might as well join in the community event, although she was far from the pep rally type of girl. She'd write it off as one more attempt to fit into the small town social fabric. Plus, it did give her a chance to be with Owen.

Ava looked skeptically back to Owen, managing a smile. They hadn't spoken since the previous day, when Noah had shown up unannounced, but if Owen was bothered by what had happened, he sure wasn't showing it. Still, Ava knew she'd be hearing about it sooner rather than later. Owen was polite, but he liked to talk about the important stuff—much to her chagrin.

Ava untied her apron. "Sure, I'm coming."

Owen waved a hand toward the door, gesturing her outside. "Come on!"

As she followed him down the sidewalk and toward the plaza, Ava was amused by how excited Owen seemed. *It's just a high school pep rally.* Then again, it had been *his* high school, and the Shiloh Sharks had been his football team. These kinds of events must be a blast of nostalgia for him.

The plaza square was already crowded with people, all decked out in blue and white. As she scanned the crowd, she recognized the shop owners from Main Street, as well as Marge Harding and Flo Finkenbaum, two ladies in town who regularly met at her cafe for their weekly Bible study. Officer Dan Harding, who was Marge's son, stood on the edge of the crowd, still in his police uniform but sporting a blue and white ball cap. Owen was greeting folks, shaking hands with the man nearest him, someone Ava didn't recognize.

"Ava!"

Ava turned, and there was Rose Robinson, her close friend from childhood summers spent in Shiloh with her grandfather, Zaidy Mel, making her way through the crowd. Ever the fashionista, she sported a sleek blue hoodie and black joggers, topped off with shiny blue eye shadow that Ava felt would have been better left in the early 2000s. In Rose's arms, baby Ellie clapped along to the drumming, which Ava now saw came from the marching band's bass drums moving toward them down Main Street.

"Did Owen force you out here?" Rose laughed, giving Ava a quick hug. "No offense, but you're not the peppiest person."

"Well, he didn't *force* me," Ava said, eyeing the crowd. "But with all this racket going on, Arcana's kind of deserted. I may as well come see what all the fuss is about."

"Oh, it'll be fun!"

Owen was still engaged in conversation with the man Ava didn't recognize. A red-haired woman Ava recognized from the checkout counter at the grocery store came to stand beside the man, linking her arm with his.

"Who's that?" Ava whispered to Rose, hoping her friend could hear her over the thumping of the bass.

Rose glanced to where Ava was gesturing. "Oh, that's Mitch Fangman. He's sort of a handyman around town, also one of the commentators for high school sports. And that's his girlfriend, Chantelle. She works at Shiloh Market; you've probably seen her around."

Ava nodded. Suddenly, Rose jerked to a start, her face drawn as she turned back to Ava.

"Ava," she hissed, drawing her friend closer. "Noah—your ex-husband. He's *here*."

"I know," Ava hissed back. "Wait—how do *you* know about that?"

"Because he's *here*. Like, right there!"

"What?!"

Doing her best to remain discreet, Rose jerked her head to her left, and Ava's gaze traveled across the crowd. Her stomach plummeted. Sure enough, there was Noah, laughing along with another man as he leaned against a building across the street.

"What is he *doing* here?" Ava hissed.

"I thought you said you knew!" Rose gave a helpless shrug of her free arm.

"I meant I saw him *yesterday*," Ava said. "He's in town for a medical conference and came waltzing right into Arcana."

"Ew! You told him to get lost, I hope!" Rose's pixie-like features screwed up in indignation.

"Sort of," Ava said, her gaze flitting to Owen, who was thankfully still occupied. "Except he's coming to Rosh Hashanah dinner tomorrow evening."

"He's *what*?" Rose looked like she was about to drop the baby. Her eyes also moved to Owen's back where they paused, then moved back to Ava.

"Yeah. It's not good."

"So, wait," Rose said, shifting Ellie on her hip. The bass drums were getting louder, now accompanied by the clatter of snare drums. "Let me get this straight. *Owen*, who's been patiently waiting for you to get it together these past few months, who saved your life, who has helped you keep your business intact, is *not* coming to your family dinner, but your cheating ex-husband *is*?"

Ava grimaced in reply.

Rose glanced again at Owen, who was finishing his conversation and maneuvering through the crowd toward them. "Does he *know*? Owen?"

"Sorry about that," Owen said, as he joined her and Rose at the edge of the plaza. "Mitch Fangman had some questions about a line of tools I carry at the shop." His expression appeared tense. Ava wondered how a discussion of tools could be troubling. But when Ellie's chubby hand reached out to swat him on the forearm, he grabbed her blue Converse-clad foot and grinned. He turned to Rose then, glancing between her and Ava. "Anyway—do I know what?"

Ava froze. She'd hoped he hadn't heard. She glanced at Rose, who looked just as flustered. "Uh—well, that Noah's here—like, at this pep rally."

It wasn't the whole truth, but it was something.

"He is?" Owen rubbed his scruffy chin, glancing around the crowd.

"Apparently. He's standing with someone—probably that friend he mentioned yesterday. God, what a nightmare," Ava moaned.

At the mention of the friend, Owen and Rose turned back to the crowd, shading their eyes to make out the man next to Noah.

"No idea who that is," Owen said with a shrug.

"Me neither," Rose said. "Must be a transplant. One of the lake people."

Rose was always dropping comments about the wealthy residents that lived on the luxury lake outside of town. Ava wasn't sure how luxurious a manmade lake in small-town Nebraska could be, but the longstanding residents of Shiloh proper sure liked to gossip about the people who lived there—which she found amusing. One of these days, she'd need to get over there and see this lake for herself.

"Anyway," Ava said, turning to Owen. "I swear I didn't know about any of this. Honestly, he scared the life out of me yesterday."

"It kind of seemed like that," Owen said. Then he shrugged his broad shoulders, as though it didn't matter. "Anyway—it's alright. Stuff happens. But I'd like to avoid him, if possible."

Ava stood on her tiptoes, straining to see over the heads of the crowd. A few blocks off, she spied the high school marching band, moving in perfect unison down the bumpy cobblestones, followed by the class floats she'd heard about, upon which the athletes rode. Each of the floats stopped at the plaza before turning down a side street, letting the burly football players and flouncy cheerleaders hop off the flatbeds. The student body gathered at the plaza, with the football team and coaches in the middle next to a line of microphone stands.

"That's Chase Wagner," Rose said, nudging Ava and jutting her chin in the direction of the football players. "The one in the middle."

"Uh... Who?" Ava raised her eyebrows at Rose. She was always the odd one out when it came to sports.

"The quarterback," Owen supplied. The crowd had gathered in tighter now, and she felt his chest warm against her shoulder. "He's thrown for 1,200 yards and fifteen touchdowns in just four games this season, off to a super great start. Word is Rhule is looking at him for this coming fall."

What was supposed to be an explanation was once again a code Ava couldn't quite decipher. This time, she turned to look up at Owen. "Sorry—Rhule?"

Owen gave her an incredulous look, then chuckled, shaking his head. His sandy blond hair fell into his eyes. "Matt Rhule. Head coach at Nebraska. It means the Huskers are looking to recruit him this year."

"Ah," Ava said, turning back to glance at the familiar-looking young man in question. Lean and solid, he was taller than the other boys around him. He looked like he could nimbly dodge anyone who might come after him, which was, Ava thought, a useful trait for a quarterback.

"Yeah, you might've seen him before, come to think of it," Rose added, pausing thoughtfully. "He also works at the grocery store. His mom was a McPherson. You know, from the apple orchard, where the fall festival is going to be this year."

"Okay, sure," Ava said, shrugging. Rose knew everyone in town, who they were related to, where their in-laws had grown up, where the in-laws of *those* in-laws had grown up, and how long the houses had been in each family. Ava could not have cared less.

As the head coach started his speech, Ava's eyes wandered the crowd. Although most of the attendees were students, Ava also recognized many of the downtown store owners, who'd done the same as she had: locked their shops and made their way outside to enjoy the change of pace. Tim Meyer from the art gallery was there, as well as Ed and Elaine Walsh, who owned Looking Glass, the wine bar next to Cafe Arcana. She also guessed by the lanyards they wore around their necks that the group of adults milling around behind the students were teachers.

"Would it kill you to look at least a *little* entertained?" Owen's whisper was sharp, yet playful, against her ear. "Even Noah looks like he's having fun over there."

Ava jerked around to glare up at him, acutely aware of the goosebumps that had erupted on the small of her back. She rubbed her arms, hissing back, "Shh. I'm listening."

"Are not." Owen smirked, raising his eyes once again to the pep talk that was still droning on.

Ava elbowed him ever so slightly, not wanting to draw anyone's attention—and certainly not Noah's. They hadn't made eye contact yet from across the crowd, and she meant to keep it that way.

Beside her, Owen clucked his tongue almost inaudibly. "I wonder what Noah thinks—seeing you flirting with me?"

Ouch.

"You know perfectly well I don't care one *bit* what Noah thinks," Ava hissed, turning toward him so that Rose wouldn't hear. She was aware of how close her face was to his chest as he towered over her.

Owen didn't say anything but turned toward the center of the plaza, settling his gaze on the coach as the speech droned on. Ava turned her attention toward the pep rally. She spotted Riley's electric blue bob on the far side of the crowd, next to a group of girls who might just as easily have been American Eagle mannequins. Just in front of her stood a tall, hoodie-clad boy in flashy Adidas shoes. Riley's attention wasn't on the coach, who was somehow *still* talking, nor was it on the cheerleaders, who now looked poised to lead the crowd in some kind of chant. Instead, she kept glancing up at the boy in front of her, who, in Ava's opinion, looked too cool for Riley to care about.

Ava nudged Rose. "Look at Riley."

"Yeah? What about her?" Rose looked annoyed. She'd clearly been listening to the coach's never-ending speech.

"She keeps looking at that guy in front of her. The one in the hoodie. Who is he?"

"Geez, you guys talk loud," Owen whispered, ducking his head between Rose and Ava. "But to answer your question, that's Trevor Phillips. Football player."

Leave it to Owen to know all the athletes in town. Ava knew Owen had played football in high school, but aside from the Huskers cap he always seemed to be wearing, she hadn't known he was such an avid sports fan. "Is he friends with Riley?"

Everyone clapped as the coach finally finished his speech. Owen then shrugged and turned toward her. "No idea. I've seen him around town with Chase and some of the other football players, and their parents are all friends, but that's about it. Why?"

"No reason."

Even from across the plaza, Ava could have sworn the girl's ears were red. Ava had the sneaking suspicion she knew where Riley's sudden desire to attend the homecoming dance had come from. The girl had offered next to no details the evening before as they'd sifted through Ava's closet, finally landing on a flouncy red number Ava couldn't even remember buying. Riley hadn't shown a lot of enthusiasm for the dress, but she'd draped it over her arm anyway and disappeared into her bedroom.

"Ava, over here!" A voice called from further down the street, and Ava turned to see who it was.

Her parents, to whom Ava had lent her car for the day, stood on the sidewalk, waving to her. Her parents were at the pep rally? She had the fleeting fear that Noah had invited them, but then her eyes fell on Juanita next to them, and she grinned.

Juanita could get anyone to do anything with that laugh of hers —even get Sara Goldberg to stand around at a pep rally surrounded by the brassy blare of trombones and the squeak of poorly played clarinets. Tugging Rose along with her, Ava made her way over to where they stood, Owen trailing behind them.

"Well, look at *you*," Mrs. Goldberg gushed, leaning down to tap Ellie on her nose. "You're so much *bigger* than the last time I saw you. How old is she now?"

"Fourteen months," Rose answered proudly. "Walking and jabbering. Her own little person."

"I would say so!" Mrs. Goldberg was in the middle of a game of peekaboo with Ellie, who was having just as grand of a time as the older woman. Without even pausing the game, Sara said in a coy voice, "Ava, your father and I haven't had a new grandbaby in quite a few years now."

Ava stiffened. It was always something, wasn't it? Her brother, Aaron, and his wife were already pregnant with their third. It wasn't like her parents were relying on Ava as their sole provider of grandchildren. She tried very hard not to look at Owen, who now stood next to her. "Yes, I'm aware. I've been kind of busy, if you hadn't noticed."

"Well, you better hop to it," Mrs. Goldberg said curtly, giving Ava a pointed look. "You're not getting any younger, you know."

"Enough." Mr. Goldberg clapped his hands. He turned to Juanita, who, to Ava's annoyance, had the audacity to look amused. "So, they're playing the Emberville Dragons tonight? Anyone know what the odds are?"

This time, Ava let out a snort. "Dad, you can barely tell the difference between a football and a basketball."

"I am *learning*," Mr. Goldberg said, crossing his arms over his chest.

"Odds are in their favor," Owen said, nodding to Ava's dad. "But not by much. It's gonna be a close one—especially with Jake Connelly being out this week."

"Oh? Is he the quarterback?" Mr. Goldberg looked fascinated, moving to stand next to Owen.

"Nah, that's Chase Wagner. Jake is our wide receiver, but he took a pretty bad hit last week and will be on the sidelines." As he spoke, Owen's eyes searched the crowd, finally landing on the players in question. He pointed them out to Ava's dad. "It'll be interesting to see how they do without him."

"Ah," Mr. Goldberg said, stroking his clean-shaven chin like he knew exactly what Owen was talking about. He paused for a minute, as though mulling things over, then asked, "I take it you'll be at the game then?"

"Tonight?" Owen grinned. "Absolutely, I'll be there."

"Well, would you mind if I sat with you? Like I said, I'm still learning the rules of the game—" Here, he shot Ava a stern glance over the tops of his glasses. "—and I'd like to ask someone questions."

"Uh..." The question had caught Owen off guard. He looked nervously at Ava, then seemed to recover his composure. He stood up straighter. "Sure thing. As long as that's alright with Ava?"

"Great," Ava said weakly. She hadn't told her parents that she'd be attending the game with Owen, and she didn't miss the sharp glance her mother threw her way. As torn as she was about the whole situation, she'd been looking forward to the time spent with Owen. *Well—maybe it's for the best.*

"Fantastic," Mr. Goldberg said, beaming.

"Michael," Mrs. Goldberg cut in. "Surely you're not intending to skip out on *kiddush* this evening..." *Kiddush* was the traditional blessing over wine recited on the Jewish Sabbath and holidays. For as long as Ava could remember, her father had said *kiddush* for the family every Friday night.

"Definitely not," Mr. Goldberg said, frowning. "I will *never* leave you hanging for a glass of wine, my dear. I'll leave for the game after." He pushed his glasses up on his nose. Then excitement dawned on his face. He began rustling in the satchel he carried slung over his shoulder. "Say—Owen. Do you know what a shofar is?"

"*No!*" Ava and Mrs. Goldberg shrieked at exactly the same moment. They shared a frantic look, at which Mr. Goldberg pouted.

"Come on," Ava's dad wheedled. "I've only got a couple days left to practice. You said 'no' at the airport, you say 'no' at the house, you say 'no'—"

"Because it's *awful*, Michael." Mrs. Goldberg laid a pitying hand on her husband's forearm.

Owen grinned in amusement. "I have no idea what that is, but now I *definitely* need to know."

Suddenly, a shout rose from across the plaza, causing them all to turn.

Shofar forgotten, Mr. Goldberg shielded his eyes from the sun as his face darkened. "Is that...?"

"Noah?" Mrs. Goldberg's voice was incredulous. "But why is he—"

A roaring bellow drowned her voice out. Ava's eyes, still searching the square for the source of the commotion, fell on Noah just in time to see another man's fist go flying toward his face. Almost catlike, Noah lurched backward, avoiding the man's swing. Even from far away, Ava saw the anger on the man's face.

"Easy, man!" Noah shouted, raising his hands to show he wasn't fighting back.

But the man swung again, and this time the man Ava had taken to be Noah's friend pushed between them, a hand on each man's chest. As he stood there, keeping the two apart like a kindergarten teacher on a playground, Ava realized that the man who'd taken a swing at Noah was none other than Mitch Fangman, the man who had asked Owen about tools earlier.

Joel Robinson, Rose's husband, came jogging down the sidewalk, followed by Officer Harding, and Ava began a brisk walk toward the action. *What the heck was going on?!*

"Hey, hey, hey," Joel said, slowing to a stop next to Noah and Mitch. "Let's everybody calm down, alright? This is a high school pep rally. You guys want to act like preschoolers, they may still have room for you at the Lutheran church daycare."

"He started it," Mitch spat, still yelling.

Noah looked incredulous. "Bro, *you* spilled your drink on *me*."

"It was an *accident*." Mitch turned to Joel and Officer Harding, jerking a shaking thumb at Noah. "And then this hotshot had to go and spit a hunk of his Snickers bar at me. I could have *died*!"

Noah snorted, folding his arms across his chest. "So dramatic, man."

Mitch's apparent girlfriend, Chantelle Svoboda—who Ava once again recognized as working at the local food market—spoke up. "He could have, though. He's got a serious peanut allergy."

"Oh, come on," Noah said, rolling his eyes. "Not from *that*.

Trust me—I'm a doctor. I know how it works. And besides, I spit it on the sidewalk, not on him."

"*Trust me—I'm a doctor,*" Mitch mimicked, his voice high, as he ran an exaggerated hand through his hair and swooped his head back.

"Not helping, Mitch," Officer Harding warned. "Now, I suggest you guys break this up and cool off. The kids want to have a good time—don't ruin it for them."

As the men moved apart from each other, trying to recover themselves from whatever had just happened, Ava's face burned with embarrassment. Noah had *spit* on someone? And even if he'd only spit on the ground as he claimed, what was he doing *spitting* in the first place? The man was just as petty and entitled as she'd remembered.

Mrs. Goldberg was already scuttling toward Noah, her husband in tow, no doubt to smooth the situation over. *No way am I going over there*, Ava thought.

She chanced a glance up at Owen, only to find him smirking.

"What's so funny?" Ava demanded, annoyed that he was, apparently, finding humor in the incident.

"All of it," Owen chuckled, waving a hand. "These two jerks go making a spectacle of themselves over spilling drinks and spitting candy bars. It's like watching a preschool reality show."

"Hilarious," Ava said dryly.

Joel approached the group, taking Ellie from Rose's arms. He flashed a wary smile at them all. "I don't know about you guys, but I could do with a cup of coffee after that ordeal."

"For sure," Ava said. The thought of being inside Cafe Arcana, away from the drama that seemed to follow her since yesterday afternoon, was a godsend. "Come on."

Then, grabbing Owen's wrist and Rose's elbow, she steered the both of them back toward Cafe Arcana, with Joel and Ellie bringing up the rear. As they made their way down the sidewalk, Ava glimpsed her mother, still chatting with Noah, watching them from across the street. Ava let her hand drop from Owen's wrist. She would have to be careful. They didn't need any more drama.

5

The streets near the Shiloh football stadium were packed with cars when Ava and her dad drove in that evening. Although it took her a few rounds to find a spot, she was at least glad for her Chicago-honed parallel parking skills.

As she killed the engine and removed her seatbelt, she looked across the car to her dad. Her eyes narrowed, looking him up and down. "Did you bring the shofar?"

Mr. Goldberg scoffed. "Really, Ava. Like I would bring that to a *football* game."

"Well, you had no problem whipping it out in the middle of the airport," Ava said, exiting the car. She let the door slam behind her and raced to catch up to her dad, who was already several strides ahead of her, his lanky figure striding down the uneven sidewalk.

As she fell into stride next to him, he turned to look at her, chuckling. "I'm pretty sure you're not allowed to blow the shofar on Shabbat. And anyway—give me a little credit—I wouldn't embarrass you *that* bad in front of Owen."

"What?" Ava was caught off guard.

Her father waved a spindly hand. "I happen to be a pretty smart guy, but it doesn't take a rocket scientist to see you've got a thing for him."

Ava was silent. She had no idea what to say. The two of them had never spoken about her love life, and certainly not since her divorce. It seemed somehow strange—taboo even—to be discussing someone other than Noah with her father.

"I like him," Mr. Goldberg continued, shoving his hands in his pockets as they walked. "He's nice. Fun, respectful. One heck of a talented baker."

"Yeah." Ava just nodded. Neither of them needed to say what they both already knew: Owen could be a saint, but he still wasn't someone she could pursue. She wondered why her father was bringing it up at all.

Mr. Goldberg sighed. "Well, hang in there, kid. Tomorrow's dinner won't be as bad as you think."

Easy for him to say. He wasn't the one who was going to have to somehow explain to a love interest that her ex was coming to dinner when *he* wasn't.

As they approached the stadium, the football field came into view down below. Cheerleaders from both teams milled around, getting in some practice kicks on their respective ends of the field before the game got going. The stands were already crowded. Although fans had shown up for both teams, the sea of blue and white caps and shark-emblazoned hoodies was staggering. At once, Ava understood the logic behind the home field advantage.

Ava and her dad paid the entrance fee, then shimmied into the crowd. Voices emanated from all sides, the sounds of casual chatter and raucous laughter enveloping them as they came to stand at the top of the bleachers, looking down at the field below. Ava pressed her phone to her ear, waiting for Owen to answer, and breathed in the buttery, tantalizing aroma of fresh popcorn that drifted from the concession stand.

"Hang on—I see you." Owen's reply was short, and the line clicked off.

"He says he sees us," Ava relayed to her dad, who was squinting through his glasses to better search the crowd. She leaned toward him, also peering through the hordes of people. Suddenly, she stiffened. "You have *got* to be kidding me."

There, in line for concessions, stood Noah, scrolling through his phone and laughing at something the man next to him—the same one from the pep rally—was saying. Ava prayed he wouldn't look up. *How dare he.*

Mr. Goldberg's gaze followed Ava's, and his brow creased. "Interesting."

"That's one word for it," Ava said, snorting. "Well, whatever. I've got a word for him: *Schmu—*"

A touch at the small of her back made her jump. When she turned, Owen's lopsided grin towered above her.

"Take it easy," he said, laughing. He dropped his palm from her back and reached out to shake her father's hand in greeting. "And who are we looking at?"

"No one," Ava snapped. Noah really had some nerve, showing up to *her* town's football game, but she wouldn't acknowledge his presence any further. As far as she was concerned, Noah was ordering room service at the Omaha Hilton.

"Oh, Noah seems to have shown up with that friend of his," Mr. Goldberg said, sighing.

Ava glared at her father. *Great.*

Although Ava could have sworn she saw Owen flinch, his

expression remained unruffled. "Well, he's certainly ballsy. I'll give him that."

"Yes, and as I was about to say," Ava cut in, "he's also a *schm*—"

"Ava! Owen!" Rose's voice broke through the din of the crowd, and Ava looked up to see her and Joel waving from the bleachers a few rows down.

Rose, clad in a plaid flannel jacket, patted the seat next to her. But Owen was already on his way to where Joel and Rose sat, giving Ava's elbow a tug before he yanked her along. Mr. Goldberg brought up the rear.

Ava sat in the middle between Owen and Rose. Joel waved to her from his seat on the other side of his wife. "These benches are *cold*," Ava whined.

Mr. Goldberg, on the other side of Owen, fixed her with a playful, pouting look. "Boo hoo. Poor baby!"

Owen smothered a smirk. Instead, he turned toward Mr. Goldberg and pointed across the field. "The teams and coaches are all over there. Looks like they're ready to go."

Ava turned her attention to Joel and Rose. Determined not to let Noah ruin their evening, she decided against alerting Rose to his presence. "Too cold for Ellie?"

"Yeah, and also past her bedtime. She's at Mom and Dad's," Rose said. She wrinkled her dainty nose. "You know you're getting old when your idea of a night out is the high school football game.

"Speak for yourself," Joel put in, wrapping an arm around his wife and shooting Ava a wink. He glanced at Owen then, including him in the conversation. "Some of us have *always* come to these games. Wouldn't miss them, right?"

"Right." Owen's green eyes sparkled under the stadium lights.

Ava stared at the mayhem in the stands and the all-too-cheery cheerleaders in the glare of floodlights as she squirmed her now frosty thighs on the metal seat. This would be his idea of a night out from now on?

As a wail of microphone feedback pierced the air, followed by crackling static, Ava felt the tips of Owen's fingers lace with hers on the bench between them. She stiffened, chancing a glance at her dad, who was now squinting at the scoreboard, trying to make out the letters. Satisfied he hadn't noticed, Ava kept her hand where it was, glad for the warmth of Owen's gigantic palms—along with the small reassurance that, just maybe, things would still be right between them.

"Relax," Owen murmured, leaning toward her, his breath hot on her neck. He squeezed her hand. She could've sworn her frozen fingers already felt warmer. She smiled weakly at him.

"Alright, ladies and gentleman!" An official, yet somewhat slimy sounding voice echoed through the loudspeakers. "Welcome to Memorial Stadium—home of the Shiloh Sharks!"

A momentary surge of excitement overcame the crowd, followed by a gradual hush as the speaker continued. "Coaching your home team is, of course, the one and only Coach Callahan. Let's hear it for Coach Callahan!"

The crowd erupted in applause. Owen took his hand away for a moment to clap, gripping Ava's again as he brought it back down. Lost in the magic of the moment, Mr. Goldberg stared around in awe at the cheering, blue-and-white-jacketed students and the marching band in their stiff uniforms lined up in the stands. At the bellowing direction of the announcer, the football players ran out onto the field one by one as their names were called, beating their chests for the crowd. They were eating up the applause, using the moment to pump themselves up for the game ahead.

As the players lined up on the field, and the kicker from the Emberville Dragons backed up in preparation for kickoff, Mr. Goldberg whispered, "He's punting, right?"

"Yes," Owen said, trying hard to keep a straight face. He squeezed Ava's hand. "Let's watch."

The crowd waited with bated breath as the kicker moved forward and connected his foot with the ball, which spiraled end over end up and across the field. The Shiloh team was ready, and the Sharks swarmed the field, with the receiver catching the ball smoothly in his grasp. He made it a few yards before a Dragon twice his size sacked him.

"Okay. They've got him. What now?" Although clueless, Mr. Goldberg was enraptured by the game already. He leaned forward, elbows on his bony knees, and glanced back at Owen.

"Yeah. So, that was the kickoff, and they got him at the fifteen. That's where they'll start now to try to get a first down," Owen explained.

"And they get four downs?"

Ava suddenly remembered her father coming to one of her middle school choir concerts and throwing individual roses onto the stage at her feet after her solo. Now, she wished she could melt into the bleachers, but she had to hand it to her dad: he wasn't afraid of looking stupid. *Well, that's the perk of living life as a professor—everyone already thinks you're smart. Nothing to prove.*

"Exactly," Owen said to Mr. Goldberg, squeezing Ava's hand silently as though he'd read her mind. "You've got it."

Mr. Goldberg settled back, looking satisfied with himself, and the game continued. Throughout the first quarter, Ava was sure that her father's incessant questions would drive Owen to insanity, but Owen remained friendly and unruffled. She'd always known Owen was patient, but to spend the entirety of a football game you're trying to watch answering the never-ending questions of the father of the girl you're sort of dating—from whom she's trying to keep you a secret—took a kind of patience Ava supposed even the Pope would applaud. She was glad for the answers herself, though, as it kept her from constantly elbowing Rose, who was, not surprisingly, not so patient.

"Now, when he fails the pass like that—" Mr. Goldberg began. He was cut off by a collective gasp that went up through the crowd, causing Owen, Joel, and Rose to lean forward in unison, their necks craned toward the field.

"Dang," Owen muttered, letting go of Ava's hand to wipe his sweaty palm on his jeans. When he brought his hand back to hers, his grip was tighter than before.

Rose was murmuring, "No, no, no, no," and Joel, who still had his headphones on, was pressing the earpieces tightly as though to make sure he caught every word of the broadcast.

"What happened?" Ava asked, unsure if anyone could hear her amidst the tense chatter of the crowd.

"Dragons just intercepted," Owen said, his mouth a thin line. "And they got a good run from it. Our guys weren't expecting it. Shoot, that won't look good for Chase Wagner."

"Yeah, Fangman's going nuts over here," Joel remarked, lifting one of the headphones from his ears. "He's been rough on Chase all season, but this is something else. Here." He lifted the headphones from his ears and passed them to Owen, who sat for a moment, listening. His face was grim when he passed the set back to Joel.

"Yikes," he said, shaking his head. "I don't listen to the broadcasts. He's been like that all season?"

"Pretty much." Joel placed the headphones around his neck. "I know Chase has heard about it, too. That's got to suck, having your performance torn apart like that for the whole town."

Ava was confused. "Huh? What broadcast? I don't get it."

"Joel likes to listen to the radio broadcast during the games," Rose said. "The announcer calls out the surface stuff over the loudspeaker for us in the stands, but the commentators sit up there in the press box and give all the stats, discuss the plays. It's so people can listen on the radio or at home."

"And Mitch Fangman has been absolutely trashing our quarterback," Joel said, jumping in. "Fred Sutton, the other commentator, sometimes tries to counteract Mitch's criticism, but it doesn't help. I mean, Chase has made some dumb moves the past few games, sure, but it's been brutal. Like, he's a kid."

"Mitch Fangman?" Ava asked, recognizing the name. "Isn't that the guy Noah got into it with at the pep rally today? Chantelle's boyfriend?"

"The very same," Owen remarked. Under the glow of the stadium lights, his face darkened.

"Yeah, he's kind of a hothead," Joel said. "Both on air and off."

Ava resisted the urge to scan the crowd for her ex-husband. "Well, that and Noah was being a total *schm*—"

"Shhhh!" Owen hissed. He released Ava's hand and rubbed his palms together.

The crowd hushed to a breath as the teams set up again for the next play. The ball was now in the Dragons' possession, and they didn't have far to go to score. The quarterback yelled 'hike,' the center snapped the ball, set the play in motion, and barely a beat later, groans echoed everywhere on the Shiloh side. The Emberville quarterback shot off like a streak, dashing up the field and dodging three Sharks on the way, who failed miserably to tackle him. As he passed into the end zone, an ear-shattering roar erupted from the Emberville side of the stands, and the students all got to their feet, shouting, stamping, cheering.

"Noooo," Rose groaned. Beside her, Joel shook his head in disappointment and Owen slapped his thigh.

"Touchdown? Emberville?" Mr. Goldberg questioned, sounding scared to give voice to the unfortunate happening.

"Yes. And for no reason." Owen's mouth was a thin line, his brow furrowed. As he chewed on his bottom lip, Ava saw his dimple appear and disappear.

"But it's only one touchdown," Ava offered. "And it's only the first quarter. There's plenty of time for us to come back."

"That's true," Owen admitted, rubbing his chin with rough fingers. She could hear the callouses on his fingers scratching against his evening stubble. "It's just not great for the morale that something like this happened so early in the game."

"Well, hey, it's homecoming," Rose said, linking her arm through Joel's and snuggling closer for warmth. "That'll automatically keep the morale up. They'll be really angling to win this one."

The game continued, with Emberville completing their touchdown with a field goal. On Shiloh's next possession, the stand-in wide receiver took what looked to be a brutal sacking, and the ball was turned over faster than Ava thought possible. After another touchdown for the Dragons and another fumble for Chase Wagner, to which Owen clucked his tongue and shook his head, the ref called the game for halftime.

"Snacks anyone?" Owen asked, slapping both palms on his knees and getting to his feet. "I was holding out hope for the Wiener Schlinger making its way over here, but now I'm craving a Frito pie."

At the start of the game, Rose had pointed out the giant hotdog-shaped machine manned by a guy at the foot of the bleachers. Every once in a while, he'd hold the machine up and sling a half dozen foil-wrapped hot dogs into the screaming, waving arms of the crowd. An interesting thing to watch, but Ava noticed as a man on the other end of the bleachers from her unwrapped his hotdog that they were Fairbury franks. Although the famous franks were all beef, she didn't care for them. The bright red dye—probably an homage to the Huskers —stained her fingers and made you look like a little kid with Jell-O mouth. She was silently thankful the wiener-slinging man had passed her friends by.

"Sounds amazing," Mr. Goldberg said. He turned to Ava, holding a crisp ten-dollar bill out to her. "I don't think I can brave that crowd, but if you want to bring me back some popcorn, I wouldn't be mad."

Rose elbowed Ava. "Get me a Frito pie, will you?"

Ava wrinkled her nose. "What even *is* that?"

Owen snorted as Ava stood up to join him. "You're going to say it's gross."

"Well, *is* it gross?" Ava asked, laughing, as she and Owen made their way to the center stairs, pushing past the hordes of people as they climbed. Ava could feel Owen's palm on the small of her back, keeping track of her in the crowd.

The line for the concessions was long, as everyone else had

had the same idea. Ava couldn't imagine what the line for the women's bathroom was like. She stood next to Owen in the line, rubbing her hands together to keep them warm. The late September night was chilly, and she wished she'd brought gloves.

"Give me those," Owen said, clamping his huge hands around hers to completely envelop them. He smiled. "Don't look so shocked—your dad's not here."

Ava glanced around. "I know, but…"

Owen gave her hands a quick rub, then let them fall from his grasp. He shoved his hands in the pockets of his Carhartt jacket. "Your dad's cool. I think we're getting along."

"You are. But that's not the problem. I *told* you, it's not about them *liking* you—"

"Yeah, yeah, yeah. Trust me, I got it." Owen waved a hand to stop her explanation. He nodded his head toward the gap that had appeared in the line, signaling for her to step forward. "We'll figure it out."

"Yeah." Ava didn't want to say what she was really thinking: she wasn't sure they *would* figure it out. Then a question dawned on her. "So, what's the deal with you and Mitch Fangman?"

"Deal?"

"Yeah, you look pissed every time someone mentions him— including when you were talking to him at the pep rally today. What were you guys talking about?"

Owen raised an eyebrow at her. Then, smirking, he stepped behind her and wrapped his solid arms around her shoulders. He said into her ear, "Nosy."

Ava's ears burned as she wriggled herself free of his grasp. She shook him off, already missing how warm he'd been and pushing the thought down. Had anyone seen? "Yes. I *am* nosy."

A fleeting expression of something like hurt crossed Owen's face, quickly replaced by amused resignation. He sighed, crossed his arms over his chest, and rocked back on his heels. He looked her straight in the eye. "Well, while you and Rose were so fervently discussing the fact that your ex will be joining you for dinner on Saturday, as I've already said, Mitch was asking me about a brand of tools I carry at the store."

An icy fist clenched Ava's stomach. "You heard."

"How could I not? You guys aren't exactly the picture of discretion."

A buzzing erupted from Owen's jacket pocket. Drawing out his phone, he glanced at the screen, frowning.

"Hey, I gotta take this," Owen said to Ava, his brow still furrowed. "You go ahead and order, and I'll join you in a few minutes, alright?"

Without even waiting for a reply, Owen pushed past Ava and disappeared into the crowd, leaving her staring after him.

Great, Ava thought grumpily. Not only did she have no clue what this thing she was ordering was supposed to be, but Owen also seemed to think she had four hands to carry it all.

Now alone in the line, Ava gazed around at the throngs of people surrounding her. Down below, she saw that the marching band had taken the field. The crowd seemed indifferent, however, and it was impossible to hear anything save for the occasional blast of a lone trumpet over the roar of the chattering crowd. The band looked like sad ants, marching in their rigid uniforms for an audience who'd forgotten they were there.

"Neeeext," came the voice from the concession counter, gesturing Ava forward.

The woman who stood in front of the register looked tired, drained. Almost as fast as Ava listed off her order, the woman pushed the snacks toward her: a greasy bag of lukewarm popcorn for her dad, a bottle of Mountain Dew, and two paper dishes that looked to Ava like someone had thrown up in them for Owen and Rose.

Just as Ava was trying to figure out how to carry everything, Owen reappeared by her side. Although he flashed her his signature grin, Ava noticed he seemed flustered somehow, his eyes distant.

"Sorry about that," he said to Ava, tucking the Mountain Dew under his arm. "Had to take care of something."

Ava was about to ask Owen just what he'd had to take care of, but she stopped herself. Knowing Owen, he'd take her prying as an opportunity to do some prying of his own—which was the last thing she wanted, what with the situation with Noah. No, she'd just have to keep her curiosity to herself.

As they left the concession stand, Ava pointed to the paper dishes Owen held in his hands. "What *is* that?"

"Frito pie," Owen said, as though it were the most natural thing in the world. "It's Fritos, topped with chili. A true midwestern delicacy. We even had it in our school lunches."

Ava swatted him. "Oh, stop."

Owen broke into laughter, the previous tension he'd radiated dissipating. "I'm serious! They served it with cinnamon rolls."

"Hey, what's that?" Ava asked, jerking to a stop.

Owen followed her gaze. On their left were the stairs that led up to the press box, and on the second step from the top, something glinted. A piece of glass? The lights from the concession stand didn't reach the press box stairs—a real safety hazard, Ava thought. Those stairs looked awfully shaky, and something on them would make them even more dangerous.

"Dunno," Owen said, chewing his lip. "A quarter? Piece of foil? Literally anything?"

"I guess..." Ava said, her voice trailing off. "But it's weird, no? That it's glinting like that?"

"Not really," Owen said, doing his best to shrug with his hands full of Frito pie. "Anyway, let's go. The snacks are getting cold."

"It'll only take a second," Ava said, already on her way up the rickety press box steps. "I just want to make sure it's not glass or something."

Owen heaved a sigh in reply, but he followed Ava just the same.

As Ava neared the object at the top of the steps, it once again caught the light. Seeing that it was most definitely *not* glass, she picked it up and turned it over. Whatever it was appeared to be some kind of laminated card. It must have been the shiny plastic that had caught her eye beneath the stadium lights. The words *GOLDEN PASS* were printed in bold across the front.

Owen joined her on the step, glancing at the card. "Oh, that's one of those cards you can get if you're over sixty. They let seniors in for free to all the sporting events."

"Dang. Don't tell my dad," Ava joked.

"Here," Owen said, balancing both Frito pies in one hand. He took the card from Ava with the other. "I'll just leave it with the guys in the press box and they can try to get it back to its owner."

He opened the door, and Ava stood behind him as he stuck his head inside, glancing around.

"Fred? Mitch?" Owen stood for a moment, then turned back to Ava, frowning. Then, glancing back inside the press box, said, "Nobody's answering. I'm gonna see if he's—oh, *no*."

Owen sucked in a sharp breath. Ava felt herself tense behind him, her heart beginning to race.

"What?" Ava asked, alarmed at the expression of shock that had overtaken Owen's handsome features. "What's wrong?"

Without answering, Owen flung the door open wide, bounding into the room. Still clutching the Frito pies, Ava stood on the top step of the stairs for a moment, craning her neck after Owen. Gingerly, she stepped inside.

At first, Ava thought the press box was empty. Fluorescent lights buzzed overhead, file cabinets stacked up along the wall nearest her. To her left, the entire upper half of the front of the press box was made of windows, overlooking the field below. In front of the windows was a polished desk; pens and binders lay open next to what appeared to be a roster of names. This was where the announcers sat, giving them a prime view of the game below as they recounted its happenings to the crowd and radio listeners. But then her gaze flicked to the rest of the room, where Owen was now kneeling down next to Mitch Fangman, who was sprawled in the middle of the carpeted floor.

"*What* the—"

Her shriek was cut off by the splat of the Frito pies as they dropped from her hands. With chili and soggy Fritos now splattered at her feet, Ava stood frozen.

"Stay there," Owen warned, holding a hand out to stop her before she moved any closer.

"What *happened*?" Ava hissed, her heart pounding in her chest. She wasn't close enough to make out the details, but

Mitch wasn't moving—at all. He was dangerously still, and the look on Owen's face was concerning. "Is he alive?"

Owen was silent a moment. She could see him with his first two fingers still tucked up under the man's chin, checking for a pulse. Then, still not saying anything, he gave a clipped shake of his wavy head. His face was grim.

"Are you *kidding* me, Owen?" Ava moaned, feeling weak at the knees. It had barely been three months since the last time someone in town had died, but at least *that* time, she hadn't had to be the one to stumble across the body.

"Yeah, I'm definitely kidding," Owen said, the sarcasm in his voice biting. "He's just conked out for a nap."

"Stop," Ava said, her voice weak. She looked down at the chili that was now soaking into the carpet around her feet.

Owen whipped his phone out, punched 911. "Yeah, hey. Owen O'Kelly. I'm up at the stadium, up in the press box, and we've got someone unresponsive—I mean, dead." He paused for a moment, listening, and Ava could only hear the faint buzz of the 911 operator on the other end of the line. Then Owen said, "Yeah. I did that. And I'm sure—unfortunately." He hung up.

"They're coming right out." Owen shoved his phone back into the pocket of his jeans. "Shut the door—so no one else walks in and has to see this."

Dazed, Ava pushed the door shut. She felt guilty for thinking it, but being in a closed room with a corpse was an eerie feeling. Scarier still, and something she could hardly allow herself to think of, was the question of *what* had happened to Mitch. *Joel's been listening to his commentary all night, for goodness' sake!*

Owen stepped around Mitch's lifeless body and bent to pick

up the now empty cardboard dishes Ava had dropped, doing his best to scoop up the splattered chili and Fritos with the edge of the paper bowl. His face was solemn, worried, and Ava couldn't stand the silence between them.

"Did he have, like, a heart attack?" Ava asked, more to break the silence than anything.

Her gaze moved to Mitch's lifeless body. Sprawled out across the carpet on his back, his legs were bent at awkward angles, his hands hooked into little claws now resting near his chest. Although his eyes were open and glassy, his brow smooth and unstrained, the tight, pursed hold of Mitch's unmoving lips gave him the appearance of someone who'd been under great strain in his final moments. But aside from the utter stillness of Mitch's body, there was no apparent cause of death.

"I dunno," Owen said. He shoved the paper dishes into the trash, then moved to the windows and looked down over the crowd, still milling around. "But when I checked his pulse, his neck looked... I dunno, kind of weird. Like, it had weird marks."

Ava's throat closed. She glanced back at Mitch's body, lying there on the floor, and then back at Owen. "Like, he was stran-gled? Like, somebody killed him?"

"Ava, I don't *know*," Owen said, blowing out his breath in exasperation. He drummed his callused fingers on the top of the desk, clearly wishing they could leave, go sit back in the bleachers, and go back to their night. But they both knew they couldn't—they'd found a body. They'd have to stay there until the police showed up—and Ava was already dreading the look on Chief Greathouse's face when he saw she and Owen were tied up in yet another death.

Just then, the doorknob rattled, and the door swung inward.

"Ava?" Rose's dainty head poked around the side of the door.

Her dark eyes landed on Owen and Ava, standing together at the front of the press box, and her expression turned mischievous. "Looks like I walked in on something. And here I thought something had happened. I should've known better than to use Find My Friends on two lovebirds when they're gone for more than ten—"

Suddenly, Rose froze. Her eyes darted to the other side of the room, where they stopped. "What the *hell*, you guys!"

Owen groaned, and Ava rushed forward to yank Rose into the room, slamming the door shut behind her. "He was like this when we got here. Greathouse is on his way."

Rose looked frantically around the room, her round eyes wide. "Is he okay? Should we be doing something? I—I took CPR when I was a lifeguard—"

"He's dead," Ava said flatly, wishing Rose hadn't come up there. It would be bad enough having to explain things to Greathouse. But weren't there other announcers who would be coming back? Eventually, more people were going to come flooding into the press box. There was no getting around it— halftime wouldn't last forever.

"Dead?!" Rose shrieked, backing up into one of the filing cabinets. She looked with terror at Mitch's body. "But how?"

"We don't know," Owen said grimly. "It looks suspicious, though, if you ask me. And the fact that none of the other announcers or commentators have shown up yet..."

God. Ava hadn't even thought of that. Where *were* the other announcers, anyway? Had some sort of argument broken out during halftime? Had one of the other commentators lost control and taken off?

More voices sounded beyond the door.

"Excuse me," a man's voice said as the sound of boots

tromping up the outside steps filled the press box. "What do you *mean* someone is unresponsive? I was just up here twenty minutes ago, and I can assure you everything is perfectly f—"

Someone opened the door, cutting off the voice. A man Ava didn't recognize stood in the doorway, hand still on the doorknob. Over the man's shoulder, Ava could see Chief Matt Greathouse, his mustache wagging as he all but shoved the man back out of the way and burst through the door. The chief's gaze fell first on Mitch Fangman, taking in the grim scene, and then on Ava, Owen, and Rose. He heaved a sigh. Then he knelt down next to the body and held two fingers to the side of Mitch's neck. Releasing his pressure, he fixed his gaze on Mitch's neck.

"Mitch!" The man Ava didn't recognize lunged forward with the same look of frozen shock that Rose had just worn two minutes earlier. Greathouse stood and held him back. She wondered if this was the other commentator. "What's going on?!"

"We got up here about ten minutes ago, Chief, and this is how we found him," Owen explained, looking down at Mitch's body. Ava now noticed the marks that Owen had mentioned on the dead man's neck.

"What are *you* two doing up here?"

"We found this senior pass," Ava said. "It was on the steps leading up to the press box, so we thought we'd drop it off with the guys up here to return it to its owner."

"And what were you doing before that?"

Ava shrugged, trying hard not to look at the man lying lifeless on the floor. "We were getting concessions. Rose was in the stands, and she came looking for us."

Greathouse looked between Ava and Owen. "You and O'Kelly were together the entire time?"

"Yeah. He stepped out of line for a phone call but—"

Owen's gaze jerked to Ava's. "Only for a second. And he means here, in the press box."

Ava nodded, "Oh, right, we've been together since we found him."

Greathouse turned sharply to the man Ava now realized must be Fred Sutton. "What time did you leave the press box?"

Fred glanced at his watch, his expression frantic. "I don't know—right after the quarter ended. I was already out back when I heard Mitch announce the marching band."

"What were you doing out back?" Greathouse pulled a tiny notepad out of his back pocket and flipped it open. His mustache wagged as he scribbled something.

"Seriously, Matt?" Fred looked startled.

"Protocol," Greathouse replied, sighing. His shoulders heaved. The promise of an evening spent watching the football game had dissipated.

Fred sighed. He looked around the room, as though another glance might clear up some of his confusion. "I was taking a smoke break. Sometimes I wait for Mitch, but this time I went out there ahead of him."

"So, when you left the room, it was just Mitch still here, right?"

Fred shrugged, but nodded. "Yeah. Just a normal night."

"Did Mitch seem upset about anything?"

"Other than the way the game was headed?" Fred ventured a laugh, but no one returned it. Everyone stared wide-eyed back at him, waiting to get his side of the story. "No, he seemed fine! If something was bothering him, he sure didn't say."

"Hmm." Greathouse grunted in reply, getting to his feet. "Well, we'll have to get the coroner in here, but I'd say it looks like Mitch met with foul play."

"Wait," Fred said, holding a hand up to stop the chief. "Hold up. You don't mean…"

"That's exactly what I mean," Greathouse said. "You see those marks on his neck? And the unplugged microphone over there?" He nodded in the direction of the desk. "I'd say Mitch was strangled, and that cord right there's the murder weapon."

Although Owen had already voiced his concerns over the manner of Mitch's death, neither he nor Ava had noticed the microphone. As Ava glanced at Owen, a cold wave of fear flooded through her. Somehow, seeing the tool that had likely strangled Mitch to death made the whole thing seem more sinister.

"Say," Greathouse said, his eyes looking suddenly thoughtful. He stroked his mustache, moved his gaze to Ava. "Officer Harding said Mitch got into it with some city slicker at the pep rally today. He said he thought the guy might've been your ex, Ms. Goldberg—from some of the whispers he heard around town."

Ava swallowed hard. Her throat felt tight, the air in the room exceedingly hot. When she spoke, her voice was feeble. "Chief, you don't think *Noah*—"

"I don't know what I think," Greathouse cut in. "Do you know where your ex, this Noah, is tonight?"

From the corner of her eye, Ava saw Owen glance at her. She kept her eyes on Greathouse, clearing her throat. The silence in the room was deafening as the others waited for her to speak.

"Yes," Ava said. "Noah's here. He's at the game."

"Hmm." Greathouse stroked his mustache.

Beside her, Ava felt Rose grab her hand and squeeze. The gesture was comforting, but only mildly so. There was no way Noah could've killed someone—was there? And over something as stupid as spilling a drink? Or spitting a mouthful of Snickers?

"What about Chantelle? Mitch's girlfriend?" Fred asked, giving Greathouse a pointed look. "Anyone know where she is?"

Greathouse shook his head. "I don't think there's any way she could've done this. Even if she'd used the microphone cord to strangle him, there's no way she could've overpowered him enough to even get to that point. Mitch was a fairly big guy. I don't think *any* woman could've done this."

They were silent a moment, all staring at each other as they processed what might be fact or just a bias about a woman's strength.

"Well," Greathouse said, flipping his memo pad closed. "I'd better let the coaches know what's happened—and I'll be looking into all possible leads, of course." He adjusted his belt and hiked up his pants, which were now sagging from having knelt down. He looked sternly at the others in the room, then pointed a finger to let them know he meant business. "I'll be in charge of letting the family know about the death, so you all better keep your traps shut. Understood? And I'll be contacting you all later for questioning."

They all four nodded, but Ava wasn't sure how they'd be able to dodge the questions. The second half of the game would be called off, and the crowd in the stands—both Shiloh *and* Emberville fans—would be left to fear the worst. News moved fast in Shiloh—there'd be no hope of containing the news of a murder.

6

The stadium was a frenzy of questions, of people all talking over each other, desperate to find out what mysterious occurrence had caused them to call off the game. An ambulance had arrived, with EMTs swarming the place, and by the time Ava, Owen, and Rose had convinced Joel and Mr. Goldberg that they needed to leave, a small crowd had formed at the foot of the press box stairs.

"Ava!"

A familiar voice cut through the chaos, and Ava tore her gaze away from the spectacle. Noah was hurrying toward her, shimmying through the throng of people still milling anxiously near the ticket booth, many looking for refunds that would never happen. His face was dark, shadowed with worry.

"Ava, are you okay? What's going on?"

"I'm fine," Ava said, her voice weak. She could feel Rose and Owen staring at her, and she knew what they were thinking. But she couldn't address that—not now—or she'd break down into pieces. If Noah turned out to be a suspect, let Greathouse break the news.

"We can't say much about what's going on," Owen said, taking over. "But it's probably best we all get out of here."

Noah turned his gaze to Owen. He studied the taller man for a moment, dark eyes snapping. "That so? Well, I guess I'll get going then. Ava, Mike—see you tomorrow."

Ava's dad murmured his agreement, tossing Noah a quick wave as the man turned and disappeared into the crowd.

Ava, Owen, Mr. Goldberg, and the Robinsons made their way out the gates, breaking out of the crowd onto a quiet street.

"Okay," Joel said, his tone impatient. He turned to Owen and Ava as they walked. "What happened? Last I knew, you two were off getting snacks. Next thing, the game's off and we're all being hustled out of the stadium!"

"One second," Owen said, keeping up his brisk walk. "We'll tell you when we're further down the street—but you can't say anything to anyone yet, okay? Not until Greathouse informs the family."

"Informs the family?!" Joel looked aghast.

"I hope you two didn't have anything to do with this," Mr. Goldberg remarked, casting a playful, yet still somewhat suspicious glance at Ava and Owen as his long, lanky legs strode down the sidewalk. He pulled his jacket tighter around him.

"Ha." Ava was glad for her father trying to lighten the mood, but it hit a bit too close as this was the second murder she'd gotten tied up in since moving to Shiloh four months earlier.

As they reached the end of the block next to where their cars were parked, Owen slowed. A wisp of his tousled hair rustled in the evening breeze.

"We found Mitch Fangman dead in the press box," he said, his eyes solemn in the glow of the street lamps.

Mr. Goldberg sucked in his breath. Joel's face went stony. *At least*, Ava thought grimly to herself, *this time Joel has an alibi.* The last time someone was murdered in Shiloh it was Joel who'd fallen under suspicion.

"Mitch Fangman," Mr. Goldberg said, eyes narrowing in thought. "Isn't that the guy Noah had the argument with this afternoon?"

"Yes," Ava said curtly. She shot her dad a look. She couldn't let herself think about *that* yet.

"Well, what happened?" Rose asked. Her gaze flicked back toward the direction they'd come, as though wishing she could peer through the darkness. "Why were you even up there—in the press box, I mean? You were supposed to be getting snacks."

Ava shifted on her heels. "We were coming back from the concession stand, and I saw something on the press box stairs. It turned out someone lost some kind of ID, so we were just going to return it to the guys inside. And then there was Mitch —in the middle of the floor, not moving. Apparently strangled."

Joel let out a low whistle. He shook his head. "Man, that's *rough*. I wondered when he didn't come back on the air after the dance team finished performing."

"So he did announce the dance team?" Ava asked. "If he announced the dance team, but didn't come back on the air after..."

Owen caught her drift, continuing the thought. "Then it means he must've been killed while the dance team was performing."

"Well, where were the others?" Mr. Goldberg asked. "Isn't there another guy up there, the one who announces plays over the loudspeaker?"

Ava shrugged. "He told Greathouse he was on a smoke break. I don't know the guy, but he seemed pretty shocked when he opened the door and saw Mitch was dead."

"Fred Sutton," Owen supplied. "He smokes like a chimney, so that part of his story I believe for sure. I can't imagine him *killing* anyone, but then again, I couldn't fathom last July when—"

"Stop." Ava held up a hand. Owen had been about to bring up Audrey Wilson's murder, with whose killer Ava herself had had a close call. Months had passed since that night, but the event was still triggering—especially considering current circumstances. "I don't want to talk about that. One murder at a time."

Owen nodded. He pulled his key fob out of his pocket and unlocked his pickup. The headlights blinked in the darkness. "I guess we'd better be getting on home. I'm sure we'll hear more tomorrow. Greathouse said he'll want us to answer some more questions, Ava, so be prepared."

"That poor man's family," Mr. Goldberg mused.

"And the kids," Joel added. "I mean—these high schoolers have been waiting all semester for their homecoming weekend, and now to have it ruined..."

"Do you think they'll still have the dance?" Ava asked, thinking of Riley.

"I would think so," Rose said. "I mean, it happened at the football game, but it doesn't really involve the kids or the school. They'll probably try to keep things as normal as possible for the kids."

"Gosh, I wish we hadn't been the ones to walk in on that," Ava moaned, unlocking her car and starting toward it. She was vaguely aware of Owen's hand on her back before it fell away.

"No kidding," Owen agreed. "Two murders is too much for a lifetime—let alone within three months. At least this time we all have alibis."

A murmur of agreement went through the group. A brief memory of Owen having disappeared to answer a call before they left for the concession stand popped through Ava's mind, but she pushed it down. He had only been gone a few minutes, and surely he'd seen other people who could vouch for him if it came to it. They had nothing to worry about.

"Alright," Joel said, stretching. "We parked at Rose's mom's house, so we're going to keep walking. But we can't break the news to Rose's mom since Greathouse said not to say anything yet. We'll just say the game was cancelled for an unknown reason."

Rose grimaced. It was clear she agreed. "See you soon."

Owen, too, excused himself for the evening and bounded across the street to his pickup. Ava watched as he stepped up inside the cab, slammed the door, and gave her a two-fingered wave over the steering wheel. Although he couldn't see her in the dark, she smiled back. As she and her father got into her tiny sedan, neither speaking as they listened to the rumble of the engine start up, she knew he was thinking what she was thinking: Sara Goldberg would needle them about their early arrival home, and once they gave in and told her the reason...

Well, she was going to come unglued.

7

———

"What do you *mean* someone died?" Sara Goldberg's voice was sharp. She took three mugs down from the cupboard, closing the door with an icy precision that was scarier than if she had slammed it. She looked at her husband and daughter across the counter, waiting.

"That someone died," Mr. Goldberg repeated calmly. It was clear he'd broken bad news to his wife before. "The game broke for halftime, and one of the commentators was found dead before the third quarter started. I guess someone went in there during the break and, well..." He gave a sad, helpless shrug of his shoulders that said: *What are you gonna do?*

Mrs. Goldberg looked sharply at Ava. "And what do *you* know about it?"

"What do you mean?" Ava swallowed. They'd decided on the ride to try to frame it as though news of the murder was common knowledge to everyone at the game, but her mother had seen right through it.

Mrs. Goldberg scoffed. "Well, I remember that Greathouse guy—he may be inept, but I'd be shocked if he's going around sharing that specific of information with the public yet."

Ava and her father shared a look. Ava sighed.

"Alright. *Yes*, I happened to be there when the body was found, but I promise that this time—"

"I *knew* it," Mrs. Goldberg shrieked, clanging the end of her sugar spoon against the sink. She set the spoon in the sink and took a sip of her tea, glaring at Ava from over the rim of her cup. "And let me guess—that bearded lumberjack with the boots and grease-stained jeans was there, too?"

Mr. Goldberg looked confused, but Ava knew without a doubt that her mother was referring to Owen. Although she'd tried to downplay their friendship, her mother wasn't dumb. She'd been watching.

"Okay, *first* of all," Ava said, her tone snide. "He's not a lumberjack. He owns a hardware store, and he doesn't even have a beard." Recognition had now dawned on Mr. Goldberg's face. "Secondly, he happened to be there too—as was Rose, for that matter—but this has nothing to do with any of us. Okay? Not a single *thing*."

Mrs. Goldberg sniffed. "I knew that man was bad news, Ava. I would have warned you, but you're always griping on me about meddling in your life, and this time I thought, 'No, I'll just let her take care of herself', and now—"

"Whoa, there," Mr. Goldberg said, holding up his hands to stop his wife before she dug herself any deeper. "Let's all just take a breath now. This is a tragic incident that we've been tied up with by chance, and I'm sure the police have everything under control."

"I doubt it," Ava and Mrs. Goldberg muttered in unison, then scowled at one another from across the kitchen counter.

Mr. Goldberg sighed. He smoothed the top of his wiry hair, then fiddled with his glasses. He wiped the lenses with the corner of his shirt, which had somehow come untucked throughout the course of the night. "Well, regardless, there's nothing we can do about it tonight. Why don't we all just take a breather, hit the hay early? Things will be clearer in the morning."

Ava knew her father was right. No amount of arguing, accusatory comments, or defense tactics would change what had happened. Mitch Fangman was dead. She'd seen him with her own eyes, lying there on the thin carpet of the press box, empty eyes staring up toward the ceiling. Tomorrow, she and Owen would meet with Greathouse. They'd give him their story, tell him what they'd seen, and go on their merry way.

And Noah? There was no denying that his altercation with Mitch at the pep rally looked bad, but Ava was sure that once Greathouse started his investigation, Noah's polo-clad friend would vouch for his presence. Easy peasy. It was terrible about Mitch, but she hadn't even known the guy.

"Where's Riley?" Mr. Goldberg asked, glancing around the kitchen.

"She's at the parking lot."

"What, like stranded there?" Mr. Goldberg asked, perplexed.

Ava gave a tight laugh. "No, the kids all hang out there after the games. Or so I've heard." Having Riley live with her had been a learning experience for Ava, but she felt they had a good relationship. She trusted Riley to be smart as she came out of her shell and started having friends for likely the first time in her young life.

Mrs. Goldberg clucked her tongue, leaned back against the

dishwasher. "I'm glad you know what it's like raising teenagers now. I just wish we'd gotten a baby along the way somewhere."

"Wow, okay. That is *not* what I need right now," Ava said, her voice weary. She didn't have the strength tonight to fight with her mother about her perceived shortcomings as an adult.

There was a soft rap at the door. Ava and her parents glanced up, looking at each other.

"Never mind," Ava said, crossing the kitchen to open the door. "Riley must've gotten a ride home—"

She stopped. It was Noah who stood outside on the doorstep.

"Hey," he said. "Can I come in?"

Ava regarded him a moment, then moved aside, giving an exaggerated, sarcastic sweep of her arm toward the kitchen. "Make yourself at home. Oh, wait—you already have."

"Very funny," Noah shot back. Still, he stepped into the kitchen. "Do you all have any idea yet what's going on? My buddy Ray said—"

"Mitch Fangman's dead," Ava blurted out.

Noah stared at her. "I'm sorry—come again?"

"One of the commentators—the one you got in the fight with. We found him dead in the press box."

Yes, she knew she wasn't supposed to be spreading the news of Mitch's death around—but, at this point, did it really matter? This was *Shiloh*. The whole town was sure to have heard in the next half hour. Besides, Ava knew her mother could never keep such news a secret from her ex-son-in-law. May as well get it over with.

"Oh, *Noah*," Mrs. Goldberg yelped, sinking onto a bar stool. "*You* were there, too? Ava didn't mention—"

"I didn't mention it because I didn't want you to *worry*," Ava said with an exasperated groan.

"I'm already worried!"

"Well, you'd have been *more* worried if I'd told you that the chief of police thinks Noah might've killed Mitch!" Ava exploded, the tension of the evening finally snapping inside her.

The room went dead silent, all eyes on her.

Noah's face had gone pale. "Wait—what? They think I killed Mitch?"

Ava didn't know if she could believe his surprised reaction or not. She'd believed his lies before and look what that had gotten her. "I mean, you *are* the guy who just got into a fight with Mitch, like, six hours ago, and now he turns up dead—and you *were* in the vicinity."

"Oh, that's just ridiculous," Mrs. Goldberg said, waving a hand as though that settled the matter. "Noah wouldn't kill anyone."

Ava's face was grim. "Well, *somebody* killed Mitch Fangman."

"Maybe that's true," Noah acknowledged. "But that someone was not me. That'll be clear if the Shiloh police question me. Everything's going to be fine."

"Yes," Mrs. Goldberg said with a nod. "I'm sure it will be— and we'll all go into *yontef* with clear heads and happy hearts."

"Absolutely," Mr. Goldberg said, punctuating his wife's sentiment with an emphatic nod.

Casting a weary smile around the room, Noah moved toward the door. "Well, I guess I'll be heading back to Omaha. I just wanted to make sure you all were okay. What time should I plan to be here tomorrow for dinner? Should I come early to—"

"No, we won't need any help," Ava said, jumping in before her mother had the chance to offer. "Dad's making brisket, Mom's in charge of the sides, and I'm headed to the orchard in the morning to pick our apples for dessert. Please don't come before seven."

Clearly ready to argue, Mrs. Goldberg snorted, but Noah only shook his head, a small smile on his lips. "Sounds good."

Ava opened the door, gesturing him outside ahead of her.

"Hang on a sec," Noah said, pressing a hand to the door to keep Ava from closing it behind him. He leaned in, his voice low. "I didn't want to say this in front of your mom, but... Ray says that friend of yours—the baker—owns the hardware store in town. Ray's also on the zoning board and said there are rumors your friend was set to face competition soon."

Ava scoffed. "Competition? What are you talking about?"

"Mitch Fangman." Noah met her gaze, and even in the darkness, she could read the concern on his face. "Ray says Mitch Fangman put in the paperwork to open an ACE downtown. He told me after the pep rally."

Something in Ava's stomach clenched. She pushed it down, fighting to keep her face smooth, unperturbed. "Okay. Thanks for the information."

Noah let his hand fall from the door. As he moved to make his way down the sidewalk, he turned once more. "I'm not making any accusations, Ava, but if you think I'm the only one with a motive, you'd better think again."

The next morning, Noah's words still echoed in Ava's mind. All night long, she'd tossed and turned, her brain spinning, trying to tamp down the tendrils of doubt that had crept in.

What did *Noah* know about the goings on in Shiloh, anyway? His friend was most likely mistaken, and besides, even if it *was* true that Mitch had been planning to open his own hardware store downtown, that was hardly a motive to *kill* someone. Greathouse would understand that. Still, Ava knew she wouldn't be able to wait until Owen picked her up for the apple orchard to talk to him about what Noah had told her.

Throwing on a slouchy maroon t-shirt, Ava grabbed her favorite pair of suede ankle boots from the closet and hustled to the kitchen to put on a pot of coffee. Sara Goldberg was already there, seated at the table with a cup in hand. Mrs. Goldberg looked up as her daughter entered the room.

"Oh, there you are," Mrs. Goldberg said. She took a sip of her coffee. "Your father's not up and around yet, but we thought we might venture into Omaha for services before coming home to cook this afternoon.”

“Services?” Ava slid a filled coffee filter into her Mr. Coffee and flipped the switch. “Rosh Hashanah’s not til tomorrow night.”

Mrs. Goldberg gave a little cough. “*Shabbat* services, Ava. It’s bad enough I have to do my Rosh Hashanah cooking this year while it’s still technically Shabbat, so the least I can do is show up at temple.”

“Oh, right,” Ava said. In truth, she’d forgotten it was Shabbat—her mind was too tied up in what had happened last night to think about much else. “Okay, sounds good.”

For a moment, there was only the sound of the gurgling coffee pot and the gentle tapping of Mrs. Goldberg’s nails on the table. She seemed to be waiting for something.

“You’ll be joining us, right?” Mrs. Goldberg asked.

There it is. From the too light tone of her mother’s voice, Ava knew the question was one that, for her mother, had only one acceptable answer. Ava drew in a breath, praying for calm. She didn’t need an argument with her mother on top of everything else.

“Well, as nice as it sounds,” Ava began, pouring a stream of silky coffee into her travel mug. “I think I’ll have to miss out this time. Like I mentioned last night, I’m going to the apple orchard this morning—”

“Don’t you think the apple orchard can wait until early afternoon?”

“No,” Ava said flatly. She snapped on the lid of her mug. “I don’t. The apples are for a dessert tonight. I’ll go for Rosh Hashanah, though—promise.”

Mrs. Goldberg's eyes narrowed, but she said nothing. She took another sip of her tea.

"Anyway," Ava continued, pulling on her boots and slinging her purse over her shoulder. "I'm headed out. You can keep the coffee pot on for Dad and Riley—there's plenty. Good Shabbos."

With that, Ava pulled the front door shut behind her, strode down the sidewalk, and took off toward Shiloh on her bicycle. She couldn't remember when exactly she'd stopped regularly attending synagogue services, but it had been *way* before moving to Shiloh. In the depths of her divorce depression in Chicago, she'd become rather anti-social and anti-just-about-everything. Moving to Shiloh had been like a new lease on life. Now, truth be told, she felt a little guilty about missing services, but if she couldn't even find the motivation to make it to services when she'd needed it most and when the *shul* was right down the street in Chicago, she definitely wasn't going to drive forty-five minutes to Omaha. Besides, after Zaidy Mel died, religion had turned stale. She just chose not to think about it.

Ava slowed to a stop outside Owen's store. Although she wasn't to meet Owen until nine o'clock, she knew he usually got to his store early on Saturdays to get things in order before one of his employees showed up to take over. Before she'd gone to bed the night before, she'd debated sending Owen a text, asking him outright whether what Noah had told her was true. But tone was hard to convey over text, and she wasn't sure how Owen would react to knowing his name had come up in a conversation she'd had with her ex-husband, so in the end she had decided against it. Better to wait and speak to him about it in person.

Looping her bike lock around a nearby rack, Ava gave herself a quick glance in the reflection of the next-door shop window. She smoothed her long, windswept hair. *Eh. That's as good as it's gonna get.* It wasn't as though Owen's hair ever looked very polished. She set her hand on the doorknob and stopped. Through the front shop window, she could see Owen standing behind the counter, back leaned up against the wall and arms crossed over his broad chest. *Is that...?*

Ava's stomach clenched, but she didn't have to look twice to know she'd seen right the first time. Chief Greathouse stood inside scribbling something on a small notepad as his gigantic mustache twitched above pursed lips. Although she hadn't yet opened the door, he sensed her presence and looked up, his hand paused mid-scribble. Owen looked up, too, and Ava could have sworn his face fell. He looked to Greathouse, who sighed, then waved Ava in with a beefy hand.

"Morning, Ava," Greathouse nodded to her, his voice clipped. He clearly wasn't thrilled she'd dropped by.

"Hi," Ava said.

She stood in the middle of the shop, glancing between Owen and Greathouse, waiting for one of them to explain to her what was going on. After all, she and Owen had stumbled across Mitch's body together—if Greathouse had asked Owen to meet this morning to get a statement, wouldn't he have also contacted Ava? The moment of silence seemed to drag on forever, and Ava, whose brain couldn't stop shouting the words Noah had said the night before, felt her stomach turn over.

Owen looked to Greathouse, who clicked his pen closed. Then, dropping the pen into the pocket on the front of his shirt, Greathouse cleared his throat, addressing her. "You already know Mitch Fangman was murdered last night. I'm gathering more details, and since you mentioned there was a period of time when Owen left your presence last night—"

"Uh—to take a phone call, yeah," Ava cut in, alarmed. She didn't like where this was going.

"Right," Greathouse said, nodding. She got the feeling he was placating her. "To take a phone call. Anyway, since there *was* that brief period of time for which his presence can't be vouched, I had to come talk to him about it. Especially in light of other circumstances."

Ava was indignant. "Are you kidding me? Lots of people wandered around during halftime without companions to vouch for their every minute. So, what, he leaves to take a phone call, and you think he *faked* it to go upstairs and murder the commentator? And anyway, *what* other circumstances?"

"Ava, he's just doing his job," Owen said, his tone warning her to quit while she was ahead. "He's right to be examining all leads."

"That's what he said this summer," Ava retorted. "Only that time it was Joel Robinson under suspicion. Who's going to be next? Me?"

Greathouse clucked his tongue. "Slow down, little lady. Listen to your boyfriend on this one."

Ava was on the verge of reminding Greathouse that Owen was *not* her boyfriend but figured that argument wouldn't win her any points with anyone in the room.

"Anyway, it's fine," Owen continued, arranging things idly on the desk behind the counter. "I showed proof of the phone call, and the person who called me will vouch for me that I was on the line the entire time."

"Okay." Ava studied his face, trying to piece together why on earth he looked so solemn. "Who *did* call you, anyway?"

Greathouse glanced at Owen, one silver eyebrow raised. Owen rubbed the back of his neck. His eyes flitted up to the ceiling. "I'd rather not talk about that right now, Ava."

Something in her gut clenched, but she took care not to show it in her face. *Surely it wasn't a girl... right?* Then again, she was the one taking great pains not to define their relationship. It would serve her right if Owen had finally had enough. Still, her eyes narrowed as she studied him. "Why not?"

"Because it's stressful, and I don't want to get into it." Owen's voice was firm, his jaw set. When his green eyes sparked like that, she knew there was no changing his mind.

She sighed. "Fine. You're off the hook. *For now*."

Owen snorted. He didn't look happy. "Yeah, whatever."

"Well, speaking of phone calls," Greathouse said, stroking his mustache. "There was no sign of Mitch's phone at the crime scene, and we couldn't find it at his house, either. Did either of you see a phone inside the press box when you discovered the body last night? Or, for that matter, did you happen to think of anything else out of the ordinary you might've seen? Anyone behaving suspiciously? Anyone lurking near the stairs to the press box who maybe shouldn't have been there?"

Owen shook his head. "I only know what I told you, chief."

Ava shrugged. "I don't know, either. There were a lot of people around—any number of them could have been hanging out by the stairs, and I wouldn't have thought anything of it." She thought back to the touch of Owen's palm on her back as he guided her into the concessions line; her mind hadn't exactly been on her surroundings. "Was Chantelle Svoboda in the press box at all last night?"

"I told you—there's no way it was a woman. But no, she didn't say anything about it when I spoke with her again this morning to see how she was holding up." Greathouse grunted, shaking his head and snapping his memo pad closed. He stuffed it into his shirt pocket alongside the pen. He turned back to Owen. "Anyway, I'm going to need to speak to—" Here, he glanced at Ava. "—the person who called you last night. Can you give me that number?"

"Sure." Owen took a moment to scroll through his phone, then passed it to Greathouse, who took a screenshot of the contact and passed the phone back.

"I sure do hope this person can vouch for you," Greathouse remarked, giving his head another shake. "It has unfortunately occurred to me that perhaps you 'stumbled' across Mitch's body on purpose—to give yourself an excuse if we found your fingerprints inside the press box. It doesn't look great that you knew about the ACE branch going in on Main Street—you know what I mean?"

Ava jolted awake. *The ACE branch...?* Was what Noah had said true?

"I know what you mean," Owen said, pressing his lips together. "But the part about the fingerprints is ludicrous. You know me, Matt. You know that even if Mitch had come in here and thrown a torch inside this store, I'd *never* have—"

"Yeah, yeah, yeah," Greathouse said, waving a stubby hand. "I knew Joel Robinson, too, when all the signs pointed to him murdering Audrey last July. But it doesn't change the facts of the case."

"Well, one fact is that my contact will vouch for me," Owen said, nodding his chin toward Greathouse's phone. "You call and see."

Greathouse only grunted in reply. He moved toward the door. "Alright, I'll leave you two lovebirds alone."

Ava bristled at the inference but murmured a goodbye as the chief tromped out the door and made his lumbering way down the sidewalk. She turned to Owen, ready to speak, but he beat her to it.

"You weren't supposed to be here until nine."

"Well—surprise," Ava said, shrugging off the rebuff. "I'm here. And we need to talk."

Owen sighed, ran a hand through his hair. "Alright. Where do we start?"

"Well, first off, what's this about an ACE branch? Noah showed up at my house last night claiming you knew about—"

Owen's face darkened. "Oh, *Noah* told you, huh?"

"Is it true?"

"It is, but—"

"Okay, and you were going to mention this to me *when*?" Ava was indignant.

Owen threw his hands up. "It had zero to do with you!"

She blinked. He'd seldom discussed his business with her, and it wasn't like they were married—so he was right. "Fair enough," Ava finally said. She drew a breath, and they were both quiet a moment. Then, she said, "But now Mitch is dead. And Greathouse seems to think you had a motive."

Owen waved a hand. "My so-called absence in the concessions line will be vouched for."

"Are you *sure*?" Ava narrowed her eyes at Owen. She knew better than to ask again so soon who his mysterious phone call had come from. Just like him not telling her about the ACE situation, it really wasn't her business if he had other relationships.

"I'm sure," Owen said.

"Okay, well—what do we *do*? I found that golden pass on

the stairs leading up to the press box. I wonder if they could tell who—"

The funky bass line of the Seinfeld theme rang out in the silence of the shop. Extracting her phone from her pocket, Ava glanced at the screen, fully intending to ignore any guilt trippy texts from her mother. Instead, she frowned.

"It's Noah."

Owen sighed, gazing up at the ceiling. "Well, you'd better answer it."

Although Noah was the last person she wanted to talk to this morning, he'd only called her twice since their divorce had been finalized. If Noah was calling, it must be for a good reason. Ava swiped to answer the call.

"Hello?"

As she stood with the phone to her ear, listening and humming her monosyllabic responses, Owen watched her. His gaze was dark, questioning, as he listened to the low hum of Noah's voice on the other end of the line.

After a moment, Ava brought the phone away from her ear and jabbed at the screen to end the call. She looked up at Owen, her face drawn.

"Greathouse wants to have a chat with Noah about last night—and apparently *my* cafe is the perfect spot for that conversation."

9

—————

"Can we make this quick?" Ava asked, setting a mug of coffee in front of Chief Greathouse. She sank down at one of the neighboring tables, casting a weary glance at Noah and the chief to her left.

"It'll take how long it takes, Goldberg." Greathouse shot her a look over the rim of his mug.

"It's fine, Ava," Noah said, waving a slim hand.

"Fine for you, maybe, but I have a business to run. Besides, why do I need to be in on this interview, anyway? And why on earth are you doing it here?"

Despite the casual smile on Noah's face, Ava could read the worry behind it. Owen stood near the front bay windows, his back leaned against the wall and arms crossed over his chest. His face was unreadable, and so far, he'd said nothing.

Greathouse continued with a click of his pen. "*You* two—" He jutted a chin first at Owen, then at Ava. "—are here only because Shapiro here said it'd make him more comfortable. And we're *here* because I haven't had my coffee yet this morning."

Ava was about to protest that she wasn't open on Saturdays —it was *Shabbat*, the Chief *knew* that—but the pointed glance he gave her made her think better of it. She could tell Chief Greathouse was not in the mood for any lip today.

Well, what could it hurt? At this point, Ava was pretty sure providing coffee to the under-caffeinated was a mitzvah in its own right. She set to work putting on a pot of dark roast, the preferred drink for both Greathouse and Owen.

Flipping to a blank page in his memo pad, Greathouse settled back in his chair. "Now. Shapiro. You were at the game last night, correct?"

"Correct." Noah swallowed, but his expression remained smooth.

"What were you doing there? You're not from Shiloh."

"Also correct—I'm in town for a conference. A buddy of mine from med school recently moved to Shiloh, and he invited me out to the game."

Greathouse cocked his head. "Who's your friend?"

"Ray Garrison. He lives out at Lake—"

Greathouse waved a hand, cutting Noah off. "I don't know anyone at the lake."

"He's also a pot stirrer, inviting someone to a place he knows his *ex* will be," Ava cut in, pouring some of the now brewed coffee into a mug.

"Quiet over there, Ava," Greathouse said, pointing his pen at her in warning. Then he chuckled, adding, "Although you're not wrong."

Noah looked irritated. "Alright, can we get on with this?"

"Hey, buddy," Greathouse said, lifting his hands. "You're the one who wanted her in here. Anyway—you were at the game with this Ray Garrison. What about during halftime?"

"Well, to be honest, I spent the first few minutes of halftime trying to find where Ava was sitting. I thought we could talk—smooth things over before Rosh Hashanah dinner tomorrow night."

"I'm not even going to ask," Greathouse said, shaking his head. "But go on. Did you find where Ava was sitting?"

"I found her," Noah admitted. His gaze flicked to Ava as she set the Chief's coffee down in front of him, then briefly to Owen before settling back on Greathouse. "But she was with *him*, so I decided to wait for a... more opportune moment. It was pretty chilly last night, and my coat was in the car, so instead I took the opportunity to go out and get it."

Greathouse sipped his steaming coffee. "Do you remember what time that was? And how long you were gone? Did Ray go with you out to the parking lot?"

"No, he didn't. And I can't say for sure what time it was, but I remember the marching band was out on the field when I left. When I came back in, there was some kind of dance just ending."

"And was there anyone still taking tickets when you came back in? Anyone who might've seen you leave or come back?"

Noah grimaced. "I don't know. There were some teenagers supposed to be taking tickets who were just looking at their phones—but I told Ray where I was going."

Greathouse's eyes were boring holes into Noah. "But Ray wasn't actually *with* you, correct?"

Noah held his gaze. "Correct."

"And that argument at the pep rally—what was that about?"

"Nothing. I mean, I bumped into the guy by accident, and some of my drink spilled on him. I apologized, but he just went ballistic."

"Chief," Ava said, swiping the older man's already empty mug for a refill. "With all due respect, this seems like a stretch. Yes, there are a few minutes during which Noah's whereabouts can't be vouched for, but that hardly means he went and *killed* someone during that time."

Greathouse's brow furrowed as he turned to Ava. "Alright, I'll humor you. Let's say you're correct, and Noah went to the parking lot just as he said. The fact still stands that *someone* killed Mitch Fangman. Would you rather I move on to *Owen's* whereabouts for the same time span?"

"No, I—" Ava began, her thought cutting off as quickly as it had started.

"Because as far as I can tell," Greathouse said, nodding between Owen and Noah. "These two are in the same boat. Same location, same period of time unaccounted for—"

"There have to be dozens of others at the game who can't account for their every minute," she jumped in.

"—and both *these two* have a motive."

Ava pressed her lips together, saying no more.

"Oh, come on," Noah broke in. His patience seemed to be wearing thin. "The fact that I got into an argument with this Mitch character gives me a *motive*? What motive exactly?"

Greathouse shrugged his enormous shoulders. "I don't know—to get back at the guy who mocked you in public? Right some kind of perceived wrong? Reassert your manhood to yourself? Take your pick."

"And," Owen's voice drifted from across the room, "maybe if you're lucky, you could make it look like your ex-wife's new guy did it."

Noah gave a dramatic scoff. "Now *that* is ridiculous. If you think I need to—"

"Enough! Give it a rest, you two," Greathouse interrupted, clapping his beefy hands. "This isn't third grade. Mitch Fangman is *dead*, it's my job to find out who killed him, and from where I stand right now, the two of you are my top suspects."

"But Chief," Ava protested, trying her best to avoid both Owen and Noah's gaze, "you can't just *arrest* someone because they happen to be top on your list."

Greathouse grunted as he rose from his chair. He stuffed his memo pad into the back pocket of his sagging pants. "You're right. I've got to keep digging."

On his way out the door, the chief stopped and looked back into the cafe. He heaved a sigh. Then, shooting Owen a pointed look, his eyes almost pained, he said, "Trust me, this kind of case brings me no pleasure—but you can't let a murder go unpunished just because you like someone."

With that, Greathouse was gone. Noah, Owen, and Ava sat in awkward silence, staring out at the street, and then at each other.

Noah cleared his throat. "I guess I'd better get back to Omaha. Thanks for letting us do this here, Ava, rather than down at the station."

Ava nodded, her face drawn. "Sure."

Sliding his empty coffee mug onto the counter, Noah flashed Ava and Owen a weak smile as he gathered up his keys and wallet and stepped out onto the sidewalk.

Cafe Arcana was silent.

"So..." Owen began, his smile hesitant.

"Apple picking?"

Owen blew out a sigh of relief. "Thank the lord—I was half afraid you'd say you couldn't be in a car with a murderer."

Ava flashed him a wry smile as they, too, left the shop, and she locked the door behind them. Things were weird—*too weird*—and what she needed right now was *normal*. She needed a morning with Owen to shake the tension of having Noah come barging back into her world. She needed gravel roads and golden cornfields. She needed crisp, fall air, gentle sunshine, and the promise of apple cider donuts.

But as Ava climbed into the passenger seat of Owen's pickup, Greathouse's words still echoed in her head. *You can't let a murder go unpunished just because you like someone.* She couldn't shake the feeling that, sooner rather than later, she might have to heed that very advice.

10

———

The drive to McPherson's apple orchard was a short one. Ava rolled down the window, watching the tall, rigid lines of corn roll by as Owen drove. The tassels rustled in the early morning fall breeze.

"You know I didn't do it, right?" Owen asked, his green eyes fixed on the road ahead.

"Yeah," Ava said. "I know you didn't—and I don't think Noah did, either."

"Agreed." Owen was quiet a minute. "And for what it's worth, I shouldn't have said that about him—about him getting lucky that it kind of looked like I murdered Mitch. I'm sorry."

Ava sniffed. "Well, you shouldn't have, but you weren't wrong. After all, he knew about Mitch's hardware store before I did. He brought it up when he stopped by last night. That's pretty convenient knowledge to have if you *were* thinking about offing the guy—but I still don't think he was."

"Nah. He may be an egotistical jerk, but he's not a murderer."

Ava smothered a smile. She had to admit it was an appropriate description of her ex-husband. "That being said, do you think Greathouse actually thinks *you* could've killed Mitch?"

Owen's broad shoulders shrugged against his seatbelt. "I don't know. I think he thinks it's a definite possibility—but when it comes down to it, I've got an alibi."

Ava's eyes narrowed. "Which reminds me… Mind telling me who you talked to those several minutes when you disappeared?"

"I'd rather not." Owen's face remained passive, smooth. He didn't so much as glance at her.

"Hmm." Ava leaned her head back against the seat. The more she pushed it, the more stubborn Owen would get. She'd have to figure out a different way to find out who that mysterious call had been from. After a moment, she said, "But regardless, whoever you talked to, they will corroborate it—right?"

"Right."

"So, Greathouse will be off your case then—as soon as he gets a hold of said person?" Ava couldn't help but think of the fiasco a few months prior, where Greathouse had convinced himself Joel murdered Audrey. The last thing she wanted was a repeat of *that*.

"I think so," Owen agreed. He shrugged his broad shoulders, flashed her a quick smile, the hint of a dimple peeking out from his stubbled cheek. Then, turning solemn, he said, "But listen—we can't let Noah take the fall, either."

Ava twisted around in her seat to face him. She didn't like being told what to do where Noah was concerned. "If he did it, we can."

"You just said yourself you don't think he did," Owen pointed out.

"Okay, but Noah can take care of himself. Let him and Ray —or whatever his name is—dig him out of that hole. I'm under no obligation to do him any favors."

"Definitely not," Owen said. "I'm not saying he deserves you. I'm just saying... think about it. Okay?"

"Fine," Ava snapped. She didn't want to admit that Owen had a point. After all, she hadn't wanted Joel Robinson to take the fall for a crime *he* didn't commit. Shouldn't that same sense of justice extend to the man she'd once shared her life with? The man who—like it or not—would be sitting across from her at the Rosh Hashanah dining table tomorrow? *Ugh. Don't remind me.*

Ava's gaze moved back to the window, and she watched the fields again as they drifted by. They were several miles north of town now, and the highway wound peacefully between acreages, farmhouses and barns dotting the vast landscape.

Ava tapped on her phone screen and opened Facebook. These days, the site was full of cheesy chain messages and aunts posting inspirational quotes, but it was still rife with gossip. Ava wasn't sure what it said about her, but she had a habit of opening the app whenever there was a juicy news story and scouring the profiles of the people involved. More often than not, their profiles were public, and any nosy outsider could scroll through to see the posts that filled the person's day-to-day life. Sometimes, these posts were illuminating. Other times, they were sad, full of red flags and warning signs noticed only in hindsight—too late.

"What are you doing?" Owen asked, flicking his eyes from the road to glance at Ava, who leaned against the window as she gazed at her phone.

"Looking at Mitch Fangman's Facebook profile."

"Um... Why? Were you friends with him?"

Ava shrugged. "Just because. And I don't have to be listed as a 'friend'—he has it set to public."

"*Had*. The poor guy's not alive anymore to *have* a Facebook."

"Well, unlike him, his Facebook profile is alive and well," Ava said, casting Owen a wicked grin. She looked back at the screen. "Looks like he was pretty active, too."

Owen raised an eyebrow, kept his eyes on the road as he slowed the truck at a stop sign and turned onto a gravel road. They were almost to the orchard. "What are you looking for?"

"I'm not sure. I just wanted to see what he was like. You know, what kind of stuff he was posting, who he interacted with. Whether he was one of those people who share all the political stuff."

"I highly doubt Mitch Fangman was killed over a difference in politics," Owen said.

"No, no," Ava cut in. "But you'd be surprised what you can learn about a person by scrolling through their wall."

"Wall?" Owen clucked his tongue, and his dimples made a full appearance as he grinned at her across the cab of the truck. "I think you mean feed. It hasn't been called a *wall* in, like, a decade! Come on now, Ava, you're showing your age."

Ava laughed. "Well, you knew what I meant! I'd say that dates you, too. I bet Riley wasn't even *alive* when it was called a Facebook wall."

"Something tells me Riley wouldn't be caught dead with a Facebook account. Facebook's for old people, Ava," Owen said, winking at her.

"Wow, remember when you could poke people?"

"And throw *sheep*? What the heck was that ab—"

"Shh," Ava hissed, cutting Owen off mid-sentence. "Wait."

"What, they brought back the feature?"

"No!" Ava held up a hand, her eyes glued to the screen. In the middle of scrolling Mitch's profile, she'd happened to scroll back to the top, to the most recent post—a selfie, which she noticed was posted only about ten minutes before she and Owen found Mitch dead. She clicked on the photo to make it full-size, studying the caption.

"Let's hear it for some Friday night football," she read aloud, glancing up at Owen as she did so. "Kick some butt, Sharks!"

Owen looked confused. "What are you saying to me?"

Ava jabbed a finger at her phone screen. "Mitch posted a selfie from the press box last night—7:32 PM."

Owen started to peel his eyes from the road, angling his body toward Ava's phone. "Show me."

"Not while you're driving!" Ava flicked a hand indignantly at the steering wheel. "We're almost there. No one's going to take the post down before we park."

"Fine," Owen grumbled.

The truck sped along down the gravel road, bumping over washboards that jostled them back and forth. Ava hated driving on the gravel roads in Shiloh, especially in her tiny little Civic. You never knew when a truck would come roaring over the hill and you'd have to crank the wheel just to get over and out of the way, nearly sliding off the road from the loose gravel—not to mention the rusty, dusty nails that always seemed to end up in your tires. She avoided gravel as much as she could. But Owen was a pro, maneuvering his pickup over the dusty hills like there was nothing easier. Then again, that probably wasn't far from the truth. Owen had grown up in Shiloh, had probably driven a pickup from the age of ten. That was Shiloh for you.

The lush tree lines of the McPherson farm came into view, and Owen pulled the truck into the driveway, continuing down along the lane toward the farmhouse. Although it was early, the gravel lot that served as parking was far from empty. Not only did the McPherson's own the biggest apple orchard in town, but they also crafted a huge, twisty corn maze that Ava had heard some of the kids around town talk about—so the place was busy.

Twisting in his seat, Owen glanced into the rearview mirror and stretched a long arm out to grip the headrest of Ava's seat as he backed the pickup into a spot in the shade.

"You're like my dad," Ava commented. "Backing in, when you could just as easily pull forward."

"Gee, thanks," Owen said, flicking his green eyes at her. "Just what every guy wants to hear."

"Whatever. Look at this," Ava said, shoving her phone, which was still open to Mitch's last Facebook post, into Owen's huge, callused hands.

Owen studied the photo a moment, then nodded, passing the phone back to her. "Yep. Looks like the press box. Pretty eerie, honestly, thinking about how he was going to die, like, ten minutes later. Yikes."

Ava was silent as she took the phone back, looking at the photo once more. It *was* eerie. Suddenly, something caught her eye. She tapped the photo to bring it full size again, then pinched the screen to zoom in.

"What? Is there somebody else in the background?" Owen was leaning closer now, and Ava could feel the warmth of his shoulder against hers.

"Not some*one*," she said, squinting at the screen. "But I

think there *is* some*thing*. Look at that—that cup on the file cabinet in the background."

They both sat for a moment, squinting over Ava's phone. The bright morning sun shone in through the windshield, already hot, and Owen shielded his eyes. "Okay? There's a coffee cup..."

Ava jabbed an impatient finger at the screen. "Yeah, but the lipstick ring on the rim! I don't see Mitch wearing lipstick—and certainly not that deep purple color."

"Oh." Owen craned his neck to look. "*Oh.* Dang, you're right." Owen frowned. "What are you saying? That someone else must have been in the press box that we don't know about?"

"I mean, it makes sense. Wasn't Mitch dating Chantelle Svoboda? Did Greathouse say if she was on the list of people who'd entered the box that night?"

"They were dating, yeah, but I don't think anything was said about Chantelle having been there. Anyway, even if she *was*, and if *she* left the coffee cup there on the cabinet, that doesn't help us much. It makes sense she would've been there— visiting Mitch and all."

Ava pushed open the door of the truck and clicked her seatbelt loose. She sighed, tossing her mane of chestnut hair impatiently. "Right—it's the perfect cover! And it's worth looking into."

Owen slammed the pickup door and strode around to Ava's side of the truck. He leaned a tanned arm against the hood, looking at her incredulously. "You don't actually think Chantelle Svoboda killed Mitch Fangman, do you?"

"Dunno. All I'm saying is, if Chantelle was up there in the

press box last night and didn't come forward to say so, it seems like a red flag. It's fishy."

They walked along the parking lot, gravel crunching underfoot. Owen shoved his hands deep in the pockets of his jeans. "Are you going to bring it up to Greathouse?"

Ava scoffed. "After last year? He'll tell me to stay far away from this one. Besides, he made it pretty clear last night that he didn't think a woman could've done it."

"He has a point," Owen admitted. "I'm not sure a woman—especially someone as small as Chantelle—would've been able to overpower a guy like Mitch Fangman, even with a microphone cord on her side."

Ava sighed. "Maybe. Women can be pretty strong with enough motivation, though. But hey, if I can gather some evidence for a different lead and *then* go to Greathouse with it..."

"You'll get Noah off the hook?"

"And you."

Owen squinted at her for a moment. Then, shaking his head, he placed a firm hand on Ava's back and guided her toward the farmhouse.

The orchard, which was owned, run, and operated by the McPherson family, was already full of visitors, from both Shiloh and other surrounding towns. From the looks of it, lots of folks from Lincoln and Omaha had made their way out here on a day trip out of the city. With hay-stuffed scarecrows propped up all over the place and garlands of silk red and brown leaves strung from the rafters, the farmhouse that served as a lobby of sorts screamed fall—which made sense, given that the farm would host the fall festival this coming week. Several people milled about when they stepped inside.

A middle-aged man in a plaid flannel shirt approached them, a stack of wicker baskets in one arm. He reached out to Owen with a hearty handshake. "Owen! Nice to see you in. Weird day in Shiloh—glad we can give people an activity to take their minds off things for a while."

"Weird day is right," Owen said, grimacing. He gestured to Ava. "Curtis, have you met Ava Goldberg? She owns Cafe Arcana downtown. Ava, this is Curtis McPherson—of the McPherson apple orchard."

Recognition dawned in the man's eyes as he shook Ava's hand, chuckling. "I don't believe we've met, but I've been into your cafe a time or two. I tell you what, you've got some *great* coffee—exactly what this town needed. Seems like the place to maybe meet some nice ladies, too, or so I'm hoping." He gave a little conspiratorial smile.

Ava glanced down. He wasn't wearing a wedding ring. She smiled back, checking off one more box on the list of reasons people might like her shop—a non-intimidating way to meet potential suitors. She'd never envisioned herself making *shidduchim* in Shiloh, but hey—never say never.

"You've got that blue-haired Novak girl working for you, right?"

"Uh, right," Ava said, surprised. Though Riley was a native-born Shiloh resident, she usually kept a low profile around town. "Riley's been working for me since day one. She's amazing. I couldn't keep the place going without her."

Curtis nodded. "Ah, yes. Riley—that's right. One of my nephew's friends was talking about her the other day. I wondered if that's who he meant—guess I was right. You never can tell with these high school kids. One day they're going steady—boyfriend or girlfriend's the bees' knees—and then next thing you know, it's old news. I always tell Chase—that's my nephew, Ava—'Chase, you gotta focus on football. None of this high school stuff's gonna last.'"

"Right..." Ava said, glancing at Owen for help. This guy was a rambler.

Owen caught her eye, the corner of his mouth twitching as he held back a grin. "Yep. Focus is always good. Especially when you're as good a player as—"

"That's what I'm saying!" Curtis interrupted, giving Owen a friendly slap on the arm. "He's got it *made*—but only if he puts in the work, takes things seriously. The other thing I always say—"

Suddenly, Curtis's head gave a violent jerk, and he was cut off mid-sentence by his own sneeze. Ava nearly jumped out of her skin before she realized what was happening.

"Bless you!" Ava said, grasping for her manners.

Curtis waved a hand. He fished a tissue out of his pocket and wiped his nose, his eyes watery. "Thanks. My allergies are always acting up this time of year. I think it's all the dust every-where—from the combines in the fields, these scarecrows we've got strung up around the place." He sniffed. "Could also be you, Owen. Fabric softener'll do it, too."

"Sorry," Owen said, flashing a nervous smile. "We'd prob-ably better get out of your hair."

Curtis waved a hand again in dismissal of the idea but was contradicted by the half-hearted sneeze that followed. He pressed one of the baskets he was holding into Owen's arms. "Here—take this. If you go out these doors here, the Jonagold trees are on your left and the Granny Smith are on your right. Up ahead, you'll see signs for Golden Delicious and Macintosh."

"Great, thanks," Owen said. He clapped Curtis on the shoulder. "Good luck with those allergies!"

Curtis laughed, wiping his nose again as he flicked a hand at Ava and Owen to signal them off. On their way out the door, the chatter of voices from the crowded farmhouse faded behind them. The morning sky was a rich blue, and wispy clouds floated overhead like cotton candy.

"That guy does *not* stop talking," Ava blurted out once they were a safe distance away.

Owen chuckled. "Yeah, he's always like that. My mom said it's gotten worse since his dad died a few weeks ago—I think he just needs people to talk to."

"I guess. Anyway—what kind of apples do we want?"

"Well, I know what *I* want," Owen said. "Jonagold are amazing for baking. I can't speak for you, though—you want them to eat or what?"

"I guess so," Ava said, nearly bounding in her attempt to keep up with Owen. Ava's legs were long, but they were no match for his lanky strides. "We dip them in honey. That's about all I know."

"Ah, so we've got sweet on sweet," Owen mused, flashing her a grin. "You're going to want something crisp then, and maybe even a little sour. Granny Smith might do the trick."

"That's the green kind, right?" Ava came to a halt in front of the sign that said Macintosh. She tugged a branch toward her, inspecting the fruit that hung off of it. "How do we know if they're, you know, *good*?"

Owen strode up behind her, and she felt the solidness of his chest against her back. His fingers brushed hers as he grasped the apple, twisting it from side to side. "Well, you don't see any worms, do you?"

"No..."

"And it doesn't have any mushy spots, or bruises, right?"

"Right..."

Owen snapped the apple off the branch, which flicked backward, leaves rustling. He smiled, tossing the apple into the basket Ava held. "Then it's a good one."

And so they were off, winding through the rows of trees, on the hunt for the most beautiful apples they could find. Around them were parents with small clusters of toddlers clinging to their legs and groups of middle-aged female friends, no doubt getting their fresh air in before heading off for a glass or three of wine with lunch. The grass underfoot was still green, although a lighter shade that was soon to turn to brown in the coming winter months. The first frost was yet to arrive, and although Ava enjoyed sweater weather, she found herself enjoying the morning sunshine on her bare forearms as they walked.

Somewhere between the Jonagold and Granny Smith apples, Owen turned to Ava, his eyes serious and his hands in his jeans pockets. "You know it really sucks, right? That he's in on your family dinner and I'm not?"

Ava tensed. It was the elephant in the room, and although she hadn't wanted to talk about it, she knew she had to. "Trust me, I know. It sucks for me, too. I mean, I doubt you'd like for Becky Phillips to show up at Christmas. I feel the same way now about Noah."

Owen had told her this past summer that his high school sweetheart and ex-fiancée, Becky, had called off their wedding at the last moment. Maybe Ava shouldn't have brought her up, but how else could she make him see how much she *didn't* want Noah around for Rosh Hashanah?

Owen winced. "Right. That'd be awful. But this is kind of different..."

Ava cast a nervous glance toward him, but he wasn't looking at her. His gaze trailed along the toes of his workboots as they stepped through the grass. "How so?"

"Well," Owen began, his gaze moving up to the treetops. His eyes were the same color as the foliage. "If Becky was coming to one of my family's holidays, I'd make sure as hell that you'd be there, too."

"So, you're mad you're not invited."

"I mean, kinda, yeah," Owen said, shrugging. "Not *mad*, though. Frustrated."

"That sounds like something a Jewish mother tells you when she's about to go into full-on guilt trip mode," Ava remarked, hoping to lighten up the conversation a little.

"I'm not trying to guilt trip you, Ava," Owen said, clearly not finding the joke funny. He shook his head. "I wanted to be honest with you. It hurts. I mean, come on—you're adamantly against defining whatever it is we have, and you want to keep it a secret from your parents. And then I find out that your ex-*husband* is—"

"Hold up," Ava said. She stopped, held a palm up. "Is this about Rosh Hashanah or is it about something else?"

"Wow, I really don't appreciate that tone," Owen said, looking surprised. "It *is* about Rosh Hashanah, but that's the surface level. Underneath that, it's about you not being able to make up your mind."

Ava groaned, exasperated. "We already discussed this. I *have* made up my mind. I *do* like you. We *are* a—" Here, she waved a hand as though trying to conjure up the correct word. "—a *thing*. But my mom—"

"Will never be okay with me not being Jewish?" Owen looked at her pointedly.

"That's pretty much it, yeah." Ava forced herself to maintain eye contact, but her face was burning.

"Well, how are you so sure about that? Have you talked to her about it?" Owen's gaze was sharp.

"No, but trust me—I don't have to. I went to prom with this Methodist guy in high school, and that was bad enough."

Owen threw up his hands. "That was high school! You married a Jewish guy. He cheated on you. You got divorced. Doesn't she want you to be happy, even if that means being with a guy who isn't Jewish but treats you well?"

Ava sighed. "I don't know. All I know is that I was *just* managing to win back a little of her respect—you know, with Cafe Arcana doing well. I don't want to jeopardize that."

"Right. You'd rather jeopardize us."

Ouch.

Owen was quiet, and Ava could hear his disappointment as it echoed even through the silence.

She stopped in front of an apple tree, looked up into its rich, emerald foliage. "What do you want me to do?"

"I want to come to Rosh Hashanah dinner, and I want you to be honest with your parents about us."

"God." Ava brushed the hair out of her eyes, wondering if he knew what he was asking. "Anything else?"

"Yeah, one more thing."

"What?"

"I want you to be my girlfriend."

Ava froze. "Your... what?"

Owen gave a soft chuckle. "My girlfriend, Ava. I want you to be my girlfriend."

She'd heard him correctly, of course, but still she stared at him, her pulse quickening. As a hot flush crept into her cheeks, Ava realized her insides were vibrating—whether with excitement or apprehension, she wasn't sure. Probably a mix of both. Because this was what she wanted, wasn't it? To be with Owen?

But still...

She couldn't. *They* couldn't. The situation was too complicated.

Ava's voice quavered as she spoke. "Okay, listen. The first one? Dinner? It'll be awkward, but—done. You've got it. The last two requests, though..."

Owen moved closer to her, placed a callused hand on the back of her head, and stroked her hair. "Come on. It's not just me. You want them to be true, too."

Ava moved away from him, afraid of what she might agree to with the warmth of his solid chest so close to hers. "Okay. Let's say I do wish I didn't feel I had to lie to my parents. Wish I was your ... girlfriend. But don't you think things will go a lot better if we take this slowly, let my parents get used to the idea...?"

"Really? Isn't that a cop-out?" There was a slight hint of a grin on Owen's face.

Ava swallowed. She was suddenly shy, but she forced herself to look him in the eye. "No, I mean it. Let's take it one step at a time. You'll come to Rosh Hashanah dinner tonight—but you'll promise to field any questions. We'll have to warm them up to the idea slowly. We can't just shove them off the deep end."

Owen cocked his head to the side, considering for a moment. Then he nodded. "Fine. Deal."

Ava let out her breath. She hoped he meant it. "They

already know that you helped me this summer with my business and that you're a good friend of mine. We'll say you wanted to learn more about... Jewish holidays."

Owen plucked an apple off the tree nearest them and tossed it into the basket. He looked back at her, his gaze mischievous. "I know how I can win your dad over. I'll learn how to play that horn thing."

Ava wrinkled her nose but laughed, anyway. "You may win him over with that, but you'll send *me* packing. I can barely take one shofar at my house, let alone two."

Owen grinned, raking a giant hand through the apples in the basket. He blinked up at her, a shock of wavy hair falling across his forehead. "Alright. I think we're set. Ready to head out?"

"I suppose," Ava replied with resignation, remembering with dread the cooking list her mother had written up the night before. "Let me guess—you're going to go home and bake an apple pie for tonight, now that you've got your coveted dinner invitation?"

"Actually..." Owen began, his voice sly. "Google tells me apple cake is the more traditional dessert for Rosh Hashanah. And it sounds like the way to your mother's heart is through..." He took a big breath, then belted out, "tradiiiitiooooon!"

This time, Ava laughed out loud. One thing she never thought she'd hear was Owen singing Fiddler on the Roof. She shook her head as they headed for the lobby to pay for their apple haul. "Fine. But just know, you've got your work cut out for you."

11

———

"Do you mind stopping by the grocery store?" Ava asked as they were on their way home. Owen's eyes flicked to the rearview mirror where a line of cars was piling up. They'd been stuck behind a combine for the past two hills, and what with the sea of cars headed toward Lincoln for that evening's Husker game, there was no sign of a break in the oncoming traffic.

"What's another bump in the road today?" Owen sighed.

"I'll be quick, I promise," Ava said, clasping her hands together in a pleading gesture. "I remembered I'm supposed to pick up the stuff for the *simanim*."

"The what?" Owen raised an eyebrow.

"Never mind," Ava said, waving a hand. "You'll find out tomorrow. But will you stop? I know, I should've thought of it earlier and driven myself—"

"Shh," Owen cut in. He rubbed his temple. "We'll stop. And you're fine. It's just at the dinner..."

She knew he felt confident about seeing her parents, so speculated he was having second thoughts about Noah being there. "You're tired of seeing Noah?" Ava asked, risking a glance in Owen's direction. It didn't take an astrophysicist to figure out that Owen's mood since seeing Noah that morning had been less than stellar.

"Pretty much." Finally spotting a break in the traffic, Owen flicked his turn signal on and swerved smoothly into the left lane, whipping the truck around the combine and settling them back on their way.

"Well, that makes two of us," Ava said, wrinkling her nose. "Trust me when I say there's no one I'd rather *not* see."

"Yeah? I hate to be that guy, but you're not exactly discouraging him," Owen said, his green eyes fixated on the highway in front of them. He didn't turn to look at her, and his face remained blank, unreadable.

"What do you mean?" Ava asked, a sudden flush creeping into her neck.

"I mean, you've got to enforce boundaries," Owen said. "Your mother's clearly still in contact with him, he's showing up at your place of work, he practically invited himself into your home, and you just... let him. That's not the Ava I know."

Ava was about to retort that he had no clue what having a Jewish mother could be like when a call came in over Owen's pickup stereo. Owen frowned. He pressed a button on the dash.

"Hello?"

"Owen?" Chief Greathouse's booming voice filled the cab of the truck.

"Yeah, chief. What's up? I'm driving, so you're on speaker—Ava's with me."

The chief gave a grunt, and Ava could almost see his mustache twitching. "Alright, well, I spoke to your contact, and everything seems to check out. I gotta say, though, next time you get yourself into a corner like this, I'd pick someone with a better reputation to use as your alibi."

Owen laughed harshly. "Noted."

"Anyway," Greathouse continued. "Looks like you're clear. Let's hope we can say the same for Shapiro."

"Thanks, chief. Take care."

The line clicked off.

"Well, that's good news," Ava said. "Right?"

Owen sighed. "Yeah. I wanted to avoid dragging—well, this other person—into things, but I didn't really have a choice."

Ava wanted to know *who* this other person was, but she knew asking again would only piss Owen off. She felt a bit smug that it was someone with a poor reputation. Then she frowned. Maybe that made it all the worse.

"Okay if I wait in the car while you go in?" Owen asked.

"Sure. I'll only be a minute."

As she entered the cool blast of the air-conditioned store, Ava struggled to remember what it was she even needed. While she was beyond relieved Greathouse was no longer looking at Owen, there was still the problem of Noah, and, if she was being honest with herself, this mysterious person who Owen didn't want to talk about. *It'd be just my luck if he had a secret wife all this time.* The fluorescent lights buzzing overhead did nothing to lighten her mood, just made her feel even more like she was trapped in some kind of nightmare, the grocery store an inescapable labyrinth.

Okay. Dates, squash, beets. Her mother already had the fish head covered, thankfully. What even *were* the other traditional foods they were meant to taste at Rosh Hashanah? She should have written them down. As she wandered down the produce aisle scanning the selection, she pulled up a list on the internet.

With a pang, her grandfather's kind and wrinkled face flashed through her mind. The holidays had never been the same without him. *And here I can't even remember something as small as what we need for the simanim without Google's help—Zaidy Mel would be so disappointed.*

After locating most of the items on the list—even thrilled to find pomegranates in the small Shiloh grocery store—Ava made her way to the checkout at the front of the store. A hand shot up behind the magazine racks, waving to let her know the lane was open, and she steered her cart toward it. It wasn't until she rounded the corner and narrowly missed upsetting a rack of tabloids and bubble gum that she saw who the cashier was.

"Hi Chantelle," Ava said, honestly surprised she could find her voice so fast. Her pulse sped up as she remembered the coffee cup in the back of Mitch's pre-murder selfie.

"Nice to see you, Ava." Chantelle nodded in greeting. She pressed a button to move the conveyer belt, as though reminding Ava to move things along.

"I am *so* sorry for your loss," Ava said, remembering her manners. She fixed her gaze on Chantelle for a moment, hoping her face imparted the sympathy she really did feel. She couldn't imagine what the woman was going through.

"Thanks." Chantelle looked down at her feet, her expression uncomfortable.

Ava began unloading the few items she had in her cart, setting them on the conveyer belt and watching as they jerked their way toward Chantelle. "How are you holding up? I didn't think you'd be working today."

Chantelle shrugged her thin shoulders, continued scanning Ava's items with a shake of her head. She placed the peaches on the scale, then tapped a long acrylic nail at the screen. "I'm hanging in there—they couldn't find anyone to cover my shift, and I said it was okay. Keeping busy helps."

Ava knew that to be true, from her own experience. When her grandfather died, she'd barely allowed herself to sleep that first week, so scared was she of being alone with her thoughts. It was far easier to keep on moving than stand still and let reality catch up with you.

"That's good, I suppose," Ava said. Her basket now empty, she placed it below the counter and moved toward the register, her gaze moving across Chantelle's back as she finished ringing her up.

Chantelle turned to Ava, her faded red curls swishing around her shoulders. "Your total is thirty-two seventy-five today."

As she announced the total, Ava's throat nearly closed up. She cleared it, glad for the excuse of digging through her wallet, and gladder still when Chantelle turned back around to swipe her card. There'd been no mistaking the deep purple of Chantelle's lipstick—it was the very same shade on the cup in Mitch's picture.

Ava inhaled deeply, willing her jumping heart to settle down. It didn't mean anything—not necessarily. It only meant that Chantelle had indeed been inside the press box the night before, a fact that, on its own, made perfect sense. She was Mitch's girlfriend, after all. She had a perfect explanation for being there. Perfectly perfect.

"You want your receipt?" Chantelle asked. She held up the strip of flimsy paper between her taloned fingers.

"No, that's fine," Ava replied, more breezily than she felt. She waved a hand, then gave Chantelle one final nod, trying hard not to stare at her purple lipstick, before scooping up her groceries.

As she headed across the parking lot toward Owen's parked pickup, her mind was a dust storm of furious thoughts, all spiraling around and around each other. If Chantelle had been in the press box last night—especially so close to the time Mitch had been murdered—why hadn't she mentioned it to Greathouse when he called her this morning? He said she hadn't mentioned being there. The victim's significant other was always the first to fall under suspicion—so wouldn't she have wanted to eliminate herself as a suspect? It was all so strange.

Unless—and here, Ava's breath caught at the thought of it —perhaps what Chantelle wanted was to fly under the radar for some nefarious reason. There was no getting around it. Chantelle was hiding something—and Ava wasn't going to let it go, not when Noah was still a suspect. As Owen had said, her ex-husband was a jerk—but he wasn't a killer. She'd just have to get to the bottom of things.

12

The kitchen was alive with clattering dishes when Ava arrived home. She was still thinking about Chantelle's lipstick, sifting through ideas of how she could approach Chantelle and tease any information out of her. But it would all have to wait, as the tantalizing aroma of chicken soup reminded her when she stepped through the kitchen door and headed once again to the coffee pot. Zaidy Mel might not actually care about her forgetting the *simanim*, but she was positive he wouldn't approve of skipping out on Rosh Hashanah dinner to investigate a murder she wasn't even involved in.

"Oh, not a minute too soon," Sara Goldberg said, wiping her manicured hands on a dish towel. "We were just ready to start another pot of coffee."

"Well, if there's anything I'm good for, it's coffee," Ava said, already spooning coffee into a filter. She switched on the coffee pot, then clapped her hands together. There was only one way to get Chantelle out of her mind—get her mind onto something else. "Where do you need me?"

Mr. Goldberg raised a flour-covered hand from his perch

near the stove, then used it to push his glasses further up his sweaty nose, where it left a smudge of white. "Your mother's making the matzo balls too fluffy, but she won't believe me. I told her we'd wait 'til you got here to let you be the judge."

Ava held her hands up, laughing. "Oh, no, no, no. I'm not getting involved in *that* discussion. That's a trap if I ever saw one!"

Mrs. Goldberg rolled her eyes, striding to the stovetop where a pot of simmering soup gurgled on the back burner. She lifted the lid and peered down into the soup. A delicious wave of savory goodness wafted toward Ava, and her stomach grumbled.

"Okay, fine," Ava said, relenting. "Give me a couple. I passed up the apple cider doughnuts at the orchard, and I'm starving."

Mrs. Goldberg dipped a ladle into the steaming broth and fished out a pair of fluffy dumplings, which she slid into a bowl for Ava. As Ava stabbed a fork into one of them, blowing on the still steaming ball before it reached her mouth, Mr. and Mrs. Goldberg waited with bated breath.

"So? What's the verdict?" Mr. Goldberg asked, his brown eyes shining with eager anticipation. "Too fluffy, right?"

"They're *supposed* to be fluffy," Mrs. Goldberg retorted, giving a toss of her perfectly blown out hair. "That's the point!"

Mr. Goldberg scoffed. He and his wife both waited in silence for their daughter to finish chewing.

"Just right," Ava pronounced, swallowing the last of the matzo ball and spearing the second with her fork.

Mr. Goldberg threw up his spindly hands. "Wow, I tell you what—my grandmother didn't survive Auschwitz for *this* to be how her descendants learn to make *kneidlekh*. Truly a *shanda!*"

"Oh, Michael, *please*," said Mrs. Goldberg, rolling her dark eyes, even as they shone with smug satisfaction. "The art of the fluffy matzo ball has been passed down by Jewish women for *centuries*. I promise you, your grandmother would have been kicked out of her shtetl if her *kneidlekh* had been the rocks you claim they were."

Ava clapped her hands, feeling as though she were attempting to rally a classroom of squabbling preschoolers. She cleared her throat. "It's going to be just fine. As the saying goes —two Jews, three opinions."

"Yes, except *you* forewent your opinion and sided with your *mother*," Mr. Goldberg retorted. Despite the indignant tone of his voice, there was a twinkle in his eye. "Shall I get the shofar and blow you two a victory tune?"

"No!" Ava jumped in, laughing. "You do that, and I have a feeling there won't *be* any matzo balls—fluffy or otherwise—as Mom will have thrown them all in your face."

Indeed, Mrs. Goldberg's steely expression as she surveyed her husband from across the kitchen was not one to mess with. When she spoke, her tone was cool, measured. She was obviously still basking in her triumph. "There's no need to be a sore loser, Michael. You still have your brisket."

Mr. Goldberg's eyes went wide. "The brisket! My goodness, I almost forgot! I need to get that in the oven. What time is it?"

"Just past one," Ava volunteered, glancing at her phone. All this matzo ball drama had distracted her from thinking about Mitch Fangman, but even a glance at her phone screen was enough to remind her of the mysterious Facebook selfie she'd noticed that morning. She'd already decided not to mention Chantelle's lipstick again to Owen, but if there was someone else she could bounce her idea off... "Is Riley still sleeping?"

"No, she came down for coffee soon after you left," Mrs.

Goldberg said. Her eyes remained fixed on the cup of flour she was measuring.

"Wow. I'm surprised she was up and around that early, what with the dance tonight. I lent her one of my dresses for it—not a request I saw coming."

"Yes, I know," Mrs. Goldberg said, her gaze flitting to Ava before it returned to her dough. "The dance starts at eight, but she's going to dinner with her date and some friends first. Said friends are all getting together at Summer Davis's house. Do you mind preheating the oven for the challah? It needs to bake before the brisket goes in."

Ava turned on the oven, then stood facing her mother, who was now using her hands to mix the dough. "Okay, back up. Riley has a *date* to the homecoming dance?"

"She does indeed," Mrs. Goldberg said, a tiny smile playing on her immaculately lined lips.

"Who?"

"Trevor Phillips. Apparently, he's one of Shiloh's star football players, although I couldn't for the life of me tell you anything else about the boy."

Ava chewed her lip. Wasn't that the name of the boy she'd seen Riley gazing at during the pep rally yesterday? "Interesting... Riley's going to homecoming with a star football player?"

If Ava had been shocked at the image of Riley waltzing into homecoming with a date on her arm, the image of her with some hot-stuff, chiseled ball player was even more unfathomable. Riley *laughed* at those people. Was an invitation to a dance really all it had taken to get her to buy into the hype of high school?

Mrs. Goldberg shrugged, finally looking up at Ava as her

hands continued to knead. "I guess so. You know her, though. She didn't say much else about it."

"Well, who's this Summer Davis?" Ava asked, the question coming out a bit more demanding than she'd intended. Her mother hadn't been here but days and seemed to know more about someone living under Ava's roof than she did herself.

"No idea," Mrs. Goldberg said, shaking her head so her hair fell into her eyes. "She only mentioned the name."

"You couldn't get any more out of her than that?" Mr. Goldberg asked incredulously from behind the refrigerator door as he surveyed the brisket situation. "You were gone for ages this morning."

"Gone? Gone where?" Ava turned to her mother, questioning. As far as she knew, her parents—and, she'd assumed, Riley—had been home all morning. She hadn't heard of any plans for an outing. "To the shops downtown?"

Ava's mother pursed her lips, but not before she flicked an irritated glance toward her husband. She was quiet a beat too long before she answered, and Ava didn't fail to notice it. "We checked those out, yes. That gallery's a rather nice place."

"Right," Ava said slowly, narrowing her eyes. She wasn't buying it. A quick trip to the gallery downtown wouldn't have taken *ages*—and besides, Ava seriously doubted Riley would have been very enthused about tagging along with Ava's swanky mother to visit a place she'd been in hundreds of times. There had to be more to it than that. Still, she knew pushing the issue would only make her mother more stubborn in her resolve to avoid giving an answer, so she would let it go. For now. "Well, did she say if she needs to be picked up at a certain time tonight? I'd imagine the dance will go until late..."

"It sounded like one of the girls would bring her home, but she said she'd call if anything changed."

"Great," Ava grumbled, fishing out another matzo ball from the broth simmering on the stove. "I guess I'll be staying up without even knowing if it's needed."

"Relax, honey," Mrs. Goldberg said. She made as if to lay a hand on Ava's shoulder, then drew back, realizing her hands were covered in sticky challah dough. "I can get her if need be."

"Really?" It wasn't that Ava didn't believe her mom would choose to be helpful of her own accord—just that she had a hard time picturing Sara Goldberg chauffeuring an angsty, blue-haired teenager around at midnight.

"Absolutely," Mrs. Goldberg replied with a nod. "Now, would you bring me some sort of towel? I need to cover this and let it rise. Michael, when are you starting on your brisket? I'd say you better get going if we're planning to eat at seven."

Mr. Goldberg appeared from behind the refrigerator door with an armful of packaged meat. He flapped a spindly hand at his wife. "I know, I know. I'm doing it now."

"Owen's bringing an apple cake," Ava offered, hoping she could slip in the news of Owen's invitation without dropping a bombshell. "And it's Owen—so it's bound to be good."

Mrs. Goldberg looked up. "You mean the lumberjack?"

"He's *not* a lumberjack," Ava began, already feeling the heat rising in her face.

"Well, whatever," Mrs. Goldberg said, waving a hand. She seemed to consider something for a moment, and then, to Ava's relief, went back to her kneading. "You know who I mean. Whatever he brings, I sure hope he knows not to make it with dairy products."

"Yes, he *knows*," Ava said, scowling. She crossed her arms

over her chest. Did her mother really think she'd forget to pass that on? "Trust me, the man can bake anything—even vegan stuff—and have it taste divine, so no need to worry."

"Well, I hope he puts eggs in it." Mrs. Goldberg knit her brows in disapproval. "It only needs to be *pareve*."

"I explained it all. He's got it."

"I, for one, will be anxiously awaiting the tasting of this said apple cake," Mr. Goldberg declared, setting the meat down on the counter. "I have yet to taste something that man has baked that wasn't less than divine. I'm sure my Auschwitz survivor grandmother would have agreed."

"Do you *have* to keep bringing up Auschwitz?" Ava's mother asked her husband, her voice pleading. "Please, Michael, it's a holiday."

"All the more reason to remind ourselves we survived!"

Ava swallowed a snort. "You know what they say—all the Jewish holidays can be summed up with: they tried to kill us, we survived, let's eat!"

"Exactly," Mr. Goldberg said, nodding. He pushed his glasses up on his nose with an extended pinky finger and glanced at his watch. "Now, unless you ladies need anything else from me, I've got a date with the shofar while I wait for that challah to bake. My time to practice is a-ticking."

Sara glanced at him disapprovingly. "At least take that thing out to the garage, Michael. If I have to listen to dying elephant moans all afternoon, I'll have a migraine by dinnertime."

"I second that," Ava jumped in, raising a hand. "I'd like to have it be—ah—a surprise. When we get home from services tomorrow."

Mr. Goldberg looked defeated. His bony shoulders sagged in childish disappointment as he snatched up the velvet satchel containing the shofar from the bench near the door. He tossed a playful, yet still resentful glance at his wife and daughter. "Fine, fine. You're going to be amazed tomorrow at my progress, though!"

"I'm sure we will, Dad," Ava said, placing a soothing hand on her father's arm and guiding him toward the door.

As the door clicked shut behind him, Ava sighed in relief. Bringing a smooth wooden cutting board down from the cupboard, she ran two cucumbers under a stream of water and began the work of slicing them for that evening's salad. Next to her, Ava could tell her mother was trying her hardest to keep a straight face, but the corners of her lipsticked mouth kept twitching.

Finally, Mrs. Goldberg could stand it no more. She clucked her tongue in mock irritation. "That man wants to talk *shandas*, does he? I'll tell you the real *shanda*—his godawful shofar skills! His grandmother didn't survive Auschwitz for *that* kind of shofar blowing!"

"Leave Auschwitz out of this!" Ava said, giving her mother a playful swat on the arm. But she caught Mrs. Goldberg's glance, and they both erupted into loud, happy laughter.

Of *course*, Noah would be the first to arrive for dinner—just like the stuck-up, suck-up former son-in-law he was. Ava rolled her eyes as she glanced out the dining room window, watching his sleek, cobalt rental car come sailing down the driveway. Through the tinted windshield, she could see the Ray Bans he wore, the infuriating, relaxed way he lounged in the driver's seat, one hand slung over the wheel. A scoff rose to her throat, but she caught it just in time. Her mother had come up to the window behind her, sliding the curtains aside to peer out at the driveway, and Ava didn't think it would be wise to start the dinner by pissing her mother off.

"Oh, that's Noah for you," Mrs. Goldberg chirped, smacking her lips in her reflection on the window. "Right on time."

"Ten minutes early," Ava said with a slight clear of her throat. If her mother was trying to insinuate that Owen was late, she wasn't going to let her.

Her mother smiled, unperturbed, moving briskly toward the kitchen with Ava on her heels. "Well, we can put him to work. Is the table set?"

"We're not having a guest set the table," Ava said, swiping a handful of silverware from the drawer.

Mrs. Goldberg shot her daughter a reproving look. "Noah's not a guest—he's *family*."

"Uh, I'm sorry—I must have heard you wrong. Let's try *was* family," Ava corrected, her tone sharp. She had promised herself she'd be on her best behavior tonight, do her best to get through the dinner unscathed with as little drama as possible, but her mother wasn't making things easy—and dinner hadn't even started yet.

Mrs. Goldberg waved a manicured hand, her red nails flashing. "Oh, whatever. Is, was—same thing. He has *ties*."

He certainly does, Ava thought grimly. Apparently, despite their finalized divorce, Noah Shapiro had more ties to her family than she'd realized.

A clipped, polite knock sounded at the front door, and Mrs. Goldberg rushed to answer it, escorting Noah inside with an unbridled enthusiasm that made Ava's insides recoil. But as Noah stepped into the kitchen, bringing with him a whiff of crisp cologne as he hung his folded sunglasses from the collar of his button-down, Ava felt something else in her insides—a wistful twisting she wished she could disown immediately. Noah looked good—*very* good—and divorce hadn't changed that. *Ugh.*

"*Shana tova*," Noah said, wrapping Mrs. Goldberg in a hearty embrace. Then, pulling back, his eyes met Ava's, where they rested for a moment, glimmering. "Happy new year!"

Mr. Goldberg came sailing into the room, shofar tucked under his lanky arm. He clapped Noah on the back, gazing happily around at the small trio gathered in the kitchen. "*Shana tova u'metuka!* May the year 5786 bring us peace, happiness, abundance, love—"

At this, Mrs. Goldberg's eyes flicked to Ava's, and Ava averted her gaze.

"—and lots of good coffee," Ava finished, cutting her father off.

Noah peered into the dining room, just beyond the kitchen. "Looks like we still need wine glasses. Care to point me in the right direction?"

"Just over here," Mrs. Goldberg said, linking her arm with Noah's and guiding Noah into the waiting dining room.

Ava and her father were left standing in the kitchen, watching as mother and former son-in-law walked arm in arm toward the china cabinet. Mr. Goldberg seemed about to say something, when there was a rap at the front door, this one less ceremonious than Noah's had been. Ava had been so tied up in the horror of having her ex-husband inside her home, she hadn't even seen another vehicle come down the driveway.

As always, Juanita was beaming as Ava opened the kitchen door, her face as round and cheery as a moon in a children's book. David stood behind her, a bottle of wine under each arm, and Ava ushered them inside, glad for the extra company. If anyone could lighten the tension and make the evening more fun, it was Juanita Martinez.

Juanita glanced through the doorway into the dining room, where Noah was meticulously placing wine glasses around the table. She offered him a friendly smile and a courteous wave before glancing behind her, her mouth drawn up into a slightly nervous bow. Ava followed Juanita's glance behind, only to see the screen door opening on the porch outside, and Owen stepping through it.

"Looks like we're in for a party tonight," Juanita said, fixing Ava with a pointed, yet still merry look. "Lots of new experiences!"

"You can say that again," Ava said, wrapping a loose arm around Juanita's shoulders. Although she still wasn't much of a hugger, living in Shiloh had forced her to move past her resistance when she deemed a situation worthy. And Juanita's solidarity definitely seemed to merit a hug.

Mrs. Goldberg had returned to the kitchen to greet the visitors, heels of her strapped sandals clacking on the tile floor as she strode toward them. She clasped a cool hand around Juanita's. "So nice to see you, thank you so much for coming. Shana tova!"

"Shana tova," Juanita returned with a gracious smile, her tone uncertain. She gestured to her husband, who stepped forward with an outstretched palm. "My husband, David. I think you met this past summer, but it's been a while."

"We're glad to be here," David said, beaming alongside his wife.

"Noah's just finishing setting out the wine glasses," Mrs. Goldberg said, ushering Juanita and David across the kitchen and into the dining room. "Feel free to sit wherever—"

Mrs. Goldberg stopped mid-sentence as Owen stepped into the kitchen. For a split second, she looked flustered, a hint of red coloring her already contoured cheeks, but then quickly recovered. She waved a languid hand at Owen, the corners of her red lips turning up in the gracious smile Ava knew she reserved for strangers.

"Oh, *Owen*," Mrs. Goldberg gushed. "It is Owen, isn't it? I forgot you were coming—what a pleasant surprise. Come in, come in."

Mrs. Goldberg's slight was not lost on Ava—her mother was making it clear in her own passive-aggressive way that Owen was not a fixture of the family. But if Owen took offense at her seeming lack of memory, he didn't show it, only smiled, nodded, and strode to the kitchen counter to where Ava stood, arranging the *simanim* on their plates.

"Where do you want the cake?" Owen asked, holding up a covered, two-tier cake plate from which a delightful, spicy-sweet aroma was already drifting.

"Just set it here for now," Ava instructed, pointing with her elbow to an empty spot on the counter. "We'll keep it a surprise and bring it out with dessert."

"Well, well, what have we here?" Mr. Goldberg asked as he sidled up to the pair, rubbing his palms together. "Is this that apple cake I keep hearing about?"

Owen laughed, his green eyes crinkling. "It is indeed—and without a speck of dairy in it, rest assured."

Mr. Goldberg clapped a hand on Owen's shoulder. "Ah, good man. I'm sure it'll be scrumptious."

From across the dining room, Ava saw Noah raise his gaze, his posture growing just a hair more rigid. And although her stomach was doing somersaults at the realization that Owen O'Kelly was about to have dinner not only with her *family* but with her ex-husband, she couldn't help but feel a tad bit smug at seeing Noah's discomfort. Was it the best way to be starting off her new year? Probably not—but she didn't care. *That's right. Let the man sweat.*

"Well, shall we all sit down?" Mrs. Goldberg called, eyeing the three of them. She seemed keen to put a stop to the camaraderie she saw happening between her husband and Owen, the impostor.

"Actually, I'll have you all stay standing," Mr. Goldberg said. "We've got to make *kiddush* first."

Owen shot a curious glance at Ava, one eyebrow raised. She shook her head slightly, as though to signal for him to wait. As a good half of the dinner table guests weren't Jewish, she'd already asked her father to explain the religious rituals as they performed them. And first up was *kiddush*, the blessing over the wine.

Across from Ava, Noah stood behind the chair next to his former mother-in-law, with Juanita on his other side. David and Mr. Goldberg stood at the ends of the table, with Mr. Goldberg at the head, which meant Ava and Owen found themselves across from Noah and Juanita. They all turned their eyes toward Ava's father as he opened the wine. There was a squeaking sound, followed by a delightful pop, as he pulled on the corkscrew, wiggling the cork out of the bottle. Across the table, Ava could feel Noah's eyes on her, but she refused to make eye contact.

"Now," Mr. Goldberg said, setting the cork down next to his plate. A tinge of pink was already seeping into the tablecloth. "The first thing we do at any Jewish holiday dinner is to bless the wine—which we call *making kiddush*. If I'm not mistaken, it's similar to what Catholics do for the Eucharist. I'll say the blessing—the long part in Hebrew, then a brief line in English —and we'll all say 'amen' together. Sound good?"

There was a murmur of agreement, and Mr. Goldberg poured a healthy dash of ruby wine into the ornate silver cup that stood next to his plate. He held the goblet in his palm, looked at it reverently, then gazed out at the rest of the dinner table as he began to recite the blessing. Although the words were familiar to Ava, having grown up hearing them every

Shabbat and holiday, she wasn't used to her father being the one to utter them—especially not in this house. They'd celebrated many a holiday in this very dining room, around this very table, and it had always been her grandfather who would lead the blessings, his melodious voice ringing out like a song. Ava bit her cheek, tried to concentrate on the words rather than the memories. She had enough on her mind during this dinner the way it was.

"*Baruch atah Adonai, borei p'ri hagafen,*" Mr. Goldberg said, finishing the Hebrew part of the prayer. "Blessed are you, Lord our G-d, creator of the fruit of the vine."

"Amen," murmured Ava, her mother, and Noah in unison, with the rest of the guests joining in, although just a beat too late. Next to her, Owen shot Ava a small smile, one dimple appearing.

Mr. Goldberg drank from the silver cup, then offered it to his wife. With a pang, an image flashed through her mind of Noah offering her a similar-looking cup of wine under the marriage canopy. *No. Focus.*

"Alright, time to wash," Mr. Goldberg said, clapping his hands together. His wife was already on her way to the kitchen. "Whoever wants to wash their hands before we bless the bread is welcome to do it, but do whatever you feel comfortable with."

Not surprisingly, Juanita and David nodded, staying put behind their chairs. Noah, too, stayed behind at the dinner table, explaining to the couple that it was more of a ceremonial washing than one meant for hygiene—no soap was involved. Owen, however, followed Ava to the kitchen, where Mrs. Goldberg was already standing at the sink, splashing water over each hand with a two-handled jug. He met Ava's gaze and smiled.

Mrs. Goldberg murmured a rushed blessing which Ava punctuated with a quick amen, and then, giving Owen a curious look up and down, tossed the hand towel to her daughter. She left the room.

"You've got to go first," Ava said, nudging Owen up toward the sink. "Once I say the blessing, I'm not supposed to talk until Dad blesses the challah. My mom will be shooting me death glares."

Owen looked amused. "Really? You can't talk after it?"

"Yep. Okay, hold the jug in your left hand and dump water over your right hand twice. Then change sides. Mmhm—and that's it."

"Do I have to say something with it?" Owen shook the hair out of his eyes, wiping his hands on the towel Ava passed him.

"Shh. Don't talk," Ava said, elbowing him out of the way.

"Okay, jeez," Owen hissed with a grin, raising his hands in surrender as he moved to wait behind Ava.

As Ava stood at the sink, finishing her own washing, she could almost *feel* her mother's eyes on them. Ava was just glad Noah hadn't also joined them, but then again, he never had. He wasn't very much into practicing his religion—the one tiny spot on what her mother would have otherwise called a perfect record. From the dining room, Mr. Goldberg cleared his throat. He was telling her to hurry it up.

Once everyone had returned to the table, Mr. Goldberg gestured for them to sit. He craned his neck in search of the challah, which stood waiting on Zaidy Mel's special breadboard, covered with a colorful, embroidered linen cloth. Ava reached for the board and passed it to her father. Noah followed it up with the saltshaker.

Mr. Goldberg held the breadboard high. *"Baruch atah, Adonai, hamotzi lechem min ha'aretz."*

"Amen!" came the resounding chorus of dinner guests.

These Gentiles are getting the hang of it, Ava thought to herself.

Mr. Goldberg sawed his way skillfully through the challah, then sprinkled the pile of pieces with what looked to Ava like an ungodly amount of salt. Then, popping a piece into his mouth, her father chewed, swallowed, and beamed at his guests. "Take one, pass it around!"

"You know, I always thought challah was braided," Juanita remarked as she plucked a fluffy piece of bread off the board and considered it before taking a bite.

"An astute observation," Mr. Goldberg answered. "It usually is! But at Rosh Hashanah, it's customary to shape the challah into a spiral, which symbolizes the cyclical nature of the year."

"But it's more fun to braid it," Ava pointed out.

"Regardless—this is excellent bread," Owen said.

"Thanks," Mrs. Goldberg said stiffly, trying hard to not show her pleasure at being complimented by the town baker. "Back home, I'd just drop by the bakery and buy it, but here—well, you know…"

Owen nodded. "Probably less effort to just make it, rather than go hunting around Lincoln or Omaha for it."

"I've always heard they have it in Lincoln, but never actually *seen* it," Ava put in. "At this point, I'm thinking it's just an urban legend."

"Alright, everyone," Mr. Goldberg announced, calling back the attention of the table. "Another thing that's customary at Rosh Hashanah is the tasting of the *simanim*, symbolic foods we accompany with a wish for positive outcomes in the new year."

"Oh, that's lovely," Juanita said, beaming.

Mr. Goldberg passed around a plate of apple slices, instructing everyone to dip the apples into the honey dishes scattered around the table. He held his own slice high, offering a supplication in English before taking a crisp, crunchy bite. "May it be Your will, G-d, to grant us a sweet new year."

"Amen," Mrs. Goldberg murmured.

Mr. Goldberg continued with the bowl of pomegranate seeds, wishing that his dinner guests be as full of merits as a pomegranate is of seeds, and then the dish of carrots, announcing their desire for any harsh decrees against them to be nullified in the coming year. Finally, he raised a plate containing an eerie, staring fish head over the table, declaring, "May we be the head and not the tail!"

Owen cast an amused glance at Ava, while Juanita looked blankly from her husband to Mrs. Goldberg.

Mr. Goldberg chuckled. "I know, it's a bit odd. It just means, 'Let's always hope to be ahead this year, not lagging behind.' Many of the blessings make more sense in Hebrew—they're derived from word plays on the Hebrew words for each food. For example, the word for 'carrot' is *gezer*, which sort of sounds like *g'zar*, meaning 'decree'—hence the blessing about harsh decrees being nullified."

"Interesting," Juanita mused, nodding in understanding.

"And with that—it's time to eat!" Mrs. Goldberg announced, pushing away from the table. She marched to the kitchen, a woman on a mission, and returned with a huge pot of soup, the steam still rising from it.

"I've never had matzo ball soup," Owen commented. Although it was a perfectly natural admission for a non-Jewish person from rural Nebraska, Ava still wished he hadn't said it aloud. Why out himself even further in front of her parents?

The corner of Noah's mouth twitched. He leaned forward to ladle out a bowl of soup, then handed it to Owen. "You'll have to let us know if they're fluffy enough."

"No," Ava snapped, cutting him off. She turned to Owen. "Don't take that bait. Anyway, we already had this discussion today, and it's been decided that the matzo balls are perfectly fluffy—even if *some* of us say otherwise." Here, she shot a pointed look at her father, who furrowed his brow.

The soup was a hit, and Ava was relieved to see that Owen took a second helping—a nod to her mother's matzo ball skills that wouldn't go unnoticed by Mrs. Goldberg. Also, to Ava's relief, neither of her parents saw fit to bring up the topic of Auschwitz.

After the soup came the rest of the meal, a decadent spread that made Juanita's eyes grow wide as she watched Ava and Mrs. Goldberg make trip after trip to the kitchen until the table was covered in piping hot food.

"Holy cow," David said, taking in the ungodly number of dishes in front of them. "That's a heck of a lot of food."

"Well, get ready to take some of it home with you—there's no way all this is going to fit in the fridge," Mrs. Goldberg said, looking pleased at the awe she'd been able to evoke in her dinner guests.

"So, the main dish is brisket—a Michael Goldberg special-ty," Ava said, pointing to the platter of meat next to her father. "In that glass dish near Mom is the noodle kugel—a sort of slightly sweet, noodle casserole—and next to that is the potato kugel—same thing, only savory and with potatoes instead of noodles. Over there is smoked eggplant with a drizzle of tahini, and over here we've got a chopped salad, gefilte fish, mashed potatoes, and another salad with beets and carrots."

Owen let out a low whistle. "This looks delicious!"

"Don't speak too soon, son," Mr. Goldberg said, chuckling. He laughed nervously as his wife shot him a look.

Everyone dug in, and the clatter of silverware accompanied the hum of small talk.

"So," Mr. Goldberg said. "It's nice to be spending a holiday in Nebraska again. Different, of course—but refreshing."

"Reminds me of Zaidy Mel," Ava said, feeling her shoulders relax with the flood of happy memories her grandfather's name conjured up. "He'd be happy we're still eating around his dining room table, using his challah board."

"Absolutely, he would," Mr. Goldberg agreed, fixing his daughter with a warm smile. "Remember that time he had us get up from the dinner table to watch the sunset?"

"The sunsets out here *are* beautiful," Owen said, eyes turning to the window where the sky was tinged with pink.

"Actually, that happened at a dinner in Chicago—rooftop apartment, the outline of the Magnificent Mile against the pink and purple. It was spectacular," Noah said. He cleared his throat. "I'm sure Nebraska sunsets are nice, too, though."

"Well, that's lovely," said Juanita, as though to keep Noah's words from reverberating in the silence. "That sounds like Melvin Goldberg."

Mr. Goldberg's eyes lit up. "That's right—you knew my father, too!"

Ava poured herself more wine. Noah was on a roll tonight, and she couldn't very well do anything to stop it—not unless she wanted to make abundantly clear to her mother, and everyone else, that she and Owen were more than just friends.

"I can't believe I've lived in this town my whole life and never once ran into this infamous Melvin Goldberg," Owen said, beaming at Ava's father. If Noah's comment about the sunset had bothered him, he wasn't letting it show.

"Right? He liked to get out and about, too," Mr. Goldberg said.

"Well," Noah said, "their crowds probably didn't overlap much. One a handyman, the other a professor. You know, different kinds of family lives."

Owen fixed his gaze on Noah.

"Oh? What do you mean by that?" Owen asked. His face was eerily calm, the hint of a pleasant smile playing on his lips, but his green eyes sparked.

Noah took a sip of his wine, looked Owen dead in the eye as he swallowed. He shrugged his toned shoulders and leaned back in his chair. "Just—you know—your family's circle and his may not have overlapped much. Different social spheres."

Mr. Goldberg gave a nervous chuckle. "Well, anyway. Speaking of sunsets—"

"Yes, the sky outside is *magnificent*," Juanita said, jumping in with a sweep of her hand toward the window. David nodded along.

Ava's ears burned with shame. Her whole body was tense. What was Noah doing—trying to embarrass this man he didn't even know in front of his ex-wife's family? There was no mistaking what Noah had meant by his comment, but what could she do? Kick him out? Protest, like it was some kind of schoolyard fight? She wouldn't dignify his behavior with a retort.

"Maybe we ought to go out and look at it," Ava said. At the very least, she hoped standing up from the table and a breath of fresh air would help to release some of the tension coursing through her. "You know, in honor of Zaidy."

"We haven't finished our meal," Mrs. Goldberg said. She pressed her mouth into a tight, thin line, clearly displeased with how the dinner had gotten off track. "Besides, I want to hear more about Juanita's volunteer work with Habitat for Humanity."

Ava sighed. As Juanita began to explain the project she was overseeing with Habitat, Ava dug a fork into her potato kugel and stole a glance at Owen. He was still staring at Noah, who had gone back to his beet salad and was munching away with not a care in the world. Through the dining room window, the sun sank lower in the sky, casting its melting, pink haze across the cornfields as it set behind them. The corn was still tall, stalks silhouetted against the sunset. Soon, the farmers would be out with their combines, razing the rows down into brown, crunchy stumps and leaving a cloud of dust behind them. That was one thing Nebraska and Illinois had in common—the fields upon fields of endless corn.

"I've learned so much about what goes into building a house," Juanita was saying. "We—David and I—bought our house in the '80s, and we didn't *build* it, so it's the first I've ever really known about the construction process. The plans, the contractors, the zoning, the laborers…"

Ava's mother was nodding along. "Oh, definitely. It's an ordeal—and it's *so* nice that these kinds of organizations exist, to give people who are less fortunate the opportunity to own a home. Very commendable of you, Juanita, getting involved."

Juanita shrugged. "I guess so. When David and I were newlyweds and just starting out, charities helped us a lot—

absolute *godsends*—so we're just glad for the chance to return the favor. Give back to the community a bit."

"You two live here in Shiloh?" Noah asked.

"Yes, since the late '80s—which is when we bought our house. Back then, Shiloh was sort of an undiscovered gem, and the housing prices were a steal. More than I can say *now*."

Noah nodded. "I can imagine. I mean, Chicago's always been expensive, but prices are going up there, too. When Ava and I bought our suburban house six years ago, I think we paid —what?—one and a half million for it? And now, you can barely get a *duplex* in the suburbs for that much."

Ava nearly choked on her water. She wasn't in the habit of broadcasting the kind of lifestyle she'd led before moving to Shiloh, and hearing the extent of her affluence in such concrete terms was more than a little jarring. She couldn't bring herself to look at Owen, and she only wondered what Juanita must think.

"That estimate seems a bit high," Mr. Goldberg said, giving a nervous laugh. " But yes—the suburbs are in high demand these days. I'm not sure where the influx of people is coming from. I guess people want to get further out of the city, live more of the suburban lifestyle."

Juanita, good sport that she was, simply whistled. "Wow, that's a whole different ballgame than we're dealing with here. There are some newer neighborhoods in Lincoln and Omaha where I'm sure the properties are about as high, but you won't find much of that out here. Do you still live there, Noah? In that house?"

"Yep," Noah said, draping a toned arm over the back of Mrs. Goldberg's chair. He smiled, his dark eyes shining, and looked over at Ava. "We talked about selling it during the divorce, but ultimately didn't have to—so I'm still there."

Yes—and he'd probably banged Ava's former best friend in every single room by now, if he hadn't already while they were married. Then again, though she was loath to admit it, Ava was prone to Instagram stalking, and Lexie had been conspicuously absent from Noah's stories for the past few months. That, at least, gave Ava some satisfaction.

"It's a great house," Noah continued. "The master bathroom has a jacuzzi, and Ava put in heated flooring, which has been *glorious.*"

"I'm sure it has," Ava said, forcing a smile. It was true—she'd loved that heated flooring. Too bad Noah was the one getting to enjoy it now. *You're welcome, jerk.*

"Honestly, I'm impressed at how simply you've managed to live here in Shiloh, Ava," Noah said, looking at her from across the table. "Pretty different from what you're used to."

Ava felt a flush creeping into her neck. She'd be damned if she was going to let Noah see her embarrassment, though, so she simply smiled and nodded. "Yeah, it's been great. The change I needed."

"Good for you. You needed this time to explore," Noah said. He smiled what probably looked like a genuine smile to everyone else at the table, but which Ava knew held ulterior meaning. He glanced at Owen, his smile morphing into a smirk. "Meeting new kinds of people, living the simple life."

Ava tensed. New people? Simple life? What was *that* supposed to mean? She glanced at Owen, whose eyes were no longer shining, and was about to protest when her mother hissed from across the table.

"Shh!" Mrs. Goldberg said, holding up a manicured hand for quiet. Her eyes had gone wide. "What was that?"

Everyone was still, shocked into silence by the sudden outburst. Outside, the sky was dark, save for the lingering streaks of purple still hiding a smattering of stars. And then Ava heard it, too—a slow, steady creaking coming from the opposite side of the house.

"Maybe Riley is—" Mr. Goldberg started to speak, but his wife cut him off with another hiss.

She held a finger up in front of her mouth to signal for quiet and cocked her head to the side, listening.

Ava whispered. "Riley always announces herself, and she won't be back until way late tonight. And anyway, there's no wind. It wouldn't be creaking like that."

"That's not the front door. It's coming from down the hall," Juanita hissed back, jerking her head in said direction.

"The first-floor bathroom," Ava said, whipping her head toward the noise. "The window latch is broken. I've been meaning to fix it."

"I *told* you to get those floodlights fixed in the yard," Mrs. Goldberg hissed. "If someone's come down the lane and is trying to get in, we could have seen them coming."

"Why on earth would someone break in?" Noah asked, matching their sharp whispers. "It's not like there's a Bentley parked in the driveway."

"No, but that stupid Corvette you rented is," Ava shot back. She and Noah eyed each other fiercely.

Noah broke his gaze away, scoffing. "You guys. No one is breaking in—"

Bang. The thud that echoed from down the hall was palpable. For the first time, Juanita and David looked alarmed.

Owen stood, taking care not to let his chair scrape against the hardwood floor. He glanced at Ava. "I'll go check it out."

Noah shot to his feet, moving in front of Owen. "Better let me go first. I'm a doctor—I've had emergency training."

"Right. I'm sure the burglar will desperately need some CPR," Owen said with a snort, his voice still low.

"Michael," Mrs. Goldberg cut in, her whisper sharp. She laid a hand on her husband's arm, and the look she shot Owen and Noah caused both men to shut their mouths. "Michael, go see what it is—and take David with you. We can't sit here and wait for our deaths!"

David and Mr. Goldberg looked at each other across the table, seeming to acknowledge their shared responsibility as the men of the hour, and got quietly to their feet. A scratching, scrabbling noise was now drifting down the hallway, and Mr. Goldberg jutted his chin toward it, signaling for David to follow him.

Mrs. Goldberg grabbed her husband's wrist and snatched the shofar from where it sat on the side table, waiting for the first blast of the new year. With her other hand, she shoved the horn into her husband's hands, its sharp tip pointed forward.

He looked down, frowned. "But it's—"

"I don't care how much it cost, Michael. Our lives are worth it!" Mrs. Goldberg's eyes were huge, and her husband knew that any argument would be futile. He sighed, clutching the shofar in front of him.

Mr. Goldberg crept his way down the hall, floorboards squeaking beneath his loafer-clad feet. Behind him shuffled David, and Ava brought up the rear. She could hear her mother and Juanita hanging back near the doorway. Her mother's breathing was heavy, and Ava was struck with a sudden, terrifying thought: Did Mitch Fangman's murderer have it out for *her*, too? She realized suddenly that Owen was no longer next to her.

As they neared the closed bathroom door at the end of the hallway, Mr. Goldberg drew a deep breath. There was no doubt about it—the scrabbling noise was coming from inside. Why, oh *why*, hadn't she fixed that latch when Owen brought it up to her?

Drawing a deep breath and motioning to David and Ava to pause, to get ready, Mr. Goldberg raised the shofar high above his head. Then, with a jerk of his free hand, he wrenched the bathroom door open and burst inside, letting forth an unholy, guttural shout Ava never thought she'd hear coming from her father.

From inside the bathroom, a second scream, this one higher and shriller, mingled with Mr. Goldberg's. He jerked to a stop, shofar still raised high, David crashing into him from behind. Both men's eyes were wide.

"What?!" Mrs. Goldberg shrieked from down the hall behind them. "What is it, Michael? *Who* is it?"

By now, Ava had crept forward. Craning to see around her father's shoulder, she peered into the bathroom. It took a few seconds for the sight to register, but when it did—

"Riley?" Ava asked, her mouth falling open.

14

There, standing in front of the open bathroom window, was Riley, looking just as stricken as everyone else in the house. The shimmery silver dress she wore was twisted, and one strap had fallen off her shoulder. Her blue hair was disheveled, falling into clumpy ringlets around her face.

"Hi," Riley whispered.

Mr. Goldberg glanced at the shofar he still held high above his head. Sheepishly, he lowered it.

"What is it?" Mrs. Goldberg shrieked from the end of the hall. "Who's there?"

"Riley," Ava said, locking eyes with the girl. Pushing her father and David out of the way, she clutched Riley by her bare shoulders, then moved to the window to poke her head out.

"Riley?" Mrs. Goldberg sounded alarmed. "But—but Riley's at the homecoming dance with Trevor Phillips."

"Well, not anymore," Ava said, bringing her head back inside. She wrenched the window shut.

By this time, Juanita and Mrs. Goldberg had also entered the bathroom. The small group of frazzled adults stood surveying Riley, who had backed up as far as she could into the shower curtain and was now clutching it for support. Ava caught Riley's eyes in the mirror before the girl moved her sheepish gaze down to her glittery, strappy-sandal-clad feet. Her toes were painted a fresh, electric blue—the same color as her hair. *What the—? Riley got a pedicure?*

"Alright," Mrs. Goldberg announced, her voice authoritative. She clapped her hands. "False alarm. Everybody out."

"But what about—" Mr. Goldberg began, looking confused.

"It's a false alarm, Michael," Mrs. Goldberg repeated. She fixed her husband with a blazing gaze.

"Why don't we go dish up dessert?" Juanita asked, ushering both men out of the bathroom and down the hall. She shot Ava a reassuring glance, as though to say *I got this.*

When it was only the three of them left in the bathroom, Ava pulled herself up to sit on the counter next to the sink. Her mother stood facing Riley, arms crossed over her chest, but her face kind, simply waiting for Riley to speak.

"It was a prank," Riley said finally, still unable to drag her gaze from the floor. She nudged at the bathmat with the tip of her sandal.

"What was?" Ava asked. She glanced from her mother to Riley, then back again. Mrs. Goldberg pressed her lips into a thin, straight line as she waited for Riley to continue.

"The homecoming date," Riley muttered, her voice not more than a whisper.

Mrs. Goldberg drew in a sharp breath. For only an instant, Ava saw something that looked like rage flash across her mother's face before it disappeared, replaced once again with composure.

Mrs. Goldberg cleared her throat. "Riley, do you mean to

tell me that when Trevor Phillips asked you to attend the home-coming dance with him, he did it as a *joke*?"

Riley looked up. Her cheeks were flushed pink. "We were at Summer Davis's house getting ready, and then when we were all in the car on the way to pick up the boys, they stopped in the middle of Main Street and told me to get out. Summer said I should've known that someone like Trevor would never ask someone like me to a *dance*, that it was obviously a joke, and they kicked me out and all left."

"Well, I *never*," Mrs. Goldberg sputtered. She flexed her fingers in and out, her rings gleaming in the fluorescent bathroom lighting. "How *dare* they? The absolute *chutzpah*—"

Ava doubted Riley knew what chutzpah meant, but at the tone of Mrs. Goldberg's voice, she finally raised her gaze to look at the two of them.

"Those *assholes*," Ava declared, ignoring the disapproving look her mother shot her way.

She hopped off the counter and threw her arms around Riley, who bristled beneath her but didn't pull away. The girl had never been one for hugs, and truthfully, neither was Ava—but desperate times called for desperate measures.

"It's fine," Riley said, smoothing her wrinkled dress as Ava pulled away. "I didn't even really want to go, anyway."

Ava knew this was a lie. She'd seen the shy sparkle in Riley's eye when she'd asked Ava for a dress, had noticed the way Riley looked at Trevor Phillips at the pep rally the day before.

"Well, not with *those* low-class hooligans," Mrs. Goldberg scoffed. "They're the ones who should be absolutely ashamed of themselves—and their parents, to have raised such scum."

Wow. Ava glanced approvingly at her mom. *You tell 'em.*

"Well, they're—they're probably right," Riley stammered. "I mean, I really *should* have known…"

"Oh, utter nonsense," Mrs. Goldberg barked.

She took gentle hold of Riley's arm and drew the girl toward the toilet, where she sat her down on the closed seat. Still frazzled, Riley let herself be led, and Mrs. Goldberg knelt to unbuckle the girl's shoes. She sat back on her haunches. Her eyes were stern, but not unkind, as she surveyed Riley in her disheveled state. Ava had moved back to the sink and stood watching as her mother went into full-on mom mode.

"Well," Mrs. Goldberg said, finally giving a brisk nod. "We'll take out the pins in your hair, but the curls held up nicely. You may as well stay dressed up for dessert."

"Dessert?" Riley asked, her eyes questioning. She fiddled with one of the ringlets that had fallen into her face.

"We were just about to have dessert," Mrs. Goldberg said. "The party you went to turned out to be a dud, but good news —we've got a better one here! Complete with apple cake, hot coffee, *and* decent human beings. Come on. Up you go."

She helped Riley to her feet, and the three women stood looking into the bathroom mirror. Riley was quiet as Ava and Mrs. Goldberg began their work of extracting the boatload of hairpins from her updo. When the bathroom counter was littered with pins, Ava dabbed a cotton ball moistened with makeup remover beneath Riley's eyes. With practiced fingertips, Mrs. Goldberg gave the back of Riley's hair a quick fluff, then searched the girl's face in the mirror. A small smile had appeared on her lips.

"Come on," Mrs. Goldberg said, laying a gentle hand on Riley's shoulder. "We've got apple cake and hot coffee."

"Exactly." Ava nodded her head at Riley as they moved down the hallway. With her mother a safe distance in front of them, Ava squeezed Riley's arm and whispered, "Channel your inner Queen of Swords, girl—she don't take crap from no one."

Riley just grinned in response.

15

Back in the dining room, the group gave Riley a hearty welcome as she sat down next to Ava at the table. A stern look from Mrs. Goldberg was enough to warn them all not to mention the red rings around Riley's eyes—or the fact that she'd scared them all out of their skin by climbing in through the bathroom window. Amid the bubbly chatter of Juanita and her mother as they discussed the seasonal cider the Looking Glass wine bar had released in time for autumn, Ava cut herself a hefty slice of apple cake. Owen was conspicuously absent from the table.

Noah sat across from her, arms crossed over his tightly muscled chest, nodding along to something David was saying. As though sensing Ava's gaze on him, he glanced at her. She narrowed her eyes at him, as though to ask *What did you do?* There was no way he hadn't done something that caused Owen's abrupt departure.

Mr. Goldberg, seeing his daughter's glare at Noah, said, "Owen had to get going—said to tell you he's sorry. He's got plans early in the morning, sounds like."

"Thanks," Ava said. She nodded her thanks at her father, still skeptical. Deep in conversation with David, Noah looked suspiciously innocent. *Did he say something else to Owen?*

Then again, although she couldn't help but feel annoyed at Owen for taking the bait, she knew the jabs Noah had thrown already were more than enough to make any person want to dip out. It was, of course, what she'd been dreading. Instead, Owen's delicious cake, topped with drizzles of icing, stood on the crystal cake plate in the center of the table, a stark reminder of his absence. Ava noted with disgust that Noah took not one, but two pieces of Owen's cake, wolfing them down without so much as a compliment to the absent chef.

"Not to bring up something sad at the dinner table, but I'm curious..." Noah said. "Has anyone heard what's going to happen with the ACE branch now that Mitch Fangman is... Well, won't be opening it? I bet that'd be nice to have around town."

Ava cast him a sharp glance. "We already *have* a hardware store."

Noah shrugged. "Sure, but competition's not a bad thing— and they'd probably have lower prices, being a franchise. Not many folks would complain about that."

Juanita looked uncomfortable, and David shook his head, saying, "I'd imagine it's not happening. I don't think Mitch had any business partner or anyone else going in on it with him."

"Besides," Riley said, wrinkling her nose. "That building's so run-down. It'd take a lot to get it looking decent—I don't think Owen would have even had anything to worry about."

"Really?" Ava asked, turning to Riley. "Which building is it? I only know it's on Main Street. And how do you know about this?"

Riley shrugged. "I mean, there's only one empty spot downtown—next to the post office. There's never been anything there as long as I've been alive, but Mom always said it used to be Mrs. Svoboda's bookstore."

Juanita murmured her agreement, but Ava stopped, fork midway to her mouth. Setting it down, she cocked her head. "Mrs. Svoboda's bookstore?"

"Yes," Juanita said. "It shut down in the late '90s. Mrs. Svoboda was getting pretty old by then, and I think it was too much for her to handle. She died a few years after."

"Mrs. Svoboda," Ava repeated. Now that she thought about it, she *did* remember Zaidy Mel taking her to a bookstore during one of their excursions together downtown. Could it have been the same? Ava glanced at Juanita and David, then back to Riley. "Was this lady any relation to Chantelle Svoboda?"

"Her grandmother," Juanita said. "Chantelle's dad, Gary, is Velma Svoboda's son"

"Now that I'm thinking about it..." Riley mused between bites of cake. "Chantelle used to volunteer at the library during the summer reading program when I was a kid. She used to talk about wanting to open her grandma's bookstore back up, but I never really thought about the location until now. I guess it's that spot."

"Huh..." The gears in Ava's mind were starting to whir. "Does Chantelle own the building?"

This time, Juanita shook her head. "As far as I know, Chantelle's dad—Velma's son—sold the building. I suppose they needed the money."

"Interesting," Ava said. She chewed her lip, her thoughts racing.

Chantelle Svoboda's grandmother had owned a bookstore in the same spot that Mitch Fangman, Chantelle's boyfriend until a few days ago, was planning to open a hardware store? And Chantelle had, at one time, spoken of reopening the bookstore? All this could certainly be a coincidence, but... something fluttered in Ava's stomach. She knew that feeling. She needed to follow it.

"Wait," Riley said, eyebrows furrowing. "Chantelle Svoboda was Mitch's girlfriend. Do you think..."

"No idea," Ava said, cutting her off. "I just find it interesting."

Mr. Goldberg set his fork down and pushed his cake plate away. "It's time for the moment we've all been waiting for!"

"Michael," Mrs. Goldberg said, sitting bolt upright. Her face was tight, her mouth pinched. "We don't need to hear the shofar until tomorrow. We'll hear it at services."

"Nonsense," Mr. Goldberg replied, waving a hand at his wife. He shot Ava a wink, and she stifled a groan. "Our guests are here to celebrate with us—and they won't be at services tomorrow. Let's let 'em hear the festive sounds of the new year!"

Mrs. Goldberg sighed, unable to argue with her husband's logic. Ava shared her mother's sentiment, but had to admit the shofar blasts would make for a memorable experience for their guests.

"That's the spirit," Mr. Goldberg said, flashing a grin at his wife as he got to his feet. He turned to the non-Jewish guests at the table. "Now, the sounding of the shofar—the ram's horn—at Rosh Hashanah is meant to be a wake-up call of sorts. It's meant to stir the Jewish people from our complacency of the previous year and urge us forward into a new year of renewed commitment to our values. So... Without further ado..."

Ava set her jaw, watching as her father lifted the shofar from the chair next to him and raised it to his lips. Across from her, Noah was bracing himself, and Riley was leaning forward in anticipation, eager to finally see the show unfold. Poor Juanita and David just looked delighted, unaware they were about to learn what a dying elephant sounded like.

To Ava's surprise, however, the sound that erupted from the end of the shofar was clear and long, ending in a punctuated gust. Her father's face was red, his eyes nearly crossed in concentration. As he lowered the shofar, his face broke out into a grin, eyes widening in disbelief.

"Now, how about *that*?!" Mr. Goldberg shouted, grinning around the table at the group. "Did you all hear that?"

"We did," Mrs. Goldberg assured him, nodding. She put her hands together and gave a gentle little golf clap. "Mazel tov, Michael. That was—well, it was much better than I expected."

"Yeah, you've really stepped up your game, Mr. G," Riley said. She raised an eyebrow, nodding her approval.

Mr. Goldberg gave one final trumpet sound on the shofar, this time a little warbling but not nearly as abysmal as his practice attempts had been. He placed the shofar back in its pouch.

"And that, my friends," Mr. Goldberg said, "Marks the start of 5786. May it bring us nothing but happiness, joy, and harmony."

And no more murder, Ava added silently in her head.

16

———

Morning hadn't come fast enough. All night, Ava had lain awake, staring at the ceiling fan, mind spinning with questions about Chantelle's grandmother. Even during Rosh Hashanah services with her parents in Omaha, she had a hard time keeping her mind on the liturgy. Not only was Ava sure that Chantelle had been inside the press box shortly before Mitch's murder—a fact Chantelle had conveniently kept from Greathouse—but the connection Chantelle's family had with the building in which Mitch had been planning to open his ACE hardware store intrigued her. The web of lies and connections was growing ever more complex, and Ava wanted to get to the bottom of it.

Now, as Ava stood on the front stoop of Chantelle Svoboda's dingy little house, a Tupperware container of leftover apple cake clutched in her arms, she willed her heart to stop pounding. *Act normal, natural. You're here to comfort a friend. The woman's boyfriend just died, for goodness' sake.* She pressed a finger to the doorbell and stood, fidgeting, waiting.

She *was* here to make sure Chantelle was okay, but it wasn't the *only* reason for her visit, of course. The lipstick remnants on the cup in Mitch's selfie, coupled with the fact that Chantelle's grandmother had owned a bookstore in the very building Mitch had been planning to open his hardware store in, had all but convinced Ava that there was more going on with Chantelle than the woman had admitted to Greathouse. Still, Ava decided, she would feel things out. Perhaps there was a way she could coax Chantelle into giving up more information on her own.

The door opened, and Chantelle's face appeared in the crack. The relief that broke out across Chantelle's face when she saw Ava was hard to miss, and Ava felt suddenly guilty for having an ulterior motive, but also surprised by the woman's welcome. "Ava," Chantelle said, opening the front door wide. "What a nice surprise!"

Ava beamed, squashing the mixed feelings deep into her stomach. She held up the container of apple cake. "I thought I'd drop by and see how you're holding up—and I brought you a little treat."

"How kind of you! Come in, come in."

Chantelle ushered Ava inside. The house, though run-down on the outside, had a quaint, cozy sort of interior, with cushiony rugs lining the creaky hardwood floor of the hallway and clusters of framed photographs on the walls. Chantelle led Ava to the kitchen, where she pulled out a chair for her at the table.

"Can I get you something to drink?" Chantelle asked. "Coffee? Sun tea? Believe it or not, there's still enough sun these days to make it, but not for long."

"I'll never say no to coffee," Ava said. She set the container of cake on the table and removed the lid. The sweet, spicy smell of apples and cinnamon wafted into the kitchen.

"Perfect. I'll have a cup myself." Chantelle plugged in the Mr. Coffee that sat on the counter next to the sink and pulled a can of Folgers down from the cupboard. "I'm not very gourmet around here—I hope you don't mind."

"Not at all," Ava said, still smiling. Truth be told, she *was* a bit of a coffee snob—which was to be expected from someone who owned a coffee shop—but her own father was a fan of Folgers, and she'd grown up with the stuff. Besides, a cup of bland coffee was a small price to pay for staking out potential information about a murder.

Chantelle hit the button on the coffee machine and sat down at the table, across from Ava. She peered into the Tupperware container, and her eyes lit up. "Don't tell me Owen O'Kelly made this…"

"He did," Ava replied, her voice chipper. "He made it for our Rosh Hashanah dinner last night, and we had some left over, so I thought I'd bring it along for us to share. How are you doing?"

"Oh, you know," Chantelle sighed. "I'm hanging in there, and each day is better than the last, but it's hard. It's just such a shock, you know?"

"Mm." Ava gazed at Chantelle with what she hoped was a sympathetic expression. She had never been very good at expressing her feelings in front of strangers. There was also the added conundrum of whether Chantelle even *deserved* any sympathy. What if she'd been the one to murder Mitch? Had his death *really* come as a shock? "Have you heard anything else from Greathouse?"

Chantelle sighed. The coffee machine started to gurgle. "No. The last I heard, he was trying to narrow down who all had been in the press box that night, along with what golden passes were issued that can't be accounted for. I'd imagine that'll take some time."

Ava frowned. "What? Like, he's going down a list of golden pass holders and asking everyone to show proof that their card is in their possession?"

"I guess so," Chantelle said, shrugging again and sighing. "If someone doesn't have their golden pass, it obviously doesn't mean they killed Mitch, but it might at least give Greathouse something to work from."

"Right." Ava was still skeptical of Greathouse's theory, especially after seeing the selfie Mitch posted to Facebook before the game, but she didn't know how to bring the photo up to Chantelle without making her suspicions extremely obvious. "Well, you may have heard talk that my ex-husband had something to do with this, so I wanted to personally assure you he did *not*. He's not a model human, but he isn't a killer."

"I did hear it mentioned," Chantelle admitted. "I can't say I think highly of him, given the spat that went on at the pep rally, but it seems like a stretch to go from taunting to murder."

"Agreed."

"Anyway, I'm just taking things day by day," Chantelle said. "Mitch and I weren't together for *that* long, you know, but we'd gotten serious. We were talking about marriage."

Ava looked around the outdated, yet still homey kitchen. "Did you and Mitch live together?"

Chantelle nodded. "I moved in here with him a few months ago. This is technically his house."

"Oh, I see," Ava said.

Chantelle rose, moving to the counter to pour the coffee. She set the mugs down on the table, along with a couple of plates and forks, then sank back into her chair. "Since we weren't married, and the house isn't in my name, I'll have to move out, I guess. That's the least of my worries, though. I just want justice for Mitch."

Ava used a fork to slide a piece of cake onto a plate for Chantelle, and their eyes met. She *looked* sincere. Maybe she really *did* want to see Mitch's killer found and brought to justice. Maybe this whole thing had been a dumb idea. Besides, if Chantelle was the one who'd killed Mitch, wouldn't she have been glad that suspicion had fallen on Noah Shapiro?

"Well," Ava said, swallowing a bite of cake. It was even more delicious the second day. "I brought my tarot cards. I thought you might want a reading. You know, to make a little sense of how you're feeling, give you some encouragement as you move forward."

Chantelle's eyes brightened. "Oh, that would be fabulous! Could we?"

"For sure!"

Turning to dig through her purse, Ava extracted the velvet sachet of cards and set them on the table. Then, after finishing the last few remaining bites of her cake, she pushed the plate to the side, brushed the crumbs from her hands, and began shuffling the cards. Chantelle sat waiting, her spine straight in her chair, hands clasped in front of her. Her eyes were fixed on Ava's hands, following every movement they made as she shuffled the cards and set them in a pile in front of them.

Ava slid the pile toward Chantelle. "Cut that into three smaller piles, then stack them again however you want. We'll do a three-card spread today. I think it'll be better to keep things simple, so you don't feel overwhelmed."

Chantelle did as she was told, then leaned forward with her elbows on the table, her chin in her hands. She looked expectantly back at Ava.

"We'll do a past, present, future spread. So, the first card will represent the past, the second card will represent the present, and so on. This'll be less about predicting or explaining anything, and more about just helping you get a handle on what you're feeling. Sometimes the imagery on the cards can help us tap into our subconscious in a different way than we normally do." Ava offered Chantelle a conspiratorial smile.

Ava didn't, of course, mention the purpose the spread would have for *her*—helping her to measure Chantelle's reactions and get a feel for what had really been going on in her relationship with Mitch. Ava settled her weight forward in her chair, feeling the same tingle she always felt when she started a new tarot reading. It was like a spark that lay dormant throughout most of the day but which flared to life as soon as the cards were out. She turned over the top card and placed it in front of Chantelle, all the way to the left.

"The six of pentacles, but reversed," Ava announced." Pentacles are tied to the material world—career, finances, that kind of thing. Stability at its most basic level."

"Right..." Chantelle waited.

"So, the upright six of pentacles usually signifies an act of charity or reimbursement. Maybe someone of greater financial means is helping take care of someone with less, or maybe you receive compensation for something you've been waiting for. This card symbolizes that, although there's a gap in means between two parties, the gap is lessening, moving toward balance."

Ava paused, allowing Chantelle to absorb her explanation. Whenever she read tarot, it was almost as if the meanings just flew to her, unbridled, and she had to hang on tight, sifting through the torrent of intuition to find the words that would resonate most with the person she was reading for.

"But you said that's if it is upright," Chantelle said, frowning. "This one's reversed. What's that mean?"

"It means the gap was widening, rather than lessening. What this card is saying is that, in the past—whether that's the recent past or something much more deeply rooted—you felt there was an imbalance of material means that wasn't getting any more balanced. Maybe getting worse."

"Hmm," Chantelle said. She looked pensive, as though thinking back. "To be honest, I always felt envious of Mitch, of how easy things were for him, especially financially. I mean, he had a *house*, a car, made extra money on the weekends at the football games. He was planning to open his own business, too."

And right in the spot you wanted your business to be, Ava thought. Instead, she said, "Ah. Well, let's see what the next card says."

Chantelle drew the next card. It was another pentacles card —this time the two.

"Twos usually indicate choices and decisions," Ava said. "And since this one's in the suit of pentacles, it probably means the decision has to do with something financial or career-related. Are you worried about finances? Of having to do it alone, without Mitch?"

Or maybe you're trying to decide how callous it would look to buy that spot on Main Street for yourself. Would you arouse suspicion by snatching it up so soon after Mitch's death?

"Oh, somewhat," Chantelle said. "But, you know, we weren't *married.* We kept our finances separate, for the most part. I don't know—I'll have to think on that. Maybe I need to decide if I should take more time off work to recuperate."

"That could be it," Ava said. Inside, she thought, *Yeah, right.*

Chantelle turned over the third and final card: Justice.

Well, *that* was convenient. It was hard for Ava to fight back a smile as she surveyed the card, tracing her fingertips around its worn edges.

"Now, this one's a no-brainer," Chantelle said. She looked at the card for a moment, then, voice cracking, said, "That's all I really care about right now—justice for Mitch."

Even if it means spending your own life behind bars?

But Ava knew she had to tread more cautiously than that. If Chantelle was indeed a killer, there was nothing to stop her from grabbing a knife from a drawer and plunging it into Ava's chest right then and there. Ava hadn't even told anyone where she was going. No one would know the first place to look once they realized she was missing.

As Chantelle studied the card a little longer, Ava let her gaze drift around the room. Suddenly, her eyes stopped moving. An icy cold seized her chest. There, on the counter, was a half-empty jar of peanut butter. *Wasn't Mitch's whole problem with Noah the fact that he'd spat out a Snickers bar near him? A Snickers bar containing peanuts?*

"Chantelle," Ava said, her gaze still fixed on the peanut butter jar. "Mitch lived here too, right?"

Chantelle frowned. "Yeah..."

She stared at Ava, as though trying to decipher the sober

expression she now wore. Her eyes followed Ava's gaze, landing on the peanut butter. Even across the table, Ava felt Chantelle tense, but the woman said nothing about the jar. Instead, she asked, "More coffee?"

Ava shook her head. Chantelle had caught her looking at the peanut butter. She'd come too far; it was now or never. She drew a deep breath. "Isn't it sort of the norm to keep peanut products out of the house when someone in the household is as allergic as Mitch was?"

Her mind was racing, trying to make sense of the details. Mitch had been strangled. She and Owen had seen that clearly, and Greathouse had confirmed it. Had Chantelle somehow poisoned him *first*, then used the microphone cord to fake strangulation after Mitch was already dead? Maybe Greathouse was right in his assertion that Chantelle wouldn't have had the strength to *actually* strangle Mitch...

"Oh, that," Chantelle said, her voice a little breathless. She waved a hand. "Absolutely—but, you know, I've needed some comfort food these past couple days..."

Ava raised an eyebrow. "That's a huge jar of peanut butter, Chantelle. Like, Costco size. There's no way you ate half a jar of peanut butter by yourself in two days. Besides—you told me you'd barely been eating!"

Chantelle looked stunned. Drawing a short, shallow breath, she smiled nervously and began to stutter out an explanation. "I've barely been eating *real* food. Peanut butter is about the only thing that sounds good. I'm one of those people." She gave a nervous laugh. But the debilitating sadness that filled Chantelle's eyes was not a look that suggested the woman was about to jump up and kill her. She looked, instead, like a lost and desperate woman.

Chantelle's hand was resting on the table in front of her, and Ava reached to cover it with one of her own.

"Chantelle," Ava said. She stared at Chantelle until the woman met her eyes and held her gaze. "I want to know what happened. I found the selfie Mitch posted to Facebook at the start of halftime. There was a cup in the background, which had your lipstick stains on the rim. Why didn't you tell Greathouse you'd been in the press box Friday night?"

Chantelle dropped her gaze. She stared at the table, but she didn't pull her hand out from beneath Ava's.

"I heard about your grandmother's bookstore," Ava added, hoping a reminder of a much-loved family member might cause something inside Chantelle to loosen.

"My grandmother basically raised me. She was everything to me, and she loved that bookstore. I always said after she had to give it up that I would buy that building someday and reopen the store," Chantelle said. Her voice was quiet as she looked up at Ava. "I just haven't been able to afford it yet. And then... Mitch—"

Her voice broke, but Ava didn't jump in to continue what she suspected Chantelle had been going to say. Instead, she gave the woman's hand a squeeze and sat back in her own chair, waiting.

Chantelle finally found her voice again. "Mitch told me over a game of keno one night that he was planning to buy that place downtown. I swear I felt my world shatter, but I didn't let on like anything was wrong—I went to school with Mitch, I know how stubborn he can get. One word from someone else about what he ought to do, and he'll dig in his heels and stop at nothing to do the opposite."

"But surely as your boyfriend…" Ava wasn't following. Had Mitch really been that callous?

Chantelle sighed. "We weren't dating back then. That's *why* we started dating—because it was the only way I could think of to influence the situation. He's a good-looking guy, so it wasn't the worst, but let's just say we butted heads."

And it's looking more and more like you did more than just butt heads. You took things to another level…

"So, you started dating Mitch to try to get him to not buy the building downtown?" Ava was trying to keep everything straight.

"Right. And it killed me because he didn't even *need* that place. He could've afforded something way nicer! I guess it's like that card said—an imbalance in resources." Chantelle shrugged, looking crestfallen. "Here, I'd been saving for so long to buy that place, and here comes Mitch Fangman, swooping in to buy it out from under me."

Ava glanced at the peanut butter jar. Turning back to Chantelle, she lowered her voice, almost afraid to ask what she most wanted to know. "So—what? You went in at halftime, waited until the other announcer left, and took Mitch brownies with peanut butter or something? And then used the microphone cord to cover your tracks, to make it look like he'd been strangled?"

Chantelle shook her head forcefully, her red curls bobbing. "No! That's what I'm trying to tell you, Ava—I had nothing to do with Mitch's murder."

Ava cocked her head. What was all this about then? The peanut butter, the lipstick, feigning a relationship with him, the not coming forward to Greathouse…

"I'm not following," Ava said, frowning.

Chantelle blew out her breath. She covered her face with her hands, mumbling from behind her fingers. "I didn't kill Mitch, but I was going to." Chantelle raked her fingers down her face, then sat, slumped in her chair. Her eyes reached Ava's, and Ava saw the tears that had welled in the corners.

"I was desperate," Chantelle said, her voice pleading. "I'm sure it sounds stupid to you, but that place was my *dream*. My grandmother, she—she *raised* me—when my own mother wouldn't—and I couldn't bear to see the place go to someone else. That dream was the last connection I had with my grandma. I *needed* it. I couldn't let it die."

Ava nodded. She could feel Chantelle's desperation, could understand why the woman had felt so strongly about the building. Ava felt the same way about living in her Zaidy Mel's house. Her grandfather's house had given her a new sense of life and purpose. But she couldn't understand killing over it. Still, she let Chantelle go on.

"Last Wednesday night, Mitch came home with a contract. Said he'd take the weekend to look it over, then turn it in on Monday. Up til then, nothing I'd said or done had seemed to budge his decision at all, and I knew he'd sign that paper and it would be over. I decided the only option was to—was to get rid of Mitch."

"Oh, Chantelle," Ava breathed. Chantelle held up a hand, signaling that her story wasn't over.

"I figured the safest bet would be to make Mitch's death look like an accident—which wouldn't be hard to do with how allergic he is to peanuts. And if anyone traced it back to me, I could play dumb. So, while he was at work on Friday, I bought that peanut butter and made a batch of brownies. I even tasted them to make sure the scent and taste of the peanut butter wasn't noticeable. I had them all boxed up, ready to go, to take to him during the game, but then—" Chantelle's voice broke, and she sat for a moment, the lump in her throat moving up and down as she struggled to get a hold on herself.

"You couldn't do it?" Ava asked gently.

Chantelle nodded, and a wild sob escaped her. That was all it took for the tears to start. Ava pulled her chair next to Chantelle's and placed a hand on the woman's back. She'd never been one to display much physical affection, but the people of Shiloh had a way of demanding it from her—and so she complied.

Chantelle's shoulders heaved with her sobs, her tears pooling on the table. Ava wondered if it would be rude to offer Chantelle the hand towel that hung from the handle of the oven and decided against it.

"It's okay," Ava said. She patted Chantelle's back awkwardly. "It's really okay. No one has to know. The important thing is that you *didn't* do it, right?"

"But I was *so close*, Ava," Chantelle said, moaning.

"But you didn't do it," Ava said firmly. "It may have been at the last minute, but you got your head screwed back on straight, and you didn't go through with it. That's what matters."

Ava was not sure she entirely believed this—after all, she'd never gone about *actually* planning someone's murder—but what else could she say? A woman was sitting in front of her bawling her eyes out, and Ava couldn't very well make her feel even worse about what she'd done. Or nearly done. Chantelle didn't need any help in that arena.

"What made you decide to scrap the plan?" Ava asked.

Chantelle was quiet for a moment, sniffling as she sifted

through her thoughts. "I couldn't take someone's life—especially not someone who trusted me like Mitch did. My grandmother would've been horrified. *I* would have been horrified. I realized there's no building that would ever be worth the guilt I'd have to carry around for the rest of my life—bookstore or no bookstore."

Ava was still parsing the story she'd just been told. It seemed crazy, but then again, the world was built on crazy event after crazy event. The part that bothered her now was that, after all this, she was back to square one: she had no clue who had killed Mitch Fangman.

"So," Ava said, knitting her brow in thought. "Why weren't you honest with Greathouse about being in the press box? I mean, you didn't go through with your plan. You had nothing to hide."

Chantelle shuddered. "Are you *kidding*? Can you imagine how freaked out I was when, just hours after I'd planned to kill Mitch and couldn't go through with it, he winds up *dead*?"

Ava had to admit that Chantelle had a point. "Fair. That's pretty... coincidental."

"For a minute, I even thought—*oh god, did I accidentally take the brownies by mistake?* It really messed with my head," Chantelle said. "The last thing I wanted at that point was for Greathouse to know I was the last person to see Mitch alive. I wanted to stay far, *far* away from the entire situation."

"Well, I guess someone else did your dirty work for you," Ava remarked. "I just want to figure out *who*."

Chantelle nodded. "I know. I do, too. I've been a nervous wreck, though, since Friday—jumping every time the phone rings or someone knocks on the door. The guilt of what I was planning to do has just been eating me up."

Although she didn't say it aloud, Ava thought this feeling of Chantelle's was, however unfortunate, probably somewhat deserved. The woman had been planning to *kill* someone, after all. She *should* feel guilty. It also explained the look of relief on Chantelle's face when she opened the door and saw Ava on her doorstep.

Across the table, Chantelle drummed her long fingernails on the table. "You probably think I'm happy that Mitch is dead —that someone else went through with it—but I'm not. I never wanted Mitch *dead*—I was just desperate. And thank god I came to my senses."

Sitting back in her chair, Ava studied the woman across from her. Chantelle's eyes were rimmed with red, and she looked so utterly devastated that Ava had a hard time *not* believing her story was real. It seemed so preposterous, and yet...

"Where did you go after you left Mitch in the press box? To the stands?"

Chantelle shook her head. "I was so torn up with guilt about what I'd been about to do, I knew I'd never be able to enjoy the game. I also knew I couldn't stay with Mitch—after what I'd been planning, how could I *live* with him, face him every day?—so I went home to start packing. The only reason I stopped by the game at all was for a sense of closure, and I don't think Mitch suspected anything."

"Okay, and would you say this was towards the beginning of halftime? Or the end?"

"I was in the press box while the marching band was play-ing, and they were marching off the field when I left. I heard Mitch announce the dance team on my way out."

"So... You said 'hi' to Mitch at halftime, acted like everything was normal between the two of you. Did he act weird at all? Or did anyone say anything that might have seemed suspicious in hindsight?"

Chantelle chewed her lip, thinking back. "Mitch acted like he always does: cocky, assertive, laughing loud. No one else was in the press box by then. Fred must've gone for his smoke break. But come to think of it…"

Ava leaned forward, her pulse quickening. She tried not to let the anticipation show on her face. Was this it? Had Chantelle seen the murderer?

"I bumped into someone as I was coming down the press box stairs," Chantelle said. "I didn't get a look at the person's face—it was surprisingly dark already—but the reason I even remember it is because they—honestly, I think it was a guy—had this *smell*…"

Ava raised her eyebrows. "Like, body odor?"

"No—a good smell. Maybe some kind of cologne. But whatever it was, I caught a huge whiff as they brushed past me."

Ava felt her heart speed up. If there was one good thing she could say about Noah, it was that he always smelled good. "Okay. Did you see what this person looked like? At all?"

"Not really. Like I said, I'm pretty sure it was a man—just by the build and the haircut—"

"Which was… what?" Ava was dubious.

"Well," Chantelle said, squinting as she thought back. She studied the wall, trying to remember. "It was short, like maybe it had been buzzed a few weeks ago. And pretty light. But again, it was pretty dark coming down the stairs, so I can't be sure…"

Short. Buzzed. Relief flooded Ava's stomach. Noah's hair was dark, and he wore it long. No one would ever have described it as 'buzzed'. *But then again,* she hastened to remind herself as her chest filled with hope, *just because Chantelle saw someone climbing the press box stairs, it doesn't mean that person is automatically the murderer.*

"Chantelle," Ava said. "I don't want you to think I'm doubting you, but I don't know how else to put this: Did anyone see you leave? Or talk to you after you left the press box?"

"You're asking if I have an alibi," Chantelle said. "And I do. I nearly had a breakdown on the way out, so I called my sister just to hear someone else's voice. There will be records of that call, and the police can contact her if needed. Actually, I ended up dropping by her house to try to regain a sense of normalcy. I was there until I got the call from Greathouse about Mitch."

"Okay. Good. Because we need to take this to Greathouse."

Chantelle groaned, slumped back in her chair. Her red curls tumbled around her shoulders, and she stared at the ceiling. "I had a feeling you were going to say that. Do we *have* to?"

"Well," Ava began. The wheels of her mind were spinning. "To be honest, I guess he doesn't *need* to know you were planning to... Well, do what you were planning to do. You didn't go through with it in the end. But yes, he needs to know you were in the press box that night and that you saw someone on the stairs."

Chantelle thought for a moment, looking out the window as she avoided Ava's gaze. When she finally turned back, she said, "Would you do it? Tell him what I saw? If the Chief wants to call me, he can, but I've been kind of an emotional wreck. I just... don't want to relive that night again. It's been bad enough this morning."

Ava sighed. Although she understood where Chantelle was coming from, she wasn't sure if Greathouse would give a relayed message any credence. Then again, it was better than nothing.

"Fine," Ava said as she stood up to go. "I'll bring it up when he comes into Cafe Arcana tomorrow. But I'm telling you now: If he wants to hear it straight from the source, be prepared to answer your phone or come straight down to the station with me. No arguments."

"Deal," Chantelle said.

17

———

Despite the steady sunlight that filtered down through the trees, the early afternoon weather was crisp and delightfully cool as Ava and Riley made their way around Larkspur Lake, scanning the path for Rose. After the disaster of the previous night's dinner, the schlep to Omaha for synagogue services, and the whirlwind of her visit to Chantelle's house, Ava would be glad for a break from the chaos. Her parents had opted for an afternoon nap, which Ava was glad of, as she wanted to fill Rose and Riley in on the events of the past twenty-four hours without the risk of being overheard. There was no way Ava was going to let her mother find out she'd gone to visit a might-be murderer.

There'd also been radio silence from Owen since last night, but Ava couldn't blame him. Hearing that stuff from Noah? Being made to feel like the odd one out in front of his sort-of girlfriend and by her ex-husband? She'd have been distancing herself, too, if the tables were turned. What she needed now was a quiet afternoon for reflection.

"Over here!"

Riley and Ava spotted Rose at the same time as she called out, waving to them. Turning the stroller she was pushing around on the path, she started in their direction.

"Hey," Rose said, pushing her sunglasses to the top of her blond, curly head. In her stroller, Ellie waved a baggie of goldfish crackers in greeting. "How are you two? How'd last night go?"

Ava and Riley shared a quick glance.

"Uh," Ava began, "Last night was—eventful. And today was, too."

Rose's cinnamon-colored eyes grew round. "Uh-oh. Eventful doesn't sound very positive."

"That's correct," Ava said. She pulled out one of the zip-top baggies of breadcrumbs she'd packed in her purse and nodded her head toward the lake. "Let's get this *tashlich* party started, and we'll tell you as we walk."

Riley and Rose both squinted at her. "Oh, I'll explain *tashlich* when we get to the lake," she said.

The three of them—and baby Ellie in her stroller—stepped off the path and headed across the still-soft grass toward the water's edge.

"So, last night," Ava said. "It was me, my parents, Noah, Owen, Juanita, and David. Riley had a date to the homecoming dance, so she wasn't going to join us."

"Ooh," Rose said, shooting Riley a wink. "A date, huh?"

Riley waved a hand. "Don't get too excited. The jerk stood me up."

"He *what*?!"

"I guess it was supposed to be a prank." Riley's eyes moved to her shoes. "Asking me at all, I mean. That's what Summer Davis told me."

"Well, if whoever it is thinks *that* is funny, I'd say you dodged a bullet," Rose scoffed.

"Yeah... He keeps calling me, but I blocked his number. No way am I going to let them keep stringing me along. Anyway, I came home last night halfway through dinner, but I didn't want to bother anyone, so I tried to come in through the bathroom window—"

"And made a huge freaking clatter, which scared those of us at the table half to death. We thought someone was breaking in," Ava said, continuing the story. "My dad got up, grabbed the closest thing near him that could be used as a weapon—which turned out to be a shofar—and went to scout it out. We get to the bathroom, and lo and behold, there's Riley."

Rose chanced a laugh, glancing at Riley to make sure they hadn't offended the girl. "Well, I'm at least glad you had a nice dinner and good company to spend the evening with—rather than that jerk who stood you up."

"Yes," Riley said, shooting a small smile at Ava. "I am, too."

"Although I can't say the morale at the dinner table was very pleasant," Ava remarked. "Noah started making all these comments about the house we used to live in—how nice it was, how much I loved it, the money he made—and the trips we used to take, stuff like that. It was weird, but *then* he started talking about how Owen probably never met my grandfather because our families' social circles wouldn't have overlapped. It was pretty clear what he meant by that."

"Ew!" Rose looked aghast. Ava couldn't tell if it was from what Noah had said or from the mash of chewed-up goldfish that was now falling out of Ellie's mouth as she squawked in delight at the lake. "That's so *rude.*"

"Yikes," Riley muttered. "I haven't heard *this* part yet."

Ava sighed. "Yeah... And you know Owen—he didn't say anything. He just looked really uncomfortable, as did most of us at the table, I'm sure. My mother, of course, acted like nothing at all was wrong."

"So, what happened then?"

"Nothing. He left before dessert, told my dad he had to be somewhere early this morning. I've heard nothing since."

They came to a stop at the edge of the lake. Looking out across the rippling water, Ava unzipped the top of her bag of breadcrumbs.

"Okay, so what are these breadcrumbs for again?" Riley asked.

"We throw them in the lake, and it's supposed to symbolize casting off our sins. It's something we do at Rosh Hashanah," Ava said. She brought up a handful of breadcrumbs out of the bag and filtered them into Riley's and Rose's cupped palms. "Water's seen as a purifying element, which adds to the symbolism."

Rose looked solemn. "Are we supposed to say anything special when we do it?"

"Yeah." Ava fished around in her purse for the prayer book she'd jammed into it before leaving the house. She didn't pray often, but she'd received it as a present at her bat mitzvah and enjoyed seeing it on the living room bookshelf, another piece of her heritage in Shiloh. She flipped through the pages, landing on the one for *tashlich*. "Here it is."

Riley glanced at the page, still clutching her breadcrumbs. She wrinkled her freckled nose. "That's *way* long. Hard pass from me."

Ava and Rose both laughed. Below them, the water rippled, glimmering cool and serene in the overhead sun.

"Well, then—anything else either of you want to cast off, other than sins? I know I'll be casting off all this stuff with Noah. It's such old news, and it doesn't have a place in my life anymore."

Rose thought for a moment. "I'd like to throw off my habit of devaluing myself as a mom. I'm always beating up on myself for not doing enough, not working hard enough, not being fun enough. Blah, blah, blah. I want to get rid of that energy."

Ava nodded. "That's perfect. I love that. What about you, Riley?"

Riley studied her feet. She was quiet a moment, as though deciding whether she wanted to voice her true thoughts. "I guess... What happened last night. I'm definitely ready to let that go. Trevor Phillips is a *jerk*, and those other girls—Summer Davis, especially—are just as bad. I'm pretty sure they knew all along."

"Knew *what* all along?" Rose asked.

"That Trevor only asked me as a joke," Riley said, staring out at the lake. "They told me someone dared him, and that he didn't think I'd actually say yes—that he never thought I'd think he was for *real*. Because, I mean, how *could* it be real? Trevor Phillips? *Me*?"

Ava snorted. "Oh, please. First off, you shouldn't talk that way about yourself. Second, he has no reason to act like he's better than everyone else—he's not even that cute!"

This was not true—Trevor Phillips *was* cute—but Ava hoped Riley would take the statement for what it was: an attempt to make her feel better.

"He's alright," Riley said, shrugging. She looked down at the breadcrumbs, now growing soggy in her sweaty hands.

Ava couldn't fault Riley for being excited that one of the

most popular boys in school had asked her to attend the dance with him, but she wasn't sure she would've chosen to accept the date. Then again, Ava had always been semi-popular; she hadn't had to fight for respect among her peers. When it really came down to it, she had no idea what it was like to be in Riley's shoes.

"I was just so *excited*," Riley said, looking between Ava and Rose. "Like, for the first time, it felt like someone *wanted* me. You know?"

Ava nodded. This, she *did* understand.

"Anyway, I'm throwing *all* of last night into this lake!" Riley pushed a strand of hair behind her ears, grinning.

"Perfect—and I'm throwing away Noah's stupid attempts to lure me back in," Ava said. She stood on the shore, a fistful of breadcrumbs raised, poised for the throw. She glanced between Rose and Riley, grinning. "On the count of three, okay? One, two—"

"Three!" Riley and Rose broke in.

They tossed their breadcrumbs to the water, laughing as the breeze caught most of the pieces and they floated down only a few feet in front of them.

"Good enough," Ava said, wiping the remaining crumbs from her hands and stuffing the now empty bag back in her pocket next to the second bag. She'd have to remember to add them to the bird feeder in her yard later. She, Rose, and Riley had sufficiently cast off their negativity for the day.

As they made their way back to the path and continued around the lake, Ava relished the rustling of the leaves in the trees overhead, punctuated by the occasional flutter and flap of bird wings. It wouldn't be long before the birds, wiser than the local humans, sensed the shift in the weather and headed south to escape the impending cold. For now, though, the days were pleasantly crisp, and the sun was still bright, with just the hint of autumn chill in the evenings. It was Ava's favorite time of year.

"So..." Rose said, breaking into Ava's revelry. "You two told me about last night—but you also mentioned something about this morning being dramatic?"

Riley shot Ava a sharp glance. "Yeah, what *did* you mean by that?"

"Well..." Ava began, smiling sheepishly. "Last night, Riley mentioned something interesting about the building that Mitch Fangman was going to buy downtown."

Rose groaned. "Oh, Ava. *Please* tell me you're not prying into Mitch's murder..."

"Not *prying*," Ava said, knowing very well she was one hundred percent prying. "I've just been asking questions. Out of curiosity."

"Right." Rose did not look amused.

"Anyway, Riley said something about how there hadn't been a business in that space since Mrs. Svoboda's bookshop closed down when she was a kid."

"Uh-huh..."

"And that name rang a bell in my head. *Mrs. Svoboda.* Chantelle Svoboda was Mitch's girlfriend. Juanita confirmed that Mrs. Svoboda had been Chantelle's grandma."

Rose grimaced. "She's right. But I'm not sure I want to hear where the rest of this is going..."

"Oh, come on. Just bear with me," Ava said. "The thing is, I was scrolling through Mitch's Facebook and came across a selfie he posted from the press box, right before the game. In the background, you can see a coffee cup with a ring of purple lipstick on the rim—the *exact* color that Chantelle wears."

Rose looked less than convinced. "So?"

"Yeah, so?" Riley repeated.

"Well, given that Chantelle said nothing to Greathouse about being in the press box at all that night, it looks pretty suspicious. Why wouldn't she come forward?"

"Okay. Go on," Rose said, pressing her lips together. She waved her hand for Ava to continue.

"So, once I found out there was *another* connection between Chantelle and Mitch—"

"Duh!" Rose broke in, throwing up her hands. "They were dating! Of *course,* there was a connection."

"You know what I mean," Ava said, giving both Rose and Riley the side eye. "I mean *interesting* connections. Once I found out about Mrs. Svoboda's store, I knew I needed to—you know—ask Chantelle about it."

Rose closed her eyes and inhaled, like she was praying for patience from on high. "You're not going to say you went over to Chantelle's house to *confront* her about this, are you?"

"Well, why not?" Ava demanded, although she knew perfectly well why not. It was never a good idea to drop in unannounced at the house of a person you thought might be connected to a murder—a fact she ought to have known better than anyone at this point. "Greathouse made it clear he didn't believe a woman could've done it, and you know how he gets a bee in his bonnet with whatever theory he's decided to go with. That man has a one-track mind."

"Ava, you have to admit it wasn't the smartest move," Rose said. "What if Chantelle did have some motive or something and, well, really *did* kill Mitch? What's stopping her from killing you, too?"

Riley sniffed, apparently in agreement.

"I know, I know," Ava groaned. She *did* know it, too. "Chantelle didn't kill Mitch, though."

Rose furrowed her blond brow. "How do you know?"

"Because—" Ava stopped. Did she owe it to Chantelle to keep her story a secret? No—the woman had been planning a crazy choice, and Ava didn't owe her anything. She'd be telling Greathouse tomorrow, anyway. "She was *going* to kill him, but then backed out at the last minute."

"What?!" Riley gasped.

"She *told* you that?" Rose shrieked. "Like, just came out and admitted it?"

"Pretty much. She had this huge jar of peanut butter on her counter—half empty—and I commented on how odd it was to have that in your house when your partner is so allergic—and she just broke down, came out with the whole story."

"Good lord," Rose said.

"She said that ever since her grandmother's store closed down, she's dreamed of opening a bookstore in the same spot. I guess Mrs. Svoboda raised her, and Chantelle wanted to keep that connection alive now that she's passed. She's been saving up for a down payment on the place, but Mitch snatched it up first. Apparently, the whole reason she was even *with* Mitch was to try to coax him into opening his store somewhere else."

"Are you kidding me?" Rose looked like she didn't know whether to scoff or laugh.

Ava shook her head. "Not a bit. It wasn't until Mitch came home with an actual contract that she got desperate. She was going to take him brownies with peanut butter in them, had them all ready to go, but came to her senses at the last minute."

"Jeez, thank god! What was she *thinking*?" Rose looked stunned.

"I know. Anyway, she didn't go through with it, but she didn't say anything to Greathouse about being in the press box on Friday because she felt so guilty about the whole thing."

"I can imagine. But—do you believe her?"

"I do." Ava shielded her eyes as she looked out once more at the lake. There'd been no denying the devastation in Chantelle's eyes as she'd come clean to Ava at her kitchen table. "She says she's got an alibi, too. But this stays between us, okay? Because the next part of this story is that, as she was coming down the press box stairs, Chantelle says someone going *up* the stairs bumped into her. I'm going to tell Greathouse about it, but I really hope Chantelle will speak to him herself too. I won't mention to him that she was, in fact, planning to kill Mitch."

"Well, does she know who she saw?" Riley asked. "Can she describe the person?"

"Unfortunately, no. It was already somewhat dark by then, so all she got was a glance at the haircut and build, but she's pretty sure it was a man. She also said he smelled really good."

Rose wrinkled her nose. "Well, that rules out half the men in this town. I'd say the typical smell around here is cow manure and *eau de tractor grease*."

Ava laughed, feeling some of the tension dissipate. She was glad Rose hadn't called her out for suggesting she wouldn't tell Greathouse *all* of Chantelle's story. If Chantelle wanted to come clean, great—but it wasn't Ava's place to do it for her. Not when she'd made the right decision in the end.

"So, what are you going to do about Owen?" Rose asked,

switching gears. She studied Ava intently, as though trying to read any changes in her expression.

"Honestly…" Ava began, her voice trailing off. "I have no clue."

"You need to talk to him," Riley said.

"Duh." Ava rolled her eyes, but her face grew hot. It was simple, obvious advice, but she was feeling ganged up on. It *wasn't* a given that Ava would handle this correctly, and they all knew it.

"Seriously, though," Rose said. "Owen's a good guy, and he's patient, but he won't put up with this forever. You're going to have to figure out what you're doing. Like, are you in, or are you out?"

Ava heaved a sigh. "I know, I *know*. But it's so *complicated*!"

"Is it?" Rose pressed, cocking her head to the side to stare Ava down. "Is it really that complicated? Or are you just scared to stand up to your mom?"

Riley let out a low whistle.

Ava scoffed, folding her arms across her chest. "That's ridiculous. I'm *not* scared of her."

Rose said nothing, just nodded. They'd reached the end of the sidewalk now, and their parked cars were in sight. Rose unbuckled Ellie and scooped her up, collapsing the stroller with one hand while she gave Ava a pointed look.

"I'll talk to him," Ava said. She hoped they could be done with this part of the conversation. Her situation with Owen *was* complicated. Rose had no idea how lucky she was that she and Joel were of similar familial backgrounds.

"Good."

It took both Ava and Riley to figure out how to buckle Ellie correctly in her car seat while Rose loaded the stroller into the back of her SUV. As Rose came around the side of the vehicle, she stood for a moment, shielding her eyes from the now setting sun. Concern darkened her face.

"Be careful, okay?" Rose said, giving Ava's arm a quick squeeze. "Go to Greathouse tomorrow, and then, for the love of god, please stay *out* of this."

"I will."

"And I'll hold her to that," Riley offered.

As Rose climbed into the driver's seat and took off toward home, Ava and Riley did the same. Ava's mind was racing with everything that had happened and all the pieces of the various puzzles she was trying to sort through. There was one more thing that nagged at her, though, as she shifted the car into drive and headed down the street—something she kept forgetting to ask Riley about.

The dress Ava had lent Riley for homecoming had appeared magically back in Ava's closet that morning. And when Ava remembered back through the events of the previous night, she'd realized Riley's silver dress was not the one Ava had lent her.

"Oh, hey," Ava said, breaking the silence one last time before she and Riley pulled into the driveway. She tried to keep her voice nonchalant. "Whose dress was that you had on last night?"

Riley tensed, but her face remained smooth. "Mine."

"I thought you didn't have one," Ava said, raising an eyebrow. Riley's previous words aside, Ava had a very hard time believing Riley would have a glamorous little number like *that* lying around at home. And the *strappy little open-toed pumps*? Ava had never seen Riley wear heels, aside from a platformed combat boot.

Riley shrugged. "Your mom took me shopping."

Ava blinked. "She did?"

"Mmhm."

Ava sat back, her head against the head rest. This was news to her. Why hadn't her mother mentioned it to her yesterday? Although, come to think of it, Ava's father *had* said something about Sara and Riley being gone for ages the day before...

"Did you not like the dress I lent you?"

Riley shrugged again. "It was fine. But the one your mom helped me pick out was more my style. And honestly, I think it made your mom really happy—taking me shopping, I mean. I've never seen someone so excited about *shoes*."

"Huh."

As they plodded up the sidewalk to the house, Ava turned this new piece of information over in her mind. She still wasn't sure why her mother hadn't said anything, but the mental image of Sara Goldberg helping Riley try on homecoming dresses and pick out heels tugged at her heartstrings. It wasn't something she'd have expected from her mother. Sure, her mom had taken her shopping countless times growing up—but somehow, they always seemed to leave the store with the clothes *Sara* had picked out.

But this? This sounded different. This sounded like Sara had helped Riley shine—without taking any credit for it at all. Given that her mother had volunteered none of this information herself, Ava decided she wouldn't bring it up. But knowing what Sara had done was intriguing in itself, marking a subtle shift in her mother Ava hadn't known was there. Perhaps Ava's issues with Noah weren't the only thing she ought to cast off for the coming year. Perhaps her history with her mother, too, deserved a spot at the sandy bottom of Larkspur Lake.

18
____

The next morning when Chief Greathouse came striding into Cafe Arcana, Ava had already checked the clock a half a dozen times, willing him to arrive. Although she wasn't even sure he'd listen to her—he'd most likely just want to hear straight from Chantelle herself—she was eager to get what she knew off her chest. She'd still heard nothing from Owen, and, despite Rose's advice, hadn't yet reached out. Between the tension with Owen and sitting on Chantelle's potential lead, there was only so much waiting around she could stand. But now here was Greathouse, booming his usual "good morning" around the shop, which happened to be empty aside from Ava.

The chief slapped his beefy palms on the countertop, glancing up at the menu. It was the same song and dance every day, although Ava knew he'd always order his dark roast with a splash of cream.

"Mornin', Ava," Chief Greathouse said. His mustache quivered as he scanned the menu, his lips moving with the words.

"Hi Chief. What can I get for you this morning?"

"Oh," Greathouse drawled, as though he needed to think.

He gave the counter another slap, signaling his decision, then leaned back on the heels of his boots. "You know, I guess I'll go with the usual. Dark roast, bit of room for cream."

"You got it." Ava smiled at Greathouse, pulled a cup down off the stack next to the coffee urns. "I just brewed a fresh pot, too."

Greathouse grunted his approval. "Saw you were closed yesterday when the missus and I came downtown to grab a bite for lunch—almost forgot you had that—that whatchamacallit—the *holiday*…"

Ava smiled, suppressing a laugh. "Rosh Hashanah, yeah. It's still going on today, too, but I figured the good people of Shiloh would need their coffee more than I needed another day at home with my parents."

Greathouse, catching the whiff of sarcasm in her voice, gave an amused sort of snort. "Well, I can understand that. If I had to spend two days at Christmas with my mother-in-law, it wouldn't be a pretty sight. Plus, you've got that ex floating around—weird situation, if you ask me."

"Well, I *didn't* ask you," Ava said, suppressing an eye roll as she snapped the lid onto Greathouse's coffee and slid it across the counter to him. "But now that you mention it, where's the investigation at? Any progress narrowing down the list of Golden Pass holders?"

Greathouse fixed a stern eye on Ava as he handed her his credit card. "That's police business, little lady. What's it to you?"

Since the moment she'd moved to town, "little lady" had been Greathouse's name for her, and by now she knew he meant it affectionately rather than in a patronizing way. Even so, it took everything within her not to snarl. Complaining wouldn't get her very far with Greathouse at the moment, and what she needed was information.

"Well, that ex that's floating around hasn't exactly been cleared yet," she said, looking at the chief pointedly. She handed his card back to him, then took a deep breath. It was now or never. "And actually, I've been hearing some things, and I thought maybe you should know about them…"

Greathouse snapped to attention. "What? What things have you heard?"

Ava took a rag from the sink and scrubbed at the already clean counter. "It might be nothing, honestly…"

Once again, Greathouse looked at her sternly. He took a slurp of his coffee, trying to hide his wince at how hot it was. "Well, I'll be the judge of that. Spit it out."

Ava glanced around, although she already knew no one else was in the shop. "I spoke with someone who was near the press box stairs during halftime."

Greathouse's tone was sharp. "Yeah? Who?"

"Well…" Ava cocked her head, hesitating. This was tricky territory. It seemed Chantelle hadn't come forward yet, and Ava wasn't sure of the best way to break the news.

The chief glared at her. "You better spill what you know, Goldberg—or else I may be tempted to think you're coming up with some kind of unprovable nonsense to get that city boy ex of yours off the hook."

"What?! No—no, it's not that at all. It's just—" Ava stopped. She was only making Chantelle seem more suspicious by beating around the bush. May as well come out with it. "It was Chantelle Svoboda. She bumped into someone on the press box stairs."

The chief's bushy eyebrows furrowed. "Chantelle Svoboda? She wasn't up at the press box."

"She was," Ava said, trying to keep her tone even. "She went up there to see Mitch while the band was playing. She's understandably pretty shaken up by Mitch's death, though, and she was too distraught to talk with you about it until now."

"Hmmph," Greathouse grunted, taking a sip of his coffee. "Well, what'd she see? Bumping into a person isn't much to go off."

"She can tell you the specifics herself, but what she told me is that she was coming down the press box steps as the band was marching off the field, and someone bumped into her. She didn't get a good look at a face, but she thinks from the buzzed haircut and build that it was a man. Whoever it was seemed in an awful hurry, didn't even stop to apologize."

Greathouse grunted again, but Ava could've sworn she saw a light in his eyes switch on.

"Buzzed haircut, you say?"

Ava shrugged. "That's what she said."

"Interesting." Greathouse stroked the ends of his mustache as he stared out the window. "That don't sound like your ex, does it?"

"Nope," Ava said, shaking her head once. Although she was so furious with Noah for how he'd treated Owen that a part of her thought maybe she ought to let him get what he deserved... She couldn't stand to see an innocent person accused of such a horrible crime. Noah was a jerk, but he wasn't a murderer.

Greathouse rapped his knuckles on the counter. "Alright, well, I'll give Chantelle a call. And *if* what you're telling me is true, it seems your former man is in the clear. It also seems your golden pass theory has gone kaput."

"What? Why? Who's on your list of unaccounted-for golden pass holders?"

"Well, not counting Clyde McPherson, who died last month, there's only Eunice Caldwell and Walt Kincaid. Eunice isn't a man, nor does she have a buzzed head—and Walt's not going to be making it up any stairs anytime soon, as much as I hate to say it."

Ava groaned. "Really?"

"Really, really. I'm not ruling anything out yet, but my guess is that golden pass has nothing to do with Mitch's murder. It's probably been there for ages."

"Hmm..."

Chief Greathouse tipped his coffee cup at Ava in salute, as if that settled it. Pulling at his belt loops, he hoisted up his pants around his ample middle and lumbered toward the front door. The bell atop the door jingled as he opened it, but he stopped in the doorway to nod farewell at Ava.

"Your parents still in town?"

"Yeah, they fly back late this afternoon. Dad's got to teach tomorrow."

Greathouse said. "And the city slicker? He still here, right?"

"Yes, in Omaha. I think he's had his fill of Shiloh for a while," Ava said with a wry smile.

Greathouse grunted. "Good. You don't need me to tell you this, but there's a reason that guy's in your past. You can do a whole lot better. For one thing, Owen would *never* wear that much cologne."

"Right," Ava said, rolling her eyes as Greathouse winked.

"Anyway, Goldberg. I don't want to hear anything else about you interfering with this murder investigation," he said. "I mean that. It's for your own safety, you hear?"

"I hear," Ava said.

She watched him walk outside, the door swinging shut behind him and his words still ringing in her ears. He wasn't wrong. Noah *was* in her past for a reason, although it wasn't the cologne.

Cologne.

Ava straightened. Why hadn't she thought of it before? If Chantelle could identify what the man she'd bumped into at the homecoming game had smelled like, there was a chance she could pinpoint the cologne he wore and give Greathouse another lead to narrow down his search.

Ava reached for her phone. As much as she hated to admit it, she had a favor to ask of her ex-husband. After all, there was no one who knew cologne better than Noah Shapiro.

Noah was standing by the Von Maur perfume counter, one slim hip leaning against the pristine glass, when Ava and Chantelle approached. Ava set her handbag on the counter and nodded to Noah to acknowledge the fact that he'd shown up. He gave her a little squeeze on the arm.

"Get Mike and Sara all dropped off at the airport?"

"We did," Ava said. Then, remembering her manners, she gestured to Chantelle. "Noah, this is Chantelle. Chantelle, Noah. He's the king of cologne, and he's going to help us figure out what scent that guy on the press box stairs might've been wearing—if you can remember, that is."

"I hope I can," Chantelle said as she shook Noah's hand nervously. "Although we'll have to be fast. I've got to get back to finish my shift."

"No problem." Noah flashed Chantelle a dazzling smile, his dark eyes trained on her, and Ava saw how the woman's demeanor instantly relaxed. Noah had always had that effect on women—and luckily for Ava, it no longer charmed her. She could, however, at least be glad that Chantelle was a little less jittery. That was something.

"So, where do we start?" Ava asked. She craned her neck to look down the line of glittering glass bottles that stretched along the winding counter.

"Well," Noah said, folding his arms across his chest and turning to give Chantelle his full attention. "Let's start with a few basic scents based on what you can remember, and then we'll hone our search from there. Sound good?"

Chantelle nodded.

"So, Chantelle—if you had to describe to me in just a few words what kind of scent it was that wafted past you on the press box steps, what would you say?"

Chantelle bit her lip. "Um... Spicy, I guess. That's the main thing that stood out to me. But there was also something—I don't know—*woodsy* about it?"

Noah stroked his chin. "Okay, that's two words. Got another one for me?"

"Geez, I really don't know. It smelled like the kind of thing I'd imagine men smoking cigars would wear."

"Perfect." Noah snapped his fingers. He waved his hand to the employee behind the counter, flashing her a devastating grin before he turned back to Chantelle. "That's brilliant. I know exactly what we'll start with."

Noah turned to the girl behind the counter. "Hi there. Can we trouble you for some samples? I'd specifically like to see Yves Saint Laurent M7, Dior Fahrenheit, and Tom Ford Tobacco Vanille."

The girl blushed, scurrying off to collect the requested bottles. It took all Ava had not to roll her eyes at the employee's immediate fawning, at Noah's expert knowledge of manufactured scents, all of it. Still, Noah had agreed to help, and she had to credit him that. Of course, he realized that this could help get him off the hook with Greathouse, so it really was in his best interest to be here. At least his cologne obsession was good for something.

"Here you go," the employee squeaked when she returned. She slid a handful of sample papers across the counter to Noah and stood back to watch, clearly sensing that his expertise far outweighed hers.

Noah spritzed the first cologne—Yves Saint Laurent—onto one of the papers and wafted it into the air between him and Chantelle. He breathed in, gesturing for Chantelle to do the same. He waited for her reaction.

Chantelle shook her head. "Definitely not. This one smells like incense."

Noah nodded, then followed suit with the other two scents, spritzing them onto the papers and giving them to Chantelle to sniff. With each one, she shook her head. The scent from Tom Ford was "too fruity", while the one from Dior "smelled like leather".

"Got it," Noah said, undeterred. His dark eyes scanned the shelves behind them as he rubbed his jaw, thinking. "So, you're saying it *doesn't* smell so much like leather? But the tobacco is on point?"

Chantelle looked confused. "Tobacco?"

Noah grinned sheepishly. "Never mind. Let's try another one." He signaled again to the employee, who stood watching him in awe. "Excuse me—could we also sample Herod by Parfums de Marly?"

Noah sprayed another paper with the newest cologne, and Chantelle sniffed the air as he waved it. "What do you think?"

"No..." Chantelle said, her face falling. "This one's too... I don't know, *musky*..."

Ava sighed. "Well, that's alright. We gave it our best shot."

Noah scoffed. "Please, Ava. Have a little more faith in me."

Ava shot him the darkest look she could muster, but the reprimanded look on his face was enough to make her crack a relenting smile. He'd understood the error of his words.

"Okay, touché," Noah said. "But seriously—we can get this. One more, Chantelle. Just give me one more. Was this one *any* closer?"

"Well..." Chantelle thought for a moment, giving the paper a wave and sniffing again. "Actually, maybe. For some reason, this one reminded me a little more of Christmas, and—oddly— I remember thinking that about the guy at the game..."

At this, Noah's eyes lit up. He laid a smooth hand on the countertop, drummed his tapered fingers against the glass. He flicked his gaze to Ava's, then to the employee's. "Alright, this is our last shot. Christmas is chock full of cinnamon, right? Why don't you give us... Oh, Spicebomb by Viktor & Rolf?"

The employee gave a small smile and plucked a bottle off the adjacent counter. She handed it to Noah.

Time seemed to stand still as Noah gave the grenade-shaped bottle a spritz. Even the fawning employee was invested now, clearly as interested in seeing whether this strange trio would succeed in identifying their sought-after scent as she was in gazing at Noah.

Chantelle closed her eyes, sniffed the air. She was silent a moment, and Ava swore she could hear her own heart thundering in her ears as she waited for the verdict. Chantelle inhaled again, and then, her eyes popping open, she shrieked.

"That's *it!* That's the one!"

"Seriously?" Ava asked. "You're sure?"

"Absolutely. It smells so good, I couldn't help but notice it the other night."

Noah flashed a self-satisfied grin, crossing his arms over his muscled chest and nudging Ava with his elbow. "What'd I tell you? I knew we'd get it."

"You were right," Ava conceded. She brought her eyes to his, willing herself not to look away. It wasn't comfortable being around Noah, and she was still angry about the way he'd treated Owen at dinner, but she was grateful for his willingness to help today.

"I'm going to run to the restroom before we take off," Chantelle said, laying a brief hand on Ava's arm before leaving Ava and Noah alone together in front of the fragrance counter.

"Also," Noah said, his eyes following Chantelle through the racks of clothes before turning back to Ava. "I wanted to apologize to you in person. I was awful the other night. I shouldn't have done that to you—or *him*, I guess…" He waved a hand. "I was jealous."

Ava nearly took a step back, so stunned was she at this blunt confession. In all the years she'd known Noah, she'd never heard him admit to anything even *bordering* on jealousy. He was so self-assured, so put together, so used to getting his way in everything and with everyone. Ava hadn't even known the man was capable of feeling envy.

"I know—shocking, right?" Noah said, giving a clipped laugh. He rubbed his chin. "But it's the god-honest truth. I threw what we had away, and I will *never* not regret that. That guy—Owen?—he gets you in a way I never did, and seeing that made me jealous. But also… really happy."

"Really?" Ava's voice was practically a whisper.

"Really, really. You deserve it."

Now her voice *was* a whisper. "Thank you."

"Of course," Noah said. He shot her a pained smile. "But don't ask me to apologize again for a while. Two times in one week has about killed me."

Suddenly, Chantelle was back, and Ava snapped back into the real world. "Ava, you ready to head out?"

"Yeah. Let me just take a quick photo of the cologne so we don't forget what it's called…"

"And I'm going to buy something before I meet Ray for dinner," Noah said. "Although not this stuff. I'm more of a Tom Ford kind of guy myself, and I've already had that Shiloh police chief out there suspecting me of murder—no way am I going to go around *smelling* like the suspect, too."

Ava rolled her eyes but waved goodbye, anyway. As she and Chantelle made their way out of the department store and back to the parking lot, she felt lighter than she had in a while. It could've been from sniffing too many colognes, but if Ava had to put money on it, she was pretty sure that something inside her had finally started to heal.

20

———

When Ava finally returned home after her excursion to the airport and the fragrance counter, she was exhausted. Some questions had been answered, but many still remained. For one, her mother's homecoming shopping trip with Riley. Ava had been tempted to ask about it on the way to the airport but then decided against it. Judging by the way her mother had clammed up the other day when her father had asked where she'd been gone to for so long, Sara Goldberg wanted to keep her shopping trip with Riley to herself—a sentiment Ava understood.

With Noah back in Omaha for his conference and knowing Greathouse may soon be off his tail, Ava felt better about sending her parents off back to their life in Chicago. Noah would follow as soon as his conference ended, and in another eight days it would be Yom Kippur, and another five days after that the holiday of Sukkot. Life went on, the seasons continued, and although Mitch's murderer still hadn't been caught, at least the situation with her family had calmed down. And, much to

Ava's relief, her father had not seen the need to continue practicing his shofar skills on the ride back to the airport.

Now, finally home, Ava sat down at the kitchen table across from Riley, a novel open in front of her and a mug of tea in hand, trying her best to focus more on the words she was reading and less on who it was Chantelle could've seen on the press box steps. All day, she'd racked her brain for men in Shiloh who fit the description, and there were too many to count. Now that she was also trying to remember back to how many of those men wore cologne, she was starting to go a little insane. She'd had Riley sniff the samples she'd brought home of the cologne Chantelle had picked, but the girl had determined she'd never smelled that scent in her life.

Ava had just called Greathouse to update him on the name of the cologne that Chantelle had identified and was just managing to sink into her book when her phone buzzed in her pocket. From her own seat across the table, Riley lifted her gaze from the comic book she was reading.

"Hey," Ava said, barely glancing at the name on the phone before she answered. It was Rose.

"Ava…" Rose's voice sounded breathless, but whether it was from excitement or fear, Ava couldn't tell. "Chantelle Svoboda was just in a car accident."

"Oh, no," Ava said, sliding her bookmark into place and shutting the book. "That's terrible—is she okay? Have you heard anything?"

"She's physically okay," Rose said, her voice a little shaky. "But mentally, she's really shaken up. Somebody cut her brakes."

Ava gasped. "Cut her *brakes*?"

At this, Riley's gaze snapped up. She mouthed to Ava, "*Who?*"

Ava flicked a hand at her.

"That's what they're saying," Rose said. "Joel came home from work, and he'd heard it from Chantelle's neighbor, who was there working out. He said she was downtown when she tried to hit the brakes and they didn't work, but thankfully going pretty slow when she crashed. Car's totaled regardless, but it could've been a lot worse."

"Holy cow," Ava said, gripping the phone. "And they're sure someone *cut* them? How do they know it's not just a malfunction?"

"Nah, they were definitely cut. I mean, this is all according to the neighbor, but he seemed to have a lot of details. He spoke to Chantelle himself when Dan Harding brought her home from the hospital."

"Well—do they know *who*?" Ava was doing her best to extract details from Rose while ignoring Riley, who was flailing her arms across the table and hissing at Ava to tell her *whose* brakes had been cut.

"Nope," Rose said. She lowered her voice. "But it's got to be the person from the press box stairs—the one she bumped into —who heard she ratted on them. I mean, you *did* tell Greathouse this morning, right?"

"Right—and he said he was going to speak with Chantelle himself."

"Exactly. They obviously saw her that night, too, and were probably hoping until now that she'd thought nothing of it. But now that the police likely have a better description of a person of interest and word's started getting around, it's pretty clear to *this person* who it was that told them about it. What if Chantelle suddenly remembers something else? It makes sense they'd want her out of the picture."

Ava considered this for a moment. Rose was right. Whoever it was Chantelle had seen from the back had seen *her* head-on, meaning they would know who it was that had opened their mouth and set the police closer to sniffing them out. Word got around *fast* in Shiloh. The killer would have heard by now that Greathouse was checking out a new lead.

"Yeah, there's no way this isn't connected to Mitch's murder," Ava said. "Do you know anything about what the police are making of it? Did the neighbor have any info there?"

"Not that I've heard," Rose said. "Anyway, I've got to put Ellie to bed, but I thought you'd want to know."

"Thanks," Ava said. "Talk to you soon.

Ava jabbed a finger at her phone screen, ending the call. Then, pushing her chair back from the kitchen table with a clatter, she dashed to the door, and all but sprinted down the sidewalk, Riley right at her heels.

21

———

"Chantelle," Ava hissed, her cheek pressed to the door as her knuckles rapped at the chipped, peeling wood. "Are you home? It's me—Ava."

Inside, Ava thought she heard a slight scuffling in the distance, the sound of a chair being dragged across linoleum. Chantelle had to be inside. Every light in the house appeared to be on.

"Chantelle!" Riley's voice came bellowing out from behind Ava. The girl strode forward toward the door and beat her fist against it once.

Although Ava turned to glare at Riley—so much for not causing a scene—her bellowing seemed to do the trick. Footsteps sounded on the other side of the door, and the lock rattled as the deadbolt turned. As the door opened inward, Chantelle's face appeared in the crack. She glanced curiously from Riley to Ava.

Ava said, "Sorry if we scared you—it's just—are you okay?"

Chantelle nodded, opening the door wider, then glanced around the empty block, her eyes narrowing with worry. Her head tipped in toward the house, and she stepped inside, gesturing for Ava and Riley to follow her. "Let's talk inside."

Chantelle led them down the hallway and to the kitchen, pulling out two chairs at the table. The jar of peanut butter next to the sink was gone, but Chantelle looked even more tense than the last time Ava was there—which was saying something.

"News traveled that fast, huh?" Chantelle asked, letting out a harsh sort of laugh. She sank into one of the chairs at the kitchen table.

"It's Shiloh," Ava said, by way of explanation. "Rose called me. Joel came home from work and told her about it, and he'd heard it from your neighbor, who's a regular over at New Heights."

Chantelle nodded, sighed. "Right. He was out watering the flowers when Dan brought me home. I guess I should be glad people are looking out for me, but..."

"What *happened* exactly?" Ava asked, leaning forward with her elbows on her knees.

Chantelle scrubbed a hand down her face. "I don't know! I went back to work after I saw you on my break, left my car in the parking lot like I always do, and then when I finished my shift and started for home—" Her voice broke, and she looked down, clearly trying to keep herself from falling apart.

"That's okay," Ava said gently, touching Chantelle's forearm. "I can't even imagine how shaken up you must be."

Chantelle nodded, blinking back tears. "My car seemed fine when I got there—or at least, I don't *think* anything was wrong—and I didn't notice anything weird when I got in after my shift. Not until the dang thing wouldn't brake, anyway."

Ava had a sudden thought. "No sign of the cologne you smelled at the game the night Mitch was killed?"

Chantelle shook her head, her curls falling in front of her face. She brushed them back. "No. The car was still locked and everything, too. I don't think anyone had been inside."

Riley, who had until now been listening in silence, seemed to be fitting some of the pieces together. She spoke slowly, her voice low. "Whoever it was must have known where to find your car. That you work at the market certain days. Do any of your coworkers have it out for you? They'd be familiar with your shift schedule..."

Chantelle frowned but seemed to consider this a moment. "Chase Wagner isn't my biggest fan, but we've never had any *real* problems—just squabbles over stocking duties now and then, that kind of thing. Nothing anyone would try to kill someone over." She laughed nervously, but it did nothing to lighten the mood in the room.

"Did you get promoted over anyone recently? Or anything like that?" Ava suggested. "Then again—that would have nothing to do with *Mitch*, and why he was killed."

"Right. I think I'm just collateral," Chantelle said. "Or *would* have been, if I'd picked up any sort of speed on the way home. Honestly, I'm scared to leave the house. What's to stop whoever it was from trying to kill me again? They clearly want me out of the way, even though I saw nothing other than what I already shared with you."

"Does Greathouse have anything else to go on?" Ava pressed. "Is there anything you can remember—even the *tiniest* detail—that might give him a new lead?"

"Other than the observation that whoever did it knows their way around a car? Unfortunately, no," Chantelle said, sighing.

"That's true, though," Ava said, the wheels in her mind beginning to turn again. An auto mechanic in town? With a buzzed haircut? "Ricky Birch would certainly fit that description, but I haven't heard his name come up yet."

"No, Ricky wouldn't do something like this—to me *or* to Mitch," Chantelle said firmly. "Besides, he's always planted in his seat on the fifty-yard line. Wouldn't budge if a tornado swept through. I'm sure other people will have seen him there."

"Alright," Ava said, sighing. Ricky likely smelled more like motor oil anyway. She pressed her palms to her knees and stood up. Then, hesitating, she cast a wary eye at Chantelle. "Do you want to stay at my place tonight? I know you're probably pretty rattled, wondering if whoever it was will come back and try their luck a second time..."

Chantelle flashed a grateful smile. "Thanks, but I'll manage. Greathouse didn't seem to think the suspect would strike again so soon—not with everyone's eyes peeled and alarm heightened—but I'll lock the door after you, don't you worry."

Ava nodded, and Riley stood up to follow her to the door. "Well, if you change your mind, you know where to find me."

As Ava and Riley got back into the car, the click of Chantelle's deadbolt echoing in their ears as they headed for home, she couldn't deny that she was secretly glad Chantelle had declined the offer. Although Shiloh had forced her to get better at it, socializing was still not one of her strongest suits. Her home was her sanctuary, and so many goings-on in such a short time meant that the space served as a critical haven. Still, she hoped Chantelle hadn't sensed the relief she felt.

"So, what do we do now?" Riley asked, glancing at Ava as they turned once more into the driveway and bumped over the rocks.

"*You* don't do anything," Ava said, shooting Riley a pointed look. It was bad enough that Riley had to be marginally involved because of living arrangements; Ava wouldn't let her get dragged in further. Then, seeing the disappointment in Riley's face, she softened her tone. "I mean—there's nothing we can do right now. Let's give Greathouse a little time. I'm sure he'll come up with something."

Riley just rolled her eyes. Ava couldn't blame her—no matter what she tried to project, she *wasn't* sure that Greathouse would come up with anything. She wasn't sure at all. And now Chantelle was in a killer's crosshairs.

22

"Hey," Riley said, traipsing through the front door of Cafe Arcana after school the next day and slinging her book bag over the counter.

"Oh," Ava said, looking up from the table she was scrubbing at. "Hey."

She stole a glance at her phone. Sure enough, it was four o'clock. The day had been busier than normal, and Ava brewed pot after pot of coffee, wiping down table after table. Between the non-stop rush, the racing of her thoughts since yesterday's events, and the horrifying what-if scenarios that passed through her mind each time she imagined calling Owen, she'd barely even realized what time it was. Although business would slow down now that it was late afternoon, she was still glad for Riley's company.

Riley glanced around, tying an apron around her waist. "Looks like a tornado went through here."

"It's been busy," Ava said. She flicked the dirty rag she held into the sink. Moving to pour two cups of coffee for herself and Riley, as was their daily afternoon tradition, she suddenly remembered—with everything going on, she hadn't even asked Riley how the first day back to school had gone after the horrible homecoming prank her jerky classmates had pulled on her.

She tried to keep her tone light, but she was sure Riley could still sense her hesitation. "How was school?"

"Meh," Riley said. She made a face. "Trevor stopped at my locker to talk to me, but I just turned and left. I didn't want to hear it. The girls were whispering in geometry, and then Summer started giggling when she looked back down at her book, but other than that…"

Ava put a hand on her hip. "Well, I think those kids need to be held accountable for their atrocious actions."

Riley shrugged, taking a sip of her coffee. "I'm over it."

As they stood, drinking their coffee in silence, Ava eyed Riley. The girl could say she was "over it" all she wanted, but there had been no denying the absolute betrayal in her face as she'd come tumbling through the bathroom window. There was no way she was over it, but Ava wouldn't push her further. Not today, anyway.

Inside her apron pocket, Ava's phone dinged.

She pulled it out to see one new message. *Owen O'Kelly.* A fist closed around her stomach.

Riley saw her boss's expression change. "Everything okay?"

For a moment, Ava didn't reply. She scanned the brief message.

Can we talk? Looking Glass at 6?

Ava swallowed, the tightness in her stomach now beginning to loosen. He wanted to talk. He wanted to *meet*. That was good —right?

"I think so," she said, pocketing the phone. "I mean—yes. I'll find out soon."

Riley offered her a questioning glance.

"Owen wants to talk," Ava said, sighing. She emptied the change from the tip jar into her palm to avoid having to make eye contact with Riley.

"About... the other night?"

Ava shrugged. "I guess so. He didn't say—just that he wants to meet at Looking Glass at six."

Riley glanced at the clock. "That's in less than two hours. You have to go—obviously. I'll close things up here."

"Are you sure?"

"Duh," Riley said, as though it were absolutely no question. "If he wants to meet—instead of just saying whatever it is in a text—it must be important."

"That's what I'm afraid of."

Ava dropped a fistful of quarters into the cash drawer, swapping them out for dollar bills, which she now stuffed into the tip jar. Riley stood, studying her.

"You're really worried, aren't you?" Riley asked, her question really more of a remark.

"*No*," Ava said, her tone forceful. "I'm not *worried*. I just don't like serious conversations."

"Uh-huh." Riley nodded, then tipped her head toward Ava's phone, which still lay on the counter. "Well, you better let him know you'll be there."

Determined not to let her fear show—to either Riley *or* herself—Ava swallowed her dread and shot off a reply to Owen.

Sure. See you there.

23

Ava's palms were sweaty as she pulled open the heavy glass door that led into Looking Glass, the wine bar next door to Cafe Arcana. As she stood in the entry, scanning the glitzy, dimly lit room for Owen's worn red Huskers cap, the clatter of dishes and clink of glasses enveloped her. All around her, conversation hummed, the occasional air of light laughter breaking out. Now that they'd extended their weekday hours, Looking Glass was a prime spot for I-80 commuters in search of a cocktail and a nosh after work.

On the far side of the room, Ava finally spotted the familiar sweat-stained baseball cap. Owen sat perched on a stool at the bar, his lanky legs stretched out like a too-long tape measure. His tousled head was bent over a menu. His gaze jerked up as Ava slid onto the stool next to him.

"Hey," he said, giving her an awkward nod. His fingers absently traced the edges of the menu.

Ava draped her purse over the back of the stool, trying to ignore how nervous Owen seemed. "Did you order yet?"

"Nah." He lowered his gaze once again to the menu, barely

even glancing at Ava. "No, but I'm thinking about a Moscow mule. They've got a two for one special, if you're interested…"

"Sounds great," Ava said. "Let's do it."

As they waited for their drinks, Owen fidgeted in his chair. Although she'd had every intention of waiting for him to speak first, the silence was killing her.

"Sorry about the other night," Ava said, chancing a glance at Owen, who, was busy examining the calluses on his fingers.

"That's alright." He looked up at her, his face still distressed. "I mean—it *sucked*, but I don't want to discuss it. It's done."

"Okay…" If it wasn't the disastrous dinner that Owen wanted to hash out, what on earth had he asked her to meet him here for?

The bartender set two copper mugs, each beaded with ice cold sweat, on coasters in front of them.

"Can I open a tab?" Owen asked the bartender. He handed over his ID, ignoring the questioning look Ava shot his way.

"You're opening a tab? How many drinks are you planning to *have*?" she asked, surprised. She couldn't remember ever having seen Owen drink more than a single beer, so the fact that he seemed to be settling in at the bar worried her slightly. *Is this it? Has he finally had enough, and needs the liquid courage to break the news?*

Owen gave a clipped laugh, shaking his head so a thatch of sandy hair fell into his green eyes. He held up the copper mug to Ava, against which she reluctantly clinked her own.

"I'll drink as many of these puppies as it takes for me to get this story out," Owen said.

"Story?"

Now Ava was really flustered. She narrowed her eyes at him, not sure what was coming next. A whole host of nightmares flashed through her brain—did Owen have a criminal alter ego? Was he secretly married? Had he *killed* someone? Her thoughts came barreling to a stop. *Oh, god. Mitch.*

Owen took a long swig of his Moscow mule. He placed the mug back on the coaster, aligning it to the center of the square, his mouth twitching.

"So that phone call I got at the game..." Owen began, raising his eyes to Ava's.

Ava felt her heart catch. She had been so stupid. *Here it comes—the secret wife. The girlfriend.*

"That was my brother." Owen blew out his breath, like the simple statement had been a heavy barbell he'd lifted over his head. He took another drink.

"Your—" Ava stopped herself almost as soon as she'd begun. This was *not* what she'd been preparing herself to hear, and suddenly, she didn't know how to react. "Your brother? That's who you got out of line to go talk to?"

"Yeah. He showed up at the game. Called me to let me know he was there."

A glorious wave of relief flooded through Ava's body. She barely stopped herself from laughing, realizing only from the still serious expression on Owen's face that now wasn't the time. Instead, she sipped her drink through her straw.

"Well, why didn't you just tell me that from the get-go?" she asked. "I've been imagining all these horrific scenarios in my head, like—"

She'd been about to say *some girl*, but bit back the words, embarrassed. What right did she have to question who Owen was talking to? Especially when *she* was the one with the ex-husband dropping in on family dinners.

Owen sighed. "I know. I just… didn't want to talk about it. But now I have to."

"Okay," Ava said. She settled back against the the barstool. "I'm listening."

"My brother—Jeremy—has been in jail. For four years," Owen said. His eyes met Ava's, and he held her gaze. "That's why you've never met him. He was in for drug charges, aggravated assault. They got him pretty good, but he only had himself to blame for it. We all knew it was just a matter of time."

"Who? Your parents?"

Owen shrugged. "Yeah, my parents—but all of us." He gestured around, his eyes sweeping the room. "I think if you'd asked most people in this town, they'd have told you that Jeremy O'Kelly was a ticking time bomb. And they would've been right."

"Okay," Ava said, leaning forward to sip her drink. "So, he called you during the game—and you, what? Went to see him when you got out of line?"

"Yep." Owen raked a huge hand through his hair. "He wanted money. And a place to stay."

"Like, a place to live? Wouldn't he hit up your parents first?" Ava asked, frowning.

Here, Owen laughed harshly. "He did—but they've been around this block with him before. They made it pretty clear he's going to need to prove himself before they'll give him any sort of help again, and honestly, I said the same."

"Oh." Ava wasn't sure what to say to this admission. She tried to imagine her own brother, Aaron, asking her for a place to stay, and having to turn him down. Although her brother was happily married and had never asked her for so much as a dime, the thought of turning down a relative in need was still depressing.

"Yeah, it was rough. You can see why I stepped out of line to take that call," Owen said. "I didn't even realize he'd be getting out yet, so I wasn't prepared. I nearly had a heart attack when I saw his name pop up on my phone. And then when he told me he was *at the game...*"

"I bet," Ava murmured. "I don't know how you kept that under wraps. But—okay. Your brother's out of prison, and you had to tell him he couldn't stay with you. I understand family traumas, believe me. It's okay."

"Well, not really," Owen said, shifting on his stool. His long limbs folded and unfolded like some sort of angular slinky. "I got a call from Greathouse this morning."

Ava's eyebrows shot up. She didn't even bother to hide her alarm. "Oh my god. *Owen—*"

Owen gestured for her to quiet down. She glanced around, then, leaning toward him, lowered her voice to a hiss. "Did Jeremy kill Mitch Fangman?"

"I don't know," Owen said. "But Greathouse seems to think so—and I can't say the idea is very far-fetched."

"Okay, wait," Ava said, settling back onto her barstool and crossing her arms over her chest. She tried to rein her focus back in. "Let's back up. *Why* does the chief think your brother had something to do with the murder? What did he say?"

Owen sighed. "Well, it's all pretty circumstantial so far, but he got a lead saying that someone with the same hairstyle and build as Jeremy was seen storming up the press box steps around the time that he would've been on the premises."

Ava shifted in her seat, averting Owen's eyes. "I may know something about that."

"What? You saw something that night?"

"No, no," Ava said, swirling the ice in her copper cup. She raised her gaze to his. "But I know someone who did—and she tipped Greathouse off."

Owen drew in a deep breath, studied the backs of his hands on the bar top in front of him. "Gotcha. And are you going to tell me who this person was that saw someone headed up the steps that night?"

"Chantelle Svoboda," she said, draining the rest of her Moscow mule and setting the mug onto the counter with a clatter. "Turns out she *was* at the game. Just like we thought."

Owen's eyes grew wide, his palm slapping the table. "Oh, my god—I just heard they think someone may have cut her brakes! Is it all tied in together? And how did you find out she was at the game?"

"Yes. And, well, you're not going to like it, but I went to her house and—"

Owen threw his head back and groaned. "You went to her *house*? God, Ava. I'm starting to think you've got some kind of death wish!"

"Alright, alright. Save your lectures," Ava said, tossing her long hair over her shoulder. "It was dumb, but I was *careful*."

Owen scoffed. Then, scooting his stool nearer to her, he searched her face. "What's done is done. What'd you find out?"

Ava could feel the warmth that radiated off of Owen's broad frame, and she tried to ignore it, to not lean into it. She wished she had some of her drink left so she could at least distract herself with the occasional sip. She threw a glance around the room, checking to make sure the other patrons were involved in their own conversations.

"Chantelle was planning to kill Mitch," she said, not taking her eyes off Owen's. "She wanted the building downtown—her grandma used to own the bookstore there—and Mitch wasn't giving it up. He was about to sign the contract for it as his ACE location. She got desperate, made a plan, and then backed out at the last minute."

Owen's face remained impressively neutral, but his green eyes glowed in interest. "That's what she *says*, anyway," he said, his tone challenging.

"I believe her," Ava said. "I saw her face when she told me, heard her voice. I have no doubt she's telling the truth. That's why she didn't come forward to Greathouse about being in the press box that night—she wanted to distance herself from the whole thing as much as possible. But he knows now. She spoke with him."

Owen nodded, scratching his stubbled chin. He was quiet a moment, then signaled to the bartender to bring two more drinks. He turned back to Ava, shaking his head. "I'm not even going to comment on the fact that she was actually going to *kill* him—that's too messed up to even fathom."

"I know," Ava said, grimacing. "But regardless, she was only up in the box for a few minutes during half time, and someone bumped into her on her way down the stairs. She didn't get a look at the face, but they were headed up the way she'd come."

"Greathouse told me the person of interest had buzzed hair. Light-colored. Is that what Chantelle said?"

Ava nodded. "Does that... describe Jeremy?"

Owen's face was grim. "To a tee—*but* it also describes half the men in this state."

"True," Ava conceded, unsure whether or not to feel relief. She'd never met Owen's brother, had barely even known of his existence until a few moments ago. What if it *had* been him? "So, why's Greathouse homing in on Jeremy?"

"Ah," Owen said. He chewed his lip, paused at the sight of the bartender returning, and accepted their drinks. He pushed one of the copper mugs in front of Ava. When the bartender was safely out of earshot, Owen took a sip of his drink and said, "That's the other thing. Mitch Fangman and Jeremy were class-mates—graduated together. They weren't, uh, very good friends."

Ava's eyes narrowed. "Go on."

"Well, I don't know how it all started, but as long as I can remember, Jer would come home and whine about Mitch Fangman this, Mitch Fangman that. Things started to escalate in high school, when they both liked the same girl, and she chose Jer over Mitch. Wasn't long before Jer came out of school one day to find someone had smashed in the windshield of his Mustang—old, rusty thing, but he'd saved up for ages for it. Whoever it was slashed up the upholstery, too. He could never prove it, but Jeremy was absolutely *convinced* it was Mitch Fangman who'd done it, and it started this entire back-and-forth. I think Jer planted *drugs* in Mitch's locker once. Of course, Greathouse knew all about this at the time, so when he heard Jeremy was, in fact, no longer in jail..."

"He thought maybe Jeremy had gone to get revenge on Mitch," Ava supplied, the pieces of the story falling into place.

"Basically, yeah. And I've got to admit—it's not the *most* far-fetched theory," Owen said, drumming his fingers on the counter in thought. "Then again, I can't imagine spending four years in prison, and then the first thing you do when you get out is take out an old high school rival. Seems pretty dumb to me—but there's been plenty of stuff Jer's done that I just couldn't understand. That being said… Cutting Chantelle's brakes? I don't buy it. She never did anything to him."

Ava shrugged. "Unless he did kill Mitch and recognized her when he bumped her and didn't want a witness."

Owen shook his head. "Sorry, but I don't see him doing that. I don't see him as that clever."

They sipped their Moscow mules in silence, letting the hum of the restaurant and the clatter of silverware, the tinkle of glasses, carry them for a moment. Ava was still trying to process everything Owen had said. His older brother, a convicted felon, had not only been at the scene of the crime at the *time* of the crime—he'd also had it out for Mitch Fangman. She could understand why Greathouse was suspicious, especially given Chantelle's description of the person she'd seen on the stairs.

Then again, Chantelle had smelled cologne on the person. It seemed awfully unlikely that Jeremy, so recently released from prison, would have had the money to buy the expensive cologne Chantelle had identified—or that he'd even thought to buy any. Surely the man had more urgent priorities. No, there must be something they were missing…

Suddenly, a thought dawned on her. *The golden pass.*

"Hold up," Ava said, setting her mug down a bit more forcefully than she'd meant to. She looked at Owen, her blue eyes wide. "What about the golden pass? *Someone* must have been in the press box who we still don't know about. Right? And Greathouse told me he'd narrowed the list of golden pass holders down to two people."

Owen pursed his lips, a dimple appearing in one stubbled cheek. "Yeah, I said the same to Greathouse, and got the same information in return. However, he told me that those last two people on the list have some pretty rock-solid alibis—so he's now convinced that Jeremy *stole* one of their golden passes to get into the game. You know, being straight out of prison with no money and all."

Ava clucked her tongue. "That seems far-fetched."

"As does the rest of this," Owen said, spreading his huge hands in a helpless gesture. "I just don't know what to think anymore."

Ava collapsed against the back of the bar stool, her mind racing. Owen's shady reluctance to discuss the phone call was now a moot point. The pieces were falling into place, at least as far as Owen was concerned.

Owen cleared his throat, jolting Ava out of her thoughts. He turned to her, his mouth twitching slightly, an earnestness in his green eyes. "So now you know," he said. "It wasn't some other girl who called me. I wasn't hiding anything in order to deceive you."

Ava met his eyes, feeling the flush creep into her cheeks. She forced herself to hold his gaze. "And that stuff Noah was saying the other night—all B.S. I didn't blame you for leaving."

They stared at each other a moment longer, a thread of understanding glimmering between them, before looking down to study their copper mugs.

Owen flashed her a sympathetic smile as he raised the drink to his lips. "Riley doing okay?"

Ava shrugged, glad for the change of topic. "Yeah, for the most part. I think it hurts more than she's letting on, though. Those kids are some real jerks."

"You're telling me," Owen said. "I was lucky I played foot-ball. Sports will make them leave you alone."

"Maybe Riley ought to pick up ping pong," Ava remarked, her eyes flashing with laughter. Picturing Riley, blue hair swishing at her chin and dark eyes fixed on a pinging plastic ball, was, for some reason, hilarious. Owen broke out into a grin, too, and the sound of his baritone laughter ringing out in the space was exactly what she'd needed to hear.

"So, we're good?" he asked, his smile remaining but face serious again. "I mean—relatively speaking?"

"We're good," Ava said firmly. "And tomorrow, we're going to get straight to the bottom of who killed Mitch Fangman."

Owen groaned, but didn't protest. Then, knocking back the rest of his drink, he nodded his approval. "Fine."

24

———

When Ava arrived home, Riley was waiting in the living room, leafing through a graphic novel. At the sound of the front door, she looked up, grinned.

"Well? How'd it go?"

"Well, it depends what part," Ava said, rummaging through her purse for her tarot deck and then tossing the bag onto the sofa. "Owen and I are okay. We got things worked out for the meantime. But he told me..." Ava's voice trailed off, unsure if she should divulge the new information Owen had shared with her. It was, after all, something quite personal. "Well—come sit with me. Everything's been such a whirlwind lately that I haven't even had time to sit down and ask the cards about the case. Let's see if we can learn anything new about who killed Mitch Fangman."

Ava sank into a cross-legged seat on the living room rug. She cut her deck of tarot cards, fingered their soft, worn edges, and began to shuffle. "You ready?"

"Oh, good!" Riley dropped to her knees on the other side of the coffee table, folding her hands on the glass tabletop in front

218

of her. Her dark eyes watched Ava's hands intently as they shuffled the cards, flipped them over, and started again. "I was hoping you'd suggest asking the cards about Mitch. What spread are you going to use? Celtic cross seems kind of complicated for this situation..."

"You're right," Ava said. She gave the deck one last shuffle, then set it down on the table, looking up at Riley. "I think less might be more in this scenario—something with three cards or fewer. That way, we can really focus in on only a couple facets." She thought for a moment, trying to remember what kinds of spreads her grandfather had used when he'd faced a problem. "Oh, heck. Let's wing it. The first card will be the context— energies surrounding the situation. Second card will stand for what we need to focus on, and the third card will show us the outcome. Sound good?"

"Sounds good."

Ava cut the deck twice, then stacked the three piles back on top of one another. Taking a moment to focus her energies, she drew a deep breath, felt the room still around her. She drew the top card. The seven of swords.

"Well, that's a no brainer," she announced, disappointed. She slid the card across the table.

Riley studied the card. "This one means someone's not being honest, right?"

"Yep. Nothing we didn't know already, but I guess it's nice to have it confirmed. That's our context. Shall we move on to the second card?"

Riley nodded, and Ava drew the next card, setting it down to the right of the first.

"The five of swords," she announced.

Riley squinted. "Remind me again what that means?"

"There are several ways it could go, but I tend to associate this card with conflict and disagreement. So, since it's supposed to represent where our focus should go, maybe there was some kind of conflict going on that we need to home in on…"

"Well, duh," Riley said, rolling her eyes. "Unless it's an accident, you don't just *kill* someone for the heck of it. Of course, there was a disagreement."

Despite the gravity of the situation, Ava laughed. She had to admit Riley had a point: it seemed logical that most murders were, in fact, the result of conflict. Still, she wondered if there was more to it than that. What *kind* of conflict? How major had it been? Or had it been some kind of menial squabble? She thought uneasily of what Owen had said about his brother's relationship with Mitch.

"Do you know of any longstanding feuds in Shiloh?" Ava asked, raising her gaze to Riley's. The devious grin of the man on the card, flashing above the bag of stolen swords he toted, gazed up at her menacingly, tauntingly.

Riley shrugged her thin shoulders. "Not really. I mean, my parents might know. I'm pretty young, and that seems like more of an old-timer thing. Why—do you think whoever killed Mitch did it as some sort of feud between bloodlines?"

Ava wrinkled her nose. "Well, when you put it like that, it sounds dumb. I guess I'm not thinking of anything that formal. I just wonder if the disagreement in question was something ongoing, or if it was done in the heat of the moment…"

"Could've been both. Could be the conflict was there, but the murderer never *planned* to kill Mitch."

"Well, if it's the same person, they certainly planned to kill Chantelle," Ava pointed out. "I don't think you can accidentally cut someone's brakes."

"True—but that was an act of desperation. Let's see what the last card says."

Ava nodded. "Right. The outcome."

She drew the last card and laid it face up next to the others. The Fool, the very first card in the Major Arcana, smiled up at them.

Riley groaned. "The Fool? What's that got to do with anything?"

Ava had to admit it was an excellent question. They sat in silence for a moment, staring at the three cards in front of them, as though willing some new meaning to jump out.

"Well," Ava said slowly, thinking aloud. "The Fool signifies beginnings, innocence. I guess—and this is a huge stretch—it could refer to the murderer getting a new start in the future after owning up to what he or she did."

"Oh, please," Riley said. "That's *so* corny. And anyway, no matter what kind of new start they get, there's no way you could ever call them *innocent*."

But Ava wasn't listening. A horrible thought had just flashed through her mind. *Jeremy O'Kelly*. Her stomach clenched as the thought spiraled, morphing into a jigsaw puzzle of pieces that fit together. Jeremy was fresh out of prison —not innocent, but starting again with a clean slate. He'd arrived in Shiloh to get back on his feet, to set off on the next chapter of his life—which, Ava realized with a hard swallow, was exactly what the Fool represented.

"What?" Riley asked. She was staring at Ava, her face etched with concern. "What's that look on your face for?"

Owen hadn't asked her not to say anything about Jeremy being under Greathouse's suspicion, but Ava had gotten the feeling that he wanted to keep it quiet—for his mother's sake, if nothing else. Still, she knew Riley well enough by now to know that the girl wouldn't take no for an answer. Ava's face had betrayed her, and Riley would continue to badger her until Ava gave her a satisfactory explanation.

"Okay..." Ava began reluctantly. She would see how much Riley already knew. "Do you know Owen's brother?"

Riley frowned. "Jeremy? I heard he went to jail a few years ago, but that's it."

Ava felt something in her chest loosen. Riley already knew about Jeremy's stint in prison—so that was nothing new. And, unless Jeremy was holing up in a cave somewhere, Ava guessed that most people in town were already aware of his release. If there was one thing she'd learned since her move, it was that word spread fast in Shiloh.

"Well, he's out now," Ava said, meeting Riley's gaze. "He's out of prison, he's back in Shiloh, and—this is *not* to be repeated—he was at the game the other night."

Riley's dark eyes went wide. "Oh, *shoot*. I mean—good for him for being out, but considering how he and Mitch Fangman were always at each other's throats, that can't look awesome to Chief Greathouse..."

Seriously? Did *everyone* in Shiloh keep tabs on every single feud that ever happened? Riley would have been in grade school at that time. The amount of knowledge the people of Shiloh had regarding everyone else's personal lives was absolutely unreal.

"No, it doesn't look good," Ava said, pressing her lips together. "Again, you are to repeat this to *no one*—I only know because Owen told me this evening. Currently, Greathouse has nothing to tie Jeremy to Mitch's murder except for the fact that the two guys hated each other."

"And that Jeremy was on the premises," Riley pointed out. "Then again, it seems pretty weird that the first thing you'd do when you got out of jail is go kill somebody. Like, way to get yourself locked up again."

"That's what I said, too. Anyway, when I saw the Fool card just now, I thought of new beginnings, new journeys—fresh starts—and my mind went straight to Jeremy."

Riley cocked her head. "So, you're saying that since the outcome card turned out to be the Fool, the outcome of Mitch's murder investigation will point to Jeremy O'Kelly?"

"I hope not—but I have to concede that it's possible," Ava admitted. She brushed the cards back into the pile, not wanting to look at them any longer, and placed them back in their sachet.

Riley got to her feet, pressing up from the coffee table, and collapsed backward onto the sofa behind her. "Well, if Greathouse thinks the same person who killed Mitch is also responsible for trying to kill Chantelle—which seems plausible, honestly—then he's sure as heck going to be looking hard at Jeremy. Does he have an alibi?"

Ava sighed. Her shoulders slumped as she took a seat in the chair across from Riley. She was just getting ready to speak, to say she didn't know, but that Owen seemed worried, when her phone buzzed inside her pocket. Fishing it out, she glanced at the screen. It was Owen.

So I've been trying to call Jeremy to let him know he needs to sort things out with Greathouse ASAP... but I can't get a hold of him.

"Is it Owen? What's he saying?" Riley leaned forward, her eyes flashing.

"Well... Let's just say things are not looking good."

As much as Ava hated to admit it, the situation with Jeremy

looked awfully suspicious. She'd never even *met* Jeremy O'Kelly, so had no idea what his character was like, what he was capable of. Owen did, of course, and even though he would be inherently biased, Owen admitted he wasn't sure of Jeremy's innocence. Yet no one would want to believe their own brother was capable of murder. How miserable Owen must feel.

Letting out her breath, she finally fired off a text:

I'm sure there's an explanation and you'll hear from him soon. Keep me posted, okay?

She knew it was vague, but what else could she say? *It'll all be okay?* She couldn't promise that, and she wouldn't offer empty promises. What she needed was time to think, process things. A good night's sleep would do her good—if she could fall asleep with so many thoughts racing through her head.

Ava heaved herself up from the armchair, stretching her arms overhead. Today had been too long, and if things kept up at the breakneck pace they were going, she didn't foresee tomorrow being any shorter or calmer.

"I'm going to bed," Ava said, more to herself than to Riley, as she made her way across the living room toward the stairs. "I'll see you tomorrow afternoon, yeah?"

"Sure, boss." Riley shot her a crooked smile. As she headed up the stairs to her bedroom, she reopened Owen's text, wondering if he'd replied. Nothing. Her previous text stood sullen and bare, useless, with the two check marks next to it that indicated Owen had read it. She stood at the top of the stairs for a moment, considering, then shot off another text to him before she could think better of it.

Just know I'm here if you need me.

There wasn't much she could do to fix things, but this was one promise she *could* make. And was glad to.

25

———

Wherever she went the next day, it seemed to Ava that she was constantly sniffing the air, trying to distinguish between the hundreds of scents she smelled throughout the course of the day. *Someone* in Shiloh had to wear Spicebomb by Viktor & Rolf, and it was just a matter of time before that person came waltzing her way, bringing their spicy cloud of scent with them. She just hoped she'd recognize the cologne when she smelled it. She and Chantelle had taken a couple of sample vials with them to be able to refresh their memories, but there was no guarantee Ava's nose was up to the job.

There'd been a moment that morning at the cafe when she thought she smelled it. Somewhere amidst the velvety richness of the freshly ground coffee beans and the piney scent of the wooden countertops, a different scent had suddenly stood out, clinging to the customer who was making his way across the shop and stood to survey the menu. But when Ava commented, hopefully nonchalantly, on how nice the man's cologne smelled, making up some story that her dad had worn the same one and she could never remember the name, the man had been tickled to let her know—Ralph Lauren something. Not Spicebomb.

And then there had been the host at La Fontana, when she and Riley had stopped by to grab their takeout order after work that day. Riley, who'd caught Ava sniffing in little tufts of air, had waited until the host had turned to grab their order off the back counter before casting an unamused sideways glance at Ava and giving a curt, decisive shake of her head. *No. Not it. Nice try.*

Now, as Ava and Riley sat in the car on the way home, bumping along the gravel roads, and Riley with a sack of fish tacos balanced on her knobby knees, Ava's phone rang. She glanced at Riley, who leaned forward to fish Ava's phone out of the center console.

"It's Owen," Riley announced, smirking a bit. "Should I answer it? I'll tell him you want to marry him."

Ava rolled her eyes, not even bothering a retort. She already knew Riley would be far too embarrassed to do any such thing—especially when it came to Owen O'Kelly, around whom she still clammed up. "Yes, please."

"Yo," Riley said, stabbing at the speakerphone button. "It's Riley. We're in the car. You're on speaker."

There was a moment of silence, with only static crackling in the background. They heard Owen suck in his breath, as though hesitant to talk in front of Riley. Then he said, "I think Greathouse is going after Jeremy. Like, right *now*."

Ava frowned, even though she knew Owen couldn't see her, her hands gripping the steering wheel. "What do you mean 'going after' him?"

"I mean, I think he's going to arrest him. Jeremy's been

camped out under the bridge on the edge of town. We need to get down there *stat*."

"What?" Ava was alarmed. Even through the phone, Owen's voice sounded tense and tight. Riley held the phone higher, glancing worriedly at Ava. "Why? Did something else happen?"

Again, the moment of hesitation. Ava slowed the car, turning into the driveway of her grandfather's house. The car crunched over the gravel.

Owen sighed, his voice resigned. "He tried to sell someone a joint downtown."

"Yikes," Riley mouthed from the passenger seat.

Ava grimaced, then cut the engine. "That's... not good."

"Not good at all," Owen agreed. "It's the excuse Greathouse needed to take him into custody. I'm heading down there now to see if I can talk some sense into the chief—or rather, get him to take pity on the family. My mom is going to come *unglued*. It's been—what?—five days since he got out of prison? Six?"

Ava rested her head against the seat back for a moment, trying to think what to do. Then, gesturing to Riley to go on inside, she said, "I'm coming with you. I'm dropping Riley off at home, and I'll be on my way in two seconds."

"Thank you," Owen said. She could hear the relief in his voice. There wasn't much she could do to change the situation, but at least she could offer her moral support. "Park near the bridge. I'll see you down there."

The line went dead, and Ava and Riley looked at each other. Pushing the passenger door open, Riley swung her skinny legs out, hefting the takeout bag along with her.

Riley gave a short nod, then shut the door and was on her way up the sidewalk. Ava put the car in reverse and hit the gas, wheels spinning on the gravel before she lurched backward and made her way down the driveway.

THE SUN WAS SINKING, painting the sky a brilliant mix of pink and gold, as Ava whipped her car into a parking spot near Ricky's auto body shop. Owen's pickup had just pulled in, and he got out of it, faded cap on his head. The expression on his face was so helpless, Ava felt something in her chest clench. *Moral support*, she thought, summoning her strength as she got out of the car. *I'm here for moral support.*

"Hey," Owen said.

"Hey."

In silence, they fell into step together, making their way toward the bridge and down the embankment where he said Jeremy had pitched his tent. Two police cars were parked a little way off, their lights flashing but sirens thankfully silent. The town would find out soon enough—if they didn't know already—that Greathouse had come to arrest Jeremy O'Kelly for drug possession, but at least there weren't any rubberneckers standing around gawking.

Owen's stride was brisk as he moved toward Jeremy's tent, and Ava struggled to keep up with the ground he covered with his lanky legs. Jeremy was standing outside the tent, his posture lazy. Chief Greathouse and Officer Dan Harding stood in front of him. Harding's right hand was at his hip, and Ava realized with a jolt that it was resting on his gun.

"Chief," Owen said, his deep voice cutting into the autumn evening air. When the chief turned to him, Owen raised his hands slightly in a gesture that showed he meant no harm. "Hang on."

Greathouse's voice was stern. "Owen, this doesn't concern you. You're not responsible for your brother."

"With all due respect," Owen said, his tone cautious but steady, "I may not be responsible for him, but it still concerns me. What's going on?"

Jeremy chanced a nervous glance at his brother, and Ava was struck by the resemblance. Although Jeremy was older and rougher, his skin weathered and his frame much bonier, there was no denying the two men were brothers. The glimmer had gone out of Jeremy's green eyes.

"Owen," Jeremy said, reaching out a gentle hand. His fingernails were dirty. "Go home. This is my own fault."

"*No*." Owen's tone was forceful, and a kind of rage had come across his face. "We're not going through this again. *Mom* isn't going through this again. Okay, chief?"

Greathouse sighed, exchanging a look with Officer Harding before he lumbered toward Owen. He clamped a beefy hand on Owen's shoulder, looked him dead in the eyes. "I'm really sorry for your family, kid. I know it's been rough. But the law is the law."

Owen turned to his brother, his face more severe than Ava had ever seen it. "You know this is just a surface crime to book you for Mitch Fangman's murder, right?"

A look of confusion passed over Jeremy's face. He looked from Owen to Greathouse, as though trying to make sense of what Owen had said. Suddenly, he snorted, his voice thick with derision. "You kidding me, chief? Mitch Fangman got what was coming to him, but it wasn't me who did it."

Greathouse ignored him. "This here has nothing to do with

Mitch Fangman. This has to do with you breaking a law, one I would've thought you'd do your best to adhere to so soon after serving time for a similar charge. And speaking of which—Dan, why don't you check that bag?"

Jeremy looked suddenly tense, and Ava saw the muscles in Owen's throat move as he swallowed hard. Kneeling next to a worn backpack on the ground, Officer Harding unzipped each pocket, rifling carefully through what little belongings there were inside: a toothbrush, a bottle of 3-in-1 shower soap, a packet of wet wipes, three granola bars, and a couple sets of boxers. Just when Ava thought maybe Jeremy was going to luck out this time, that the whole thing had been a mix-up, Officer Harding brought out two last items: a baggie full of a rather suspicious looking substance, and a small glass bottle which he inspected curiously.

Jeremy, who'd been watching the whole inspection, looked startled. He pointed to the bottle in Officer Harding's hands. "Hey, wait. What's *that*?"

Officer Harding frowned, passed the bottle to Greathouse to examine. As Ava watched the older man read the label, then remove the cap and sniff gingerly, her heart sank. She glanced at Owen, but his expression was unreadable, his eyes fixed on the scene in front of him—which he was powerless to stop.

"Well," Greathouse said, heaving a heavy sigh. "I reckon it's cologne—something called Spicebomb, by the looks of it. The very same cologne that Ava here mentioned our suspected killer wore at the scene of the crime, according to Chantelle Svoboda."

"But that's—that's not mine," Jeremy stuttered out, still pointing indignantly at the bottle Greathouse held in his hands. His eyes were wild, terrified.

Ava saw Owen's shoulders tense beneath his sweaty t-shirt. His eyes flicked to Jeremy's, then landed angrily on Greathouse. "That's ridiculous. He just got out of *jail*, chief. What on earth is he doing with a bottle of expensive cologne?"

Greathouse shrugged. He turned to Jeremy, took a step closer. "I don't know, champ. You tell me. What's it doing in your bag if it's not yours?"

"I don't know," Jeremy said. His voice was shaky. "I *swear*. The baggie, yes. That's mine. I'll own up to it. But that cologne... I don't think I've owned a bottle of cologne in my *life* —not since high school when Abercrombie and Fitch was a thing." He ended his spiel in a shaky laugh, as though hoping humor and a bit of nostalgia might lighten Greathouse's mood, bring them all back into calmer waters.

But Greathouse remained unmoved. He shot a pitying look at Owen, then reached into his back pocket. "Jeremy O'Kelly, you're under arrest for the murder of Mitch Fangman. You have the right to remain silent. Anything you say can and will be used against you..."

Ava didn't even hear the rest. Without another thought in her head, she rushed forward, grabbing Owen's hand and yanking him toward her. Although his gaze stayed fixed on his brother, whom Officer Harding was now handcuffing, Owen didn't resist her presence and instead let his normally strong self go slack against her. They both watched as Greathouse and Harding marched Jeremy to the cop car, opened the door, and guided Jeremy's head inside. Ava reached an arm around Owen's waist and planted a hand firmly against his middle. She wasn't going anywhere.

26

———

The flash of police lights still haunting them from the distance, Ava and Owen watched as the two cop cars made their way back up the embankment, across the bridge, and disappeared down Main Street. They stood in silence a moment, feeling each other breathe, listening to the mournful call of the whippoorwill in the darkening sky.

"Well," Owen said finally, his voice steady in the twilight. "That's that."

"For now," Ava added.

"I guess we ought to be getting home. Nothing more we can do here." Owen looked defeated, like a man who'd trained and trained for a race and still couldn't make it across the finish line. It made Ava wonder how many times Owen had been through this kind of thing with his older brother.

Her eyes moved over Jeremy's tiny campsite, his tent and cooler outlined in the half light. She couldn't help replaying in her mind the scene that had just occurred. It seemed so... odd. What *was* Jeremy, a man newly released from a prison sentence, doing with a bottle of Viktor & Rolf cologne? When a toothbrush, a bar of soap, and a package of wet wipes made up the rest of his belongings, why on earth would *cologne* be a priority?

"It seems weird," Ava said aloud, the words coming as the thoughts formed. "I think... I think the cologne was planted. I mean, that tent's not exactly padlocked."

Owen let out a sigh. He ran a hand through his wavy hair, eyes traveling upwards to rest on the treetops darkening against the sky. "Ava, I can't do this with you right now."

Ava pulled back, her arm that encircled his waist going slack. She looked up at him, but his eyes still wandered against the rooftops of the buildings downtown. "Wait—what do you mean? You don't think it was planted?"

Owen shook his head. Then, shrugging himself free of Ava's grasp, he stepped away from her. When he turned to look at her, pain clouded his eyes. "I'm sorry, Ava. I really am. This is all just... too much." He gestured helplessly to the campsite, to her, and then shoved his hands deep in his pockets. "I don't think you get how taxing this stuff with Jeremy is. It's going to rip my mom's heart out, and I don't think I have the capacity to handle it while getting my own ripped out by you."

Ava stared at him. "What are you talking about? I'm *here*. I'm not going anywhere."

Owen smiled at her sadly. "That's true. You're physically here, and for that I'm really grateful. But I don't think the rest of you has caught up yet."

"Excuse me—you mean my *mom* hasn't caught up yet."

"No," Owen said, his voice firm. "*You* haven't caught up yet, Ava. You can blame your mom all you want, but only *you* are in charge of your life. And I don't have the strength to handle my family stuff while I wait for you to make that call."

"But—"

"Stop. I mean it. If you want to go back to Noah and—and—and your amazing house or whatever, then do that. It'll hurt, but I'm not going to stop you. I want you to be happy. But right now… I've got other stuff to deal with." Owen paused, rubbing his jaw. When he continued, his eyes were gentle, but his voice was no less firm. "Ava, we both know you're using this investigation to distract yourself from what *you* have to deal with."

Ava stepped back, stunned. A pang of fury swept through her. "That's *not* true."

Owen sighed again as he turned to head back up the hill, his boots crunching on the loose pebbles. "It is, Ava. Noah's been cleared, I've been cleared. Joel's not involved this time. Why else are you still hunting around, trying to figure this out?"

"Because—because it's your *brother*," Ava sputtered. "Because I care about you!"

Owen stopped, turning back to fix her with a pointed gaze. "Okay. So show me you care. Figure out who I am to you."

And then he was gone, disappearing over the top of the hill, leaving Ava standing alone in the ravine.

She stood for a moment, gazing around at the abandoned campsite. All was silent, save for the sound of the wind rustling through the leaves overhead, rattling the branches that would soon be bare. She felt strangely empty, like some vital organ had been snatched from inside her ribcage. Her breath caught in her chest.

She had the sudden thought of running after Owen, of catching his huge hand in hers, of pulling him close to her, of pleading her case—but she knew it wouldn't help. Owen would only shrug her off. He'd made his boundary crystal clear. But his words clung to her... Was she really using Mitch's murder investigation as a way of distracting herself from the decision she knew she needed to make?

Ava stepped closer to the thin, shoddy tent Jeremy had been sleeping in. Its canvas door was unzipped, fluttering in the biting breeze. If someone had wanted to plant the bottle of cologne in Jeremy's bag, it wouldn't have been hard to get the job done. It was, apparently, also common knowledge in Shiloh that Mitch Fangman and Jeremy O'Kelly had long been on the outs—making Jeremy a logical target if the killer wanted someone to frame. The question, of course, was—who? *Who* was the killer?

Ava's gaze swept the area, taking in the blackened remnants of the campfire. Whoever it was—whoever had killed Mitch and ostensibly come to frame Jeremy—had to have been at the campsite. And, thinking back to it, Greathouse hadn't done a full sweep of the place. He'd found Jeremy, searched the bag, gotten what he wanted, and got out. It wouldn't hurt to look around, although what exactly she hoped to find was anyone's guess.

Ava set to work as best she could, scouring the place for anything out of the ordinary. The streetlights from the bridge above cast only a shadowy glow on the campsite, so she used her phone flashlight to rifle through the belongings Jeremy had left inside the tent. On one side of the tent were a couple of cans of Bush's baked beans, along with a can opener and a single fork. A musty, still damp towel had been tossed in the corner, and below it was an empty pack of cigarettes, the box crushed. Aside from the remains of the small campfire outside the tent, into which Jeremy had seemingly thrown wads of crumpled newspaper, nothing seemed to stick out. It looked like the campsite of a man down on his luck. Nothing more.

"Well, it was worth a shot," Ava muttered to herself, crouching next to the campfire ashes and poking through the newspapers with a broken stick. She tossed the stick onto the pile of ashes and wiped her hands on her jeans.

Her mind raced through the facts of the case, spinning through what she already knew for any hint of something that could help her—some unexamined tidbit, some unfollowed rabbit hole.

But she came up short. There was nothing.

Fighting the strange tightness in her chest, Ava sat back in the dirt and flung her purse down next to her, defeated. She was at a dead end—not only in the case, but with Owen. Where could she even *go* from here? Any path forward, she was blocked.

"Zaidy," she whispered. "What do I do?"

More than once, her grandfather's voice had come to her as a whisper, even saving her life. But now, as she strained to listen through the stillness, there was only silence. No sighing of wind, no murmur of other-worldly words in her ear. She was alone.

Just then, a flutter of breeze swept through, blowing the flap of Ava's purse open. As her gaze moved to the bag, goosebumps crept up along her arms. For there, revealed by the wind, was her tarot deck, snug in its sachet, waiting.

"Of course." Ava chuckled to herself, then blew a kiss to the sky.

Extracting the cards from the velvety bag, Ava shuffled them, trying to clear her mind as she did so. She wanted guidance, and the best advice came when she was free of her own preconceived notions and biases. Once she'd shuffled, cut, and re-stacked the deck, she sat up straight and closed her eyes, focusing. Then, opening her eyes, Ava flipped over the top card and held it up to the hazy glow of the streetlights.

The Strength card.

Tears pricked her eyes. The woman on the card, dressed in a flowing white robe, had bent to stroke the ferocious lion standing next to her. Ava knew this card was a symbol of resilience, representing one's ability to draw on the inner strength and calm needed to tame even the rawest of emotions. She sniffled. She'd wanted an answer, and this was it.

Her mother wasn't a lion, but she sure had claws, and her roar could be as terrifying as any wild beast's. But, just like the woman on the card, Ava knew she had to find the strength to stand up to the roar—because, although Sara Goldberg might not like it, Owen was right. Ava was in charge of her own life, and if the man she was in love with—the man who treated her as wonderfully as her mother had taught her she deserved— happened to not be Jewish... then so be it. *She* was Jewish—in her own wonderful, complicated way—and nothing Owen was or wasn't would ever change that. They would figure it out for themselves, one step at a time.

And she'd start with the first step right now.

Placing her tarot cards back in her bag, Ava pulled out her phone. She'd spoken little to her mother since her parents had returned to Chicago, but this couldn't wait. She had to make her move now, before she lost her nerve.

"Hello?" Sara Goldberg answered on the first ring.

Ava gripped the phone, trying to calm the racing of her heart. It was now or never.

"Hey, um. I've got something I need to say."

"Okay, well, that's not at all alarming…"

"I just…" She paused a moment, thinking of how to word things. Gentle, but firm. That was the way to tame the lion. Channeling the strength she knew her grandfather wanted her to find, she forged ahead. "Well, this may not be what you want to hear—and honestly, you've probably guessed it already—but Owen? He's more than a friend."

There was a beat of silence. Her mother was waiting for her to continue.

"Look, I know he's not Jewish. And he's not a doctor. I'm well aware. But I'm okay with that—and I hope you will be, too… eventually. He's a wonderful man, and I don't really know yet how things are going to work, but—but—but we'll figure it out."

Another beat of silence. As soon as the words were out, Ava sucked in her breath. She was almost afraid to move, waiting for her mother's reply. After what seemed like a lifetime, Sara Goldberg gave a little cough.

"You're right. He is a good man."

Ava was stunned. "So… So you're not *livid*?"

Her mother chuckled. "No, I'm not livid. But I will need to process."

"Processing's okay. Processing's good."

"Alright, well, I need to get back to your father. He's shopping online for Sukkot decorations, and I can see him putting the most *awful* garlands in his cart."

Ava laughed, relief blossoming in her chest at how fast her mother had returned to normalcy. "No problem. Go save the *sukkah*, Mom."

The line clicked off. Relief still pulsed in Ava's bloodstream, filling her with a kind of exuberance she hadn't felt in a long,

long time. A weight had been lifted, a wall shattered, and finally—*finally*—she'd found a path forward.

No—scratch that. She'd *made* a path forward. Ava grinned to herself, blowing another kiss to the air. She hoped Zaidy Mel was proud of her wherever he was watching from.

Getting to her feet, Ava took one last glance around the campsite. Her vision felt fresh, her mind clear. In the hazy light of the lamp post from the bridge, a flash of white several feet away from the campsite had caught her eye. Maybe the luck of the moment hadn't finished its work quite yet.

Stalking across the dirt, Ava stooped low to examine what she saw now was a torn piece of paper, fluttering against a cluster of weeds in the evening breeze. She pinched the paper between two fingers and smoothed it out. Ava frowned, eyes scanning the page—or rather, scrap, as most of it had been torn off, leaving her with only the corner. Illustrations of green, red, and yellow leaves were scattered across the white background, clearly some kind of design. What appeared to be a single corn husk was ripped clean through the middle, and the only text on the paper was a big, chunky letter *e*, the letters before it also torn off. She turned the paper over, but the back was blank. Ava glanced around, hoping the other scraps of the page might be floating around somewhere. The dirt and weeds were bare, though, the rest of the page most likely long gone in the wind by now, tumbling through the weeds or drowned in the creek.

It looked like something fall themed, whatever this page was. And although it was probably nothing, had probably blown down the ravine from one of the downtown shops, she couldn't shake the feeling that the paper was somehow tied to the cologne bottle that had mysteriously appeared in Jeremy's backpack. After all, aside from the remnants of old newspapers in the ashy campfire, there were no other bits of paper anywhere else around. It could have, she reasoned, come from an insert in one of the papers Jeremy had used for kindling— but no. That didn't make sense either. This paper was thicker than anything she'd seen in a newspaper. It was the kind of paper you'd use for a party invite, or a graduation announcement.

Ava folded the scrap of paper, shoved it in her pocket, and headed back up the incline toward her parked car. With the nights being chillier nowadays, Main Street was all but deserted, save for a few straggling cars still parked in front of the couple of still open establishments. Scarecrows were propped up against the lampposts, their grins somehow garish in the wake of the evening's events.

Getting into her car, Ava slipped her hand into her pocket and once more brought out the scrap of paper, studying the leaves and that chunky *e* one more time. Then, having burned the design into her memory, she started her car and headed for home. She'd give Owen space tonight, but tomorrow? She smiled.

She'd found the courage to tame her lion, and by god, she was going to let Owen know it.

27

"Morning, Ava!"

From her stance behind the counter, where she stood weighing out coffee beans for the day ahead, Ava glanced up to see Tim Meyer striding through the front door of Cafe Arcana. She smiled. One of her regulars every morning, he was just on time.

"Good morning," Ava said, beaming. She snapped a lid on one last container of beans and wiped her hands on her apron, making her way to the cash register where Tim now waited. "The usual, I'm guessing?"

"Absolutely," Tim said. As per usual, he was dressed to the nines, but looked effortless, like he'd simply grabbed clothes out of his closet and every piece happened to match.

"I like your tie," Ava said, eyeing the scarecrow printed thing Tim wore around his neck. It wasn't like him to be anything less than polished, so the corniness of the tie stood out.

Tim made a face, but he laughed. "Trust me, it's only to promote the harvest festival this evening. They wanted me to wear a straw hat and face paint, but I put my foot down. This tie is bad enough."

"Well, I think it suits you," Ava said, shooting him a wink as she slid his coffee across the counter.

"Oh, *goodness*," Tim laughed, groaning. "Don't tell me *that*. Anyway, are you planning to drop by the festival tonight? It's over at McPhersons—you know, County Road A."

Ava suppressed the urge to laugh. Bless Tim's heart for assuming she knew where County Road A was. Then something clicked. "Oh! That's the same farm as the apple orchard, right?"

"The very same," Tim said. He took a sip of his coffee, smacked his lips in satisfaction. "Curtis hosts a harvest festival every year, where people from around town can come set up a booth and sell whatever autumn-themed products they have— usually stuff like sweet breads, fall decor, homegrown vegetables from the garden, that kind of thing. They'll have activities for the kids—I think this year they've got face painting and corn hole—and a bonfire where you can roast s'mores. You ought to bring Owen." He winked at her.

Ava felt her neck flush as something in her chest fluttered. She still hadn't told Owen about her conversation with her mother the night before. She wasn't sure what was holding her back—after all, it was *good* news—but she wanted to find the perfect moment, word it in the best way she could. She couldn't afford to screw things up again.

Ignoring Tim's comment, Ava instead steered the conversation back to the festival.

"That sounds fun," she said, smiling. "I'll see if I can drop by, support the vendors. I could always go for a s'more."

Tim headed toward the door, then, seeming to remember

something, turned back and snapped his fingers. "They've got a corn maze, too, this year. I've been hearing Curtis talk about that since he planted it last spring."

"Huh," Ava said—because what else do you say to a corn maze? She was pretty sure she'd been in one as a child, but it hadn't exactly knocked her socks off. It was, after all, corn. And her surroundings these days were not lacking in corn.

"Yep. I haven't seen it yet, but it's supposed to be really cool," Tim said. He smiled at her from the doorway, then glanced at his watch. "Well, I'd better get to the gallery. See you around, Ava!"

The bell atop the door jangled as the door swung shut behind him, and Ava watched as he made his way across the cobblestoned street to his gallery, waving and grinning at everyone he passed.

If only I could channel some of Tim's inherent bubbliness, Ava thought. Since moving to Shiloh several months before, she'd begun to open up a bit more to the friendly, familiar ways of the locals, but there was still a distance between them she wasn't sure how to close. The incessant penchant for small talk that everyone in the town seemed to have often wore on her, and it took all her energy just to greet her customers in a way they'd deem polite. A smile and a nod was not enough in Shiloh—you were expected to remember personal details, and more than that, you were expected to *care.* That was one thing the people of Shiloh had going for them: they cared immensely.

Well, Ava thought as she straightened the tables and chairs before the morning rush of visitors began arriving, *maybe it wouldn't kill me to care a little more.* The festival could be fun, right? Maybe she'd make an appearance.

Ava dragged the sandwich board with the day's roasts

chalked onto it outside to the sidewalk, propping open the door to welcome visitors. She positioned the sandwich board at an elegant angle, then straightened, breathing in the day. The weather was beautiful, if not a little chilly, the early autumn breeze riffling through the trees. The leaves above were beginning to change color to deep, burnt oranges and warm, golden ochres. She gazed down Main Street, taking in the rustic cobblestones and the decorated storefronts. A cheery, lackadaisical scarecrow was propped against each lamppost, and hay bales topped with terra-cotta pots of soft, vibrant mums were scattered like impromptu benches at the end of each block. Downtown Shiloh was an absolute autumn dream.

Ava stopped. Her gaze had caught on a flyer taped to the lamp post nearest her, and for a moment she couldn't pinpoint why. She just knew that something about it seemed familiar. Casting a glance back inside her shop to make sure no other customers had arrived yet, she moved toward the flyer.

The headline across the top read: *OPEN OCTOBER 1!* Ava's gaze moved down, scanning the page which was covered in ears of corn and grinning black crows. Then, at the bottom, she spotted it.

HUGE CORN MAZE!

In the lower corners of the flyer, there was a design of scattered autumn leaves. There was no doubt about it—it was the same design as the scrap of paper she had found outside Jeremy's campsite. A perfect match.

She snatched the flyer and was about to head inside when a familiar voice caught her ear. Whipping her head around to glance across the street, she stopped. There was Owen, holding the boutique door open for someone with their hands full as they entered the shop.

Ava didn't even stop to think.

"Owen!"

At the sound of his name, Owen's gaze jerked up. All thought of when, how, where, and what flew straight out of Ava's mind as she broke into a run, bounding over the cobblestones in her haste to get to where he stood. She jolted to a screeching halt in front of him, breath hitching and keenly aware of the passersby pretending not to stare.

"Is... everything okay?" Owen's gaze was one of half amusement, half concern.

Ava nodded, trying to find her voice. She held Owen's gaze, her mind spinning with all the words she wanted to say. Where did she start? An apology? A declaration? All she knew was she needed Owen to stay.

"I'm done running," she blurted out.

Owen's eyebrows raised. "I see that. You've come to a panting stop in front of me."

"No." Ava shook her head. "I mean—I'm done running away from decisions I need to make. Done running after what my mom wants, after what somebody somewhere taught me *I* should want. I'm done running away from you, Owen."

Owen held her gaze for a moment, his green eyes searching. "Okay..."

"I'm in love with you, Owen," Ava said. She didn't even know where the words were coming from, but she let them come, roll out in spite of herself. She was learning to trust. "I'm in love with you—we both know it, *have* known it—and I told my mom straight out last night."

"You... did?"

Ava nodded, biting her lip. "She took it well, all things considered—but it doesn't even matter. You were right. I'm the one in charge of my life, and I make the calls. And this is one call I should've made months ago."

Owen ran a hand through his tousled hair, looking up and down the street. Then he looked back at Ava, a glint in his eye. "So... Does this mean we can finally face up to all these poor people who insist I'm your boyfriend while we lie and deny it?"

Ava grinned. "Yes."

"Good," Owen said, moving to wrap his arms around her.

Gingerly, Ava allowed her own arms to encircle Owen's waist, drawing him to her. His sweatshirt was soft against her cheek, and she breathed in his scent, savoring the moment.

When Owen drew back, he frowned, rubbing his hands down Ava's arms. "Where's your jacket? You've got goosebumps."

Ava scoffed. "No wonder my mom approves of you. Goyish or not, you've got the makings of a bonafide Jewish mother."

Owen shook his head, chuckling. Shrugging off his zip-up sweatshirt, he reached around to drape it across Ava's shoulders. As Ava slid her goosebump-covered arms into the sleeves, Owen stood back to study her, a small smile playing across his mouth.

"I feel like we're in school and you just gave me your letterman jacket," Ava said, laughing. "But it's cozy, and it smells like you. I love it."

"Good."

Suddenly, Ava remembered the flyer she'd stuffed into her pocket just a few moments before. Fishing it out, she passed it to Owen, her eyes glowing with excitement.

Owen took the paper, one eyebrow raised. "What's this? The McPhersons' corn maze?"

"Yeah. Last night, after you left the ravine, I looked around the place a little bit—"

"Snooped around, you mean," Owen said, cutting her off with a grin.

Ava waved a hand. "Whatever. I found this torn little piece of card stock with only some fall leaves and a stylized letter *e* on it. Then this morning, Tim Meyer stopped in to tell me about the fall festival happening tonight at McPhersons, and I saw the flyer for the corn maze outside. It's definitely a match for the torn paper I found."

Owen looked up at Ava, meeting her gaze. His green eyes flashed with excitement. "Well, hey. This sounds like it could be fun. Fancy a date with me to the fall festival this evening, Ms. Goldberg? I'll even claim you as my girlfriend if anyone asks."

Ava's own eyes glimmered back at him as she stood on her tiptoes to kiss his cheek. "I wouldn't miss it."

28

The fall festival was in full swing when Owen and Ava slowed to a stop on the dry, grassy lawn next to the parking lot of McPherson Apple Orchard, where the runoff of cars had already begun to park. As they made their way across the brittle grass, Ava snuggled deeper into Owen's sweatshirt, pulling the zipper up to her chin. The early evening air was chilly, but Owen's hand in hers was warm. All that was left was to find *some* kind of clue that would help them clear Jeremy's name, and everything would be golden.

She scanned the crowd, taking in the scene. Row upon row of tables stood from the farmhouse to the barn, each covered in fall decor: sprinklings of silk autumn leaves, piles of miniature hay bales, elaborate arrangements of colorful Indian corn, and an ungodly number of pumpkins and gourds. There were hand-poured candles for sale, wreaths crafted from dried corn husks, plates of homemade pumpkin bars and apple pies. Some tables were spread with beaded jewelry, others with crocheted doilies and plushies. Everywhere Ava looked, there was something she hadn't seen yet.

"They've got caramel apples," Owen said, pointing to one of the booths. "And hot cocoa and s'mores and kettle corn, too."

"They've got *everything*," Ava said. "It's like an autumn wonderland."

"Come on." Owen tugged at her hand. "Looks like the Walshes have a booth. We can get some hot apple cider."

Ed and Elaine Walsh were both at the Looking Glass booth, standing behind a table covered in wine bottles and gift boxes. As Owen and Ava approached, Elaine looked up from the cup of cider she was filling from a tall silver urn and beamed at them. "Care for some cider?"

"You read our minds," Owen said. He handed Elaine a couple of ones as she passed the steaming cup she'd just filled to someone Ava didn't recognize.

Elaine took two more cups down from the stack and began filling them. The delicious scent of cinnamon wafted through the air, and Ava breathed it in. All around them, the sounds of the festival drifted by—the chatter of excited voices, the laughter of friends, and the crunch of dry grass underfoot as everyone meandered from booth to booth. It really was the perfect night.

"It's a great turnout," Ed Walsh remarked. "I wasn't sure it would be, what with Mitch's murder and all. I figured people would be more skittish, but I guess now that they've arrested—"

"Ed!" Elaine hissed, jabbing a sharp elbow into her husband's side and shooting him a look that drew more attention than if she'd let him finish his sentence.

Ed's eyes widened. He looked at Owen helplessly. "I mean —ah—"

"It's alright, Ed," Owen said. He took the cups of cider from

Elaine. "I figured most people would've heard by now. It is Shiloh, after all."

"Well, it's too bad," Elaine said. She gave a decisive nod, as if that settled the matter.

"Agreed."

Ava asked, "So where's this corn maze?"

Elaine pointed to the far side of the grassy expanse. "There —just behind the barn. It's not my cup of tea, but our grandkids loved it."

"Great to hear," Ava said. She linked her arm through Owen's and nudged him away from the table. "We'll have to check it out."

"Thanks for stopping by," Ed said, giving them a merry wave. Ava could tell by the pitying look in their eyes as she and Owen turned back into the crowd that they hadn't forgotten about Jeremy but were kind enough not to mention him again.

"I'm sorry," Ava said, squeezing Owen's hand. "That sucked."

"Yeah." Owen's gaze scanned the festival, his jaw flexing. "That's why we're here, though. To move forward past that. And maybe also to figure something out about who killed Mitch. You did say you found a scrap of the festival flyer near Jeremy's campsite."

Ava murmured her agreement. Although she was uncertain how finding a scrap of the flyer near Jeremy's tent could mean they'd find any leads at the festival, she was hopeful. It wouldn't hurt to keep their eyes peeled.

They continued their stroll through the rows of tables. One booth let you make a cornhusk doll, and another offered free face painting—which Ava had to shove Owen past, fielding his jokes about how she could get hers painted like the "sweet little pumpkin" she was. Aside from the fact that the phrase made her gag, there was no way she was going to go running around with her face painted like a jack-o'-lantern.

"Remind me again why you didn't do a tarot booth tonight...?" Owen mused, casting her a questioning glance as they walked along. "I mean, surely they *asked* you..."

"They did," Ava said, nodding. "And honestly, now that I'm here, I really wish I'd said yes. But it's smack dab in the middle of the High Holidays—my parents were coming and I just thought it'd be too much to handle it all."

"Makes sense. There's always next year."

"Definitely. Anyway, at least it meant I was free tonight to go prowling around with you."

Owen raised an amused eyebrow. "Is that what we're doing here? Prowling?"

Ava rolled her eyes. "Oh, you know what I mean."

"I do. I'm at a loss on what to look for here, though. There are so many people."

Ava pulled out her phone. "Is there Wi-Fi? Or can you give me a hotspot? I barely have service."

"You need to switch providers," Owen said, winking. "I've got full bars. But what are you thinking? What's Wi-Fi going to help?"

"I was thinking we could find a list of the booths on the Shiloh community Facebook page. We can see if anyone's here who might have it out for Jeremy."

"I mean... The list of people in this town he's irked in some way is probably *endless*. Besides, how do we know that whoever planted the cologne in his bag chose him for personal reasons? He could've just been an easy target, living out in the open like that. And everyone who's been around here knows he and Mitch had issues."

"That's true," Ava conceded. "We don't know. But we've got to start somewhere."

Opening the Wi-Fi settings on her phone, she flicked through to the list of available networks. First on the list was *McPherson_Orchard_Guest*, and it was unlocked—bingo. As she waited for it to connect, she scanned the list of other networks. There was Owen's hotspot, which he'd just turned on, and a few other names she didn't recognize—not surprising, as the place was buzzing. The Wi-Fi icon in the corner of her screen lit up, and she was about to close out of the settings when something caught her eye.

Ava clutched Owen's arm and jabbed at the screen. "Owen. Look."

There, below her shaking finger, a weak hotspot had appeared. *Mitch's iPhone.*

"What the...?" Owen looked at her, his brow furrowed in confusion. "Well, hold up. It doesn't necessarily mean anything. There's a *ton* of people here—and not all from Shiloh. There could be any number of guys here named Mitch."

"Okay, but *still*. They never found Mitch Fangman's iPhone after he was murdered. This could be him! Or—his iPhone, rather. Whoever took it, presumably the killer, could *be here*."

Owen rubbed his jaw. "Hmm. Well, the signal looks pretty weak. What if we just..."

He took Ava's phone from her hands and started walking in one direction, pulling Ava along with him. He stopped, surveyed the screen, then veered the other way.

"The signal's getting a little stronger," he observed.

"Keep following it!"

Glancing around to make sure they hadn't drawn attention, Ava crept along with Owen as he wandered further in the direction he'd started. As they went, she sipped her cider, casting what she hoped were interested glances toward the tables behind them. If anyone approached them, they could always say they'd stepped away from the crowd to make a phone call.

"It's giving full bars now," Owen muttered, flicking his eyes toward Ava with a grin. "Which means..."

He stopped, looked up and around. Behind them was the buzz of the festival. Ahead of them, by ten or so yards, was a large barn, and beyond that, the infamous corn maze. But the signal was too strong to be coming from the still rather far-off corn maze, which meant that the only place Mitch's phone could be was—

"The barn," Ava breathed. "The signal's got to be coming from the barn."

They stood for a moment in silence, sipping their cider. The barn doors were shut, and unless some unassuming festival-goer had somehow wandered inside, Ava was pretty sure the structure wasn't open to the public. Aside from a cheery, yet weather-worn scarecrow someone had hung in the highest eave, the place was still. It clearly wasn't part of the festival.

"Well, that's that," Ava said, crumpling her paper cider cup inside her fist.

Owen eyed her. "What's what?"

"We'll just have to come back. Tonight—when everyone's gone. If Mitch Fangman's iPhone is in that barn, there's a reason, and you better believe we're going to find out what it is."

"Good god," Owen groaned. "Can't we just let Mr. McPherson know there's a maybe suspicious Wi-Fi signal coming from his barn? He can check it out for us without us having to, you know, *trespass*."

Ava considered this for a moment, then shook her head. "No. We can't risk word getting out. Whoever this killer is has got their ear to the ground and is on the move. They just went after Chantelle, and they sure as heck won't hesitate to come after us if they catch so much as a peep of what we're onto."

Owen heaved a sigh, but he didn't argue. He just plucked the crumpled cup from Ava's hand and nudged her back the way they'd come. Ava knew he knew it was pointless to protest, that she'd come by herself if he didn't agree to come along. Besides, she reasoned, they didn't have much choice. If Jeremy was going to get the fresh start he deserved—the fresh start that Owen's *mom* deserved to see—this was their shot to figure things out, set the record straight.

And unlike the Shiloh Sharks on the football field, Ava was not about to fumble.

29

The moon was high in the sky as they crept their way along the gravel roads north of Shiloh, shining white on Ava's knuckles as she gripped the steering wheel. Dark rows of cornfields stretched out on either side of the road, far more sinister in the shadows than they'd seemed during the day.

"Pull off here," Owen whispered, tapping the passenger side window. His long legs barely fit in the small space of her Honda Civic, and his knees bumped the glove box.

"Isn't it further down?" Ava wasn't sure why they were whispering, but the thought of cutting through the silence seemed wrong.

"Yeah, but we've got a better chance of getting onto the property undetected without the car. Even without the headlights, there's no way they won't see us coming down the driveway."

It was a fair point. Ava pulled off the shoulder, maneuvering nearer the edge of the cornfield. They were far enough away and still on the upward slope of the hill, meaning the parked car wouldn't be seen from the house. As Ava killed the engine, the silence fell around them like a dark cloud. Aside from the faint chorus of crickets from deep inside the cornfields, only the ticking of the engine accompanied their hushed breaths.

"Alright," Owen said, drawing in a resigned breath. "Let's do this."

They exited the car, taking care to close the doors as quietly as possible. Around them, the night was silent, save for the crunching of gravel and browning, brittle grass beneath their feet. A ripple of cold wind swept through the night, and Ava pulled Owen's sweatshirt more tightly around her, breathing in the scent of Downy and whatever it was that was uniquely Owen.

"Let's cut around by the barn," Owen suggested, hooking his thumb toward the structure looming at the west edge of the property. "Someone might see us if we walk down the driveway."

"Or the dog," Ava said, stricken with the sudden image of a vicious, barking animal running at what it took to be trespassers. And they *were* trespassers. Even without the very real possibility that the killer was hiding out at the McPherson farm, what Ava and Owen were doing was very much illegal. There was more than one reason they needed to stay hidden.

"Right," Owen agreed. "And anyway, if someone is camping out here, they won't be close to the house. My bet's on the maze."

They crept toward the barn, the faint creaking of the wind through the branches overhead an eerie accompaniment to their clandestine mission. Perhaps it was the darkness, or perhaps it was because this time she actually hoped to spot the killer himself, but this moonlit journey felt infinitely more dangerous than her run-in with Audrey Wilson's killer a few months ago. She was walking knowingly into the lion's den. Next to her, the outline of Owen's shotgun gleamed in the moonlight, and for the first time, she found she was glad he'd brought it. She just hoped he wouldn't have to use it. She also hoped Mr. McPherson wouldn't spot them trespassing on his property while toting along a gun. But Owen had insisted they have a way to defend themselves if they ended up in a fight against the killer, and she'd reluctantly agreed.

As they reached the far side of the barn, Owen held up a hand. He cocked his head toward the barn door, signaling they should look inside. The building was taller than Ava had imagined an old barn would be, the steep, splintered roof rising to a point amidst the twisted tree branches above. With the moon as its backdrop, the old barn looked sinister and eerie, a horror movie come to life. She shivered.

Owen grasped the handle of the old, splintered barn door and slid it deftly to the side. He tensed as the door emitted a loud, high-pitched scraping sound. A cloud of dust flew swirling into their faces, and Ava had to bury her face in her sleeve to keep from coughing. She heard Owen clear his throat, low and deep. He peered around the barn door, the outline of his broad chest heaving. The two of them stood absolutely still, absolutely silent, straining to determine whether someone had been alerted to their presence. Not the slightest sound rose out of the darkness. Owen turned back toward Ava.

"I don't see anyone inside," he whispered.

"Still, they could've left stuff behind," she hissed back.

Owen nodded in agreement. Even if the killer wasn't on the premises now, perhaps there was something in the barn that would provide concrete evidence for Greathouse to make an arrest—pliers that could be matched to the ones that had cut Chantelle's brakes, perhaps.

"Okay," Owen said, his tone still hushed. "Here's what we're going to do. I'll look around inside, see what I can find, and you stay out here to stand guard."

"Why can't I—"

Even in the moonlight, Owen's expression was firm. He shook his head. "There's no telling what's inside here, Ava—or *who*, for that matter. And if you stand by the door, someone might see you from inside the house."

She couldn't argue with the logic, but the thought of sending him alone into the pitch blackness of the barn was terrifying. She swallowed her fear, nodded.

"Okay, then," Owen said. "I'm going in. If you see anything suspicious—if anyone comes out of the house or something—do an owl call."

An owl call? Ava was about to ask Owen if he was serious, but he'd already disappeared behind the door. From her position outside, she could see the faint glow of his phone flashlight streaming through the darkness.

Creeping to the other side of the barn, Ava stood with her back to the rough, splintered wood. Her breaths were heavy in the silence of the night, and she focused on calming herself. Everything was fine. Owen was a big guy, more than capable of holding his own, and no one know they were there. They'd been stealthy. Besides, Owen had his shotgun with him—there was always that fact, as much as she hated to admit that this brought her a degree of comfort. They'd planned this. Everything was going to be just—

Thump.

Ava stiffened, her chest growing cold. She froze, straining to hear in the darkness. She wanted to believe she'd imagined it, but she knew she hadn't. The muffled thump had been unmistakable.

"Owen?" she hissed, barely finding her voice. Her whole body stiffened. There was a slight scuffling sound from the barn, and she willed herself to calm down. *He tripped on something—that's all.*

There was no reply to her whisper. Ava crept forward, keeping her back to the barn, and rounded the corner. The barn door stood ajar, exactly how Owen had left it. She stopped, listened, and crept another few inches forward. Silence. Then, the soft clank of metal. *What the...?*

With her heart pounding in her ears, Ava inched toward the entrance of the barn. Taking care not to lean against the rickety wooden sliding door, she peered around the edge. The barn was shrouded in darkness; Owen seemed to have turned off his flashlight. As her eyes adjusted to the darkness of the barn, she could just make out a hint of movement from across the floor. She frowned, a little annoyed that Owen wasn't answering her. *What is he doing over there?*

Drawing her phone out of the pocket of her purse, Ava tapped on the flashlight. A short stream of white light flooded the closest area of the barn floor, but all she could see was a thin layer of scattered straw and a couple of dusty sawhorses. She took a step closer, holding the flashlight up higher. Suddenly, the light fell on a dark shape lying across the floor. Ava clapped a hand over her mouth with her free hand, realizing what—who—it was. *Owen.* Owen lay sprawled, face down, across the dirt floor, his limbs unmoving. A sharp, long-nailed fist clenched around her heart, and unable to control it, she gasped.

A figure across the barn moved sharply, and it was then that Ava recalled that soft clank of metal she'd heard just seconds before. Her eyes flicked back to Owen's sprawled figure, horrific realization dawning. His shotgun was no longer strapped to his side.

"Crap," Ava whispered. In the split second it took to put the pieces together, Ava's limbs were already carrying her back out the door and around the barn. She hardly noticed as her phone fell to the ground, the flashlight continuing to stream eerily up from the dry, brown grass.

Rounding the corner of the barn, she darted behind a tree, trying to catch her breath. She glanced helplessly toward her car, wishing they hadn't parked so far away, then remembered it didn't matter anyway because the car keys were in Owen's pocket. There was no way she could run home—Shiloh proper was a good six miles away—and she doubted she'd be able to outrun anyone even if her life depended on it.

Suddenly, the sound of pounding feet erupted from the side of the barn nearest her, getting closer and closer. She had to move. Ava took off running, not even sure where was she going, just knowing she had to put as much distance as she could between herself and those terrible pounding feet. The footsteps had rounded the corner now, and they were gaining, growing louder, faster, heavier, despite each step she took. Ava pumped her arms, gasping for air. She threw a desperate glance behind her to see the bulky figure of a man hurtling through the darkness. Owen's shotgun jostled at his side, pointing up to the moon.

Until then, she'd barely realized where she was running—just knew that she had to get away. But as she ran, her gaze fell on something ahead. She had thought it was just another cornfield, but now she could see a sign up ahead, glimmering white in the dark. *The corn maze.* Somewhere she could hide.

A burst of adrenaline kicked in at the prospect of escape, and Ava sprinted faster, her legs moving more quickly than she'd ever thought possible. Despite the stitch in her side, she forced herself to keep on moving, hurtling through the dark and toward that welcome entrance sign, pointing her into the maze. As she threw herself into the maze, walls of corn rose up on either side. She could hear the bugs humming. With no more breeze to sift through the stalks, the air inside was still as death and damp on her already sweaty skin. She veered sharply to the left, taking the first turn she came across, and continuing to pound down the dusty pathways without a thought as to which way would lead her to the other side. The exit didn't matter now—all that mattered was that whoever was chasing her not know which paths she'd taken. She hoped to god they didn't have the twists and turns of the maze memorized.

Her heart was pounding, her breath coming in gasps. Against her will, she began to slow. The footsteps were still there, but they were no longer right behind her. She couldn't tell which direction they were coming from, which she hoped was a good thing.

"Alright, Ava." A winded, phlegmy voice had spoken, somewhere through the rows of corn on her left. She'd heard that voice before. Despite the denseness of the stalks between them, Ava moved away from the sound. She pressed the back of her hand over her mouth, willing herself to remain silent, while she wracked her brain to remember where she knew the voice from.

Then it came to her.

Curtis.

Curtis McPherson, the owner of the very property she was currently trespassing on.

"Yeah, I know it's you, Ava," Curtis continued. "And I know you'll recognize my voice—which means, I'm afraid, that I can't let you leave here."

Ava refused to reply, still hoping against hope that Curtis had merely thrown a wild guess to the wind. But then she remembered Owen lying unconscious on the floor of the barn. It didn't take a genius to know that the obvious accomplice to Owen's antics would be none other than Ava Goldberg.

Curtis sighed, and she heard the click of the shotgun.

"Okay," Curtis said. His voice sounded weary, but it held a sort of terrifying resolve. "You're not making it out of here, Ava. I'm sorry—really, I am. But we'll make it fast, I promise. Just show me where you are, and this can all be over."

Make it fast? Who cared whether it was *fast?* Regardless of the speed with which he killed her, she'd still be dead. That was hardly a consolation. Ava's mind was moving at lightning speed, trying to think through her options—if there *were* any. The stalks of the maze were not so packed that she couldn't fit through them if need be, but they'd definitely slow her down. And, if Curtis knew the maze as well as she feared he did, having designed and planted it himself, he was sure to be much faster than her at navigating it. If worse came to worst, a bullet shot through the rows of stalks would make it through.

Just then, she had a thought. *There's no way he can know what height to shoot at!* Her heart pounded in her chest, but overcome with sudden determination, Ava dropped to her hands and knees as silently as she could, waiting with bated breath for Curtis to speak again. Had he heard her movement?

"Don't think I can't hear you," Curtis called, his tone sounding more impatient now. "You're not far away and mark my words—I *will* find you. I created this maze. I know it inside and out, and I've got all night."

Ava didn't doubt either statement. The stakes were far too high for Curtis, and so far, he'd managed to fly under the radar. He was good at covering his tracks. The dried corn husks that covered the dirt cut into Ava's palms as she inched forward. She stopped, grimacing at the sound. The rustling was louder than she'd expected.

Curtis heard it, too. He let out a triumphant guffaw, and Ava heard crashing footsteps begin to move in her direction.

"Ah, you're over *there*," Curtis said, as nonchalantly as if he'd spotted a friend at a crowded concert. "That makes things easier."

Squeezing her eyes shut in desperation, Ava's mind flew through her options once more. Hands and knees was not going to work. She could already hear Curtis's footsteps growing closer, no doubt having figured out which path she'd taken. Pushing back up to her feet, she crouched for a moment, trying to get a grip on herself.

Then, for the first time, she spoke, her voice clear, yet shaky in the darkness, "Wait!"

Curtis chuckled. "Wait? Honey, I told you—I've got all night."

No plan in mind, only knowing that she had to do *something*, the words began to tumble from her mouth. "What are you trying to do with all this? What did Mitch do to you? And Chantelle? Heck, what did *Owen* and I do to you?"

"Oh, no one's done anything to *me*," Curtis snorted. "Chantelle, you, Owen—you three just got in the way. You're collateral damage, and that can't be helped. Mitch Fangman, on the other hand…"

"What? You wanted his spot downtown, too?"

"Oh, please," Curtis said, his voice even louder now.

Ava could hear Curtis's crunching footsteps, and she moved away from them. Maybe, she thought, if she could keep this up for long enough, this game of cat and mouse, Owen would wake up and come looking for her. It was a long shot—but it was her only shot.

"Like I said, Mitch never did anything to *me*, but he was hell-bent on ruining Chase's life, and I couldn't let that happen."

Chase? Chase Wagner? Ava's mind flitted through faces, trying to match the name. Finally, she had a hit. Something Rose had said at the pep rally. "Chase Wagner? Oh my god— he's your *nephew*."

"That's right." Curtis's voice sounded grim. "Truth be told, I never even meant to kill Mitch—just meant to go up there and put a stop to the smear campaign he was running—but the guy had too big a head. Couldn't fathom that he might not be in the right."

"In the right? About what?"

For every step Curtis took toward her, Ava took one in the opposite direction. She had a fleeting hope that maybe she'd come to the entrance or exit of the maze, but then realized that, with Curtis still holding the gun, that relief would be short-lived. Her only choice was to keep on buying time.

"Oh, you city people," Curtis spat. "You wouldn't get it, would you? I saw your folks. Your family's rich. But some of us, like my sister and her boy, haven't had the red carpet rolled out for us. My nephew was slated to have a full ride to Nebraska—

the only hope he ever had of going to college and getting out of this cruddy little town, breaking the cycle our family's been stuck in for god knows how long. And then Mitch came along."

Ava wasn't getting it. What did Mitch Fangman have to do with Curtis McPherson's nephew's college scholarship?

"I'm not sure I understand," she called, her voice dripping with sympathy that she hoped was believable. And it was—in a way. There was no denying the love Curtis had for his nephew, the desperation he felt at seeing the kid end up the way the rest of them had, and that was the kind of familial support she respected. His tactics, though? Not so much.

"His damn tirades!" Curtis roared.

There was a whack and a wild, sudden shaking of the stalks, and Ava guessed Curtis had smacked the walls of the maze with his hands. His voice still echoed through the darkness, punctuated in the stillness by only the chirping of the crickets.

"Week in and week out, the bastard wouldn't cut the kid a break. The first time it was only Chase's pride that was hurt. My sister said he came home and stomped around, slammed the door to his bedroom. But the second week, he shut himself up in the bathroom—wouldn't come out, wouldn't talk. Before you know it, the damage isn't just at home anymore. Pretty soon he's fumbling all over the field, slipping around like a sissy afraid of getting hit."

Curtis had stopped moving, and Ava held still as well, listening. Her chest heaved with the heavy, wild thumping of her heart. She didn't dare speak. It was hard to tell by the tone of Curtis's voice whether admitting the truth was calming him down or if his anger was only starting to ramp up.

But Curtis wasn't done. "The Huskers don't recruit sissies

for athletic scholarships, and I wasn't going to let some loud-mouth commentator ruin my nephew's future just because he likes to talk trash. No, sir. So last week, I'd finally had enough. I went up there during half time, told Mitch to knock it off, that his trash talking was only making things worse—and you know what he told me? He said it wasn't his problem if the trailer trash quarterback couldn't keep up with the athletes who *deserve* to get recruited. That's when I—"

Curtis's voice cut off. He drew a sharp intake of breath, as though just catching himself from saying something he couldn't take back. "Well, I guess it makes no difference if I tell you—sorry to say."

He laughed, and Ava bit back a terrified moan at the sound of it. A part of her had hoped he'd become distracted, forgotten his threat. No such luck.

"He kept on repeating those words—*trailer trash, trailer trash*. Man, I *lost* it. I can barely even remember it—it's all just a haze. At some point, I realize I've got the microphone cord around his neck and his face is going purple, and I told myself I should stop, but I kept on going. Next thing I knew, Mitch was dead. And I wasn't even sorry—still ain't. No one's going to ruin my nephew's chances at life and get away with it, least of all not while spouting that kind of garbage."

Ava was silent. This was her chance. Curtis was so wrapped up in the story, in the confession of what he'd done, that this was her chance to take small quiet steps, distancing herself from him. She hoped desperately that the hum of the crickets would drown out the rustling of any stray corn husks under-foot. To her relief, Curtis continued talking—but for how long, she didn't know.

"Now, before you start thinking I'm some evil villain—

although I guess it might be too late for that—I'll have you know that trying to off Chantelle Svoboda was never in the plan. Granted, neither was getting rid of Mitch. But Mitch deserved to die, and Chantelle—well, as much as I hate that I'll have to figure something else out for her, I gotta admit I was kind of relieved when the brake plan failed. I felt bad using Chase to find out her work schedule. Poor kid, really didn't think twice when I asked..."

Wow, Curtis really did not shut up—some personality traits were just too ingrained to overcome. Then again, Ava realized with a sharp stab of fear, he probably figured his blathering didn't make any real difference. He was going to have to kill her, regardless.

"And *you*," Curtis continued. "I was never planning to kill *you*, but then I saw your phone connect to Mitch's hotspot this afternoon at the festival. I'd gone out to the barn to grab some wire cutters, and seeing that—well, it about made me panic, I tell you. But I figured that out quick when I heard you and your boyfriend outside, planning to come back to investigate tonight. All I had to do was bide my time, waiting. Sure enough—here you are."

Ava's heart clenched. She hadn't noticed her phone had *connected* to the hotspot, notifying the person holding that phone. If she made it out of this corn maze alive, she'd have to make sure Riley never caught wind of this fact, or she would never stand a chance of living it down.

Curtis let out a throaty growling sound, as though he'd had the sudden realization that Ava wasn't answering him. She held her breath, not daring to respond. She glanced down the path she was on, saw that it curved right in just a few steps. Could that lead to the exit? Had she put enough distance between them as he talked to give herself a head start if she started running now?

Suddenly, a hot, clammy breath swept across the back of her neck, followed by the same low growl from a moment ago. She screamed, but a hand clapped over her mouth, cutting it short. Her whole body went rigid, and her eyes bulged with wild panic.

"Got so caught up in trying to figure an escape you didn't even hear me coming, did ya?" Curtis's hoarse voice spit into her ear. Frantically, Ava writhed and struggled, but his burly farmer arms gripped tightly around her entire body, no escape possible.

"You know, I'd figured to just shoot you, make it fast and painless," Curtis said. "But that brings the risk of someone hearing the shot—and we don't want that. This'll be better, and it'll be over fast. It was for Mitch, anyway."

Suddenly, Curtis sniffled then, his grip loosening for a split second. Behind her, his hand still covering her mouth, his body twitched. With no warning, Curtis drew in a sharp breath and let out a violent sneeze, immediately followed by another. In that split second, Ava rammed her elbow into Curtis's gut and wrenched herself free before he realized what had happened.

"What the..." Curtis choked, grabbed at her, then sneezed again. His whole body convulsed.

Ava ripped Owen's gun from Curtis's scrabbling palms. As Curtis lunged at her, still trying to recover from the force of the sneeze, Ava raised the shotgun like a baseball bat and swung.

Thunk!

He looked at her, dazed, his head trembling from the impact for a moment, then sank to his knees, dropping to a heap on the dusty corn maze floor.

Silence. Ava stood, too stunned to move. Panic hit—*oh god, have I killed him?*—but as she bent to examine Curtis's unmoving frame, she noticed his chest moving. Warm, joyous relief flooded her as she dropped to her knees. She had *not* killed someone. And she hadn't been killed.

All thanks to a sneeze.

She bent her head to her chest as her adrenaline surge drained, gulped in the humid air, and the scent of Owen's sweatshirt tickled her nose. Downy. Was that it? Was that what had made Curtis sneeze? She could see the headlines now: *Murderer felled by fabric softener allergy.* Before she could stop it, Ava snorted a laugh, and a crazed, throaty giggle escaped her. Horrified, she hiccuped it down.

No. Knock it off, Ava. You need to be serious. She wasn't out of the woods—well, *corn*—just yet. There was no sign of movement from Curtis, but she didn't have time to dawdle. He could wake up at any moment, and then her victory would mean nothing. She had to think—fast. She thought of her phone, lying face up in the dirt outside the barn, which may as well have been miles away.

Still clutching Owen's gun in her sweaty hands, she stuffed it under one arm, praying it wasn't cocked. She had no clue how to shoot a gun and had never cared to, but thought now that it might be a good idea to get Owen to teach her—if she got out of this alive. Owen? The image of him in the barn brought shivers—was he alive? Desperately, she dug through her purse slung across her body, then dumped the contents out on the ground. A tube of chapstick rolled into her foot. Her deck of tarot cards, a couple of hair ties, her wallet—what help would those be?

Wait. The inside pocket of her purse felt lumpy. She

unzipped it, swiping a frantic hand around inside, and brought out a baggie. A baggie full of stale, crumbling breadcrumbs. In a gleeful rush, Ava realized she'd never taken the unused bag out of her purse after returning home from *tashlich*. Thank god. She could use them to pull a Hansel and Gretel maneuver, keep track of the paths she went down as she searched for the way out of the corn maze. If this wasn't divine providence, she didn't know what was.

Casting one last cautious glance at Curtis, who remained motionless on the ground, Ava wasted no time in getting on her way. There was always the grim chance that Curtis would wake up, follow the breadcrumbs, and be back on her tail, but it was a risk she'd have to take. It was either that or remain a sitting duck, twiddling her thumbs in fear. But she wasn't about to give up. She wasn't beaten yet.

There weren't as many breadcrumbs in the second baggie as there had been in the first—the one she, Riley, and Rose had emptied into the lake on Rosh Hashanah morning—so she'd have to conserve them. All she needed was a little trail, a way to mark her progress so she wouldn't continue wandering around and around for god knew how long. Even without the threat of Curtis waking up, she needed to get to Owen. If something had happened to him—but no, she couldn't think about that now. She had to focus.

Every few yards, Ava dropped a couple pieces of bread. Although they were hard to see in the dark, with only the moon shining down overhead and the corn stalks casting long shadows across the paths, it was at least enough for her to chart her way. And, if she were lucky, the pieces were small enough and far enough apart that Curtis wouldn't even notice them.

She tried one turn, then another, and hit a dead end. Backtracking to the last split in the paths, she went the opposite direction, followed that for a few yards, and hit yet another dead end. With each towering wall of corn that sprang up in front of her, she had the urge to scream, but she bit it back. *Focus, Ava. You'll get out of here sooner or later.* She hoped she wasn't lying to herself.

Twist left, twist right, left again. Boom—dead end. Wind back, take the other turn instead. Boom—dead end. How big was this maze? Curtis should've stuck to corn maze creations, topiary design—anything other than murder—she thought. He was good at it. She was getting down to the last dozen crumbs in the bag. Her heart raced in her chest, and her palms were clammy. The gun grew heavy, and the thought that Owen might be lying there suffering—alone—was almost more than she could bear.

Ava cupped the last handful of bread pieces in her palm. In sudden desperation, she tried jumping, hoping somehow to see over the tops of the corn. How close was she to the edge of the maze? Just a glimpse of the farmhouse in the distance, the barn, the windmill—anything, really—would give her the assurance she needed that she was getting somewhere. But try as she might, the tassels of the corn were too tall, and she landed on her heels with a grim thud. That was the trouble with cornfields. They were just too tall.

She knew she had no other choice but to keep moving forward. Ava continued on her way, dropping her bread pieces even more conservatively. She was down to eight now, another fork in the road. She stopped, trying to clear her mind and feel which way was the right way. Right? Left? She breathed in.

Right.

Hearing the word nearly jolted her into a scream. She

whipped her head around, half sure that Curtis had woken and snuck up behind her again. But she was alone.

Right.

When the voice came again, this time more adamantly, she knew it hadn't come from outside. She shivered.

Alright, Zaidy, Ava thought, setting her jaw in determination. If you say right, then right it is. Without so much as a glance behind, Ava dropped one breadcrumb to mark the crossroads, and strode to the right, dropping another piece of bread a few feet along. She moved through the walls of corn, the path twisting and turning, but no other forks in the road came up, and no dead ends either. The crickets still hummed, the tassels of the corn still rustled overhead in the breeze that she'd now give almost anything to feel on her grimy, sweaty face. And still she kept on, her feet aching and her heart nearly pounding out of her chest. Just when she thought she couldn't take another step, that she'd drop into a heap in the dust, she turned a corner and—

Ava nearly shrieked with the flood of relief that came bursting through her chest. The narrow, stifling passages of the maze had opened onto a vast, moonlit lawn, and the breeze was already rippling through her damp hair. Taking a few stumbling steps forward, Ava gasped in lungfuls of crisp, clean autumn air, stripping off Owen's sweatshirt so the breeze could ripple through the fabric of her t-shirt beneath. She looked down at her clenched hand, unfurled her fingers. Only one piece of bread remained nestled in her palm.

Now able to breathe, and high on the feeling of victory, Ava broke off into a sprint toward the barn. She held the gun as far away from her body as possible to avoid accidentally setting something off as she sent up a silent prayer for Owen.

Please. Please, oh, please. The words became a rhythm as Ava's feet pounded the dry grass. Once or twice, she cast a glance back over her shoulder, but Curtis was nowhere in sight. She sprinted around the barn, rounding the corner at breakneck speed. She skidded to a stop, glancing down for her phone —she'd need it to call 911—but it wasn't there. This *was* the right barn, wasn't it? The twists and dead ends of the maze had disoriented her and had taken so much time.

Then another terrible thought struck her. Had Curtis awakened and taken a different way out of the maze and already beaten her back? *Oh, god.* He might have finished Owen off, then taken Ava's phone so she would have no way of calling for help.

A shadowy figure stood in front of her, silhouetted against the glow of moonlight through the barn's rafters. Ava jumped back, her nerves already ripped to shreds. The figure rushed her and strong arms wrapped around her, their shoulders shaking, sobbing.

Owen. Thank goodness.

After a moment, Ava felt his arms loosen, push her gently away. She looked up into Owen's face, saw the faint traces of tears there as he wiped them away with the back of his hand. He grinned at her, looking as though he could barely believe it, and rubbed the tops of her arms beneath his huge, rough palms.

"Thank *god*," Owen said, clutching her to him once more.

"You're telling me."

Once again, Owen pulled away from her. He studied her face, drawing a delicate thumb down her cheek. "Are you hurt?"

Ava shook her head. Even in the darkness, his eyes glowed

green. "I'm okay—just rattled." She reached up to squeeze his hand. "Are *you* hurt?"

"I don't think so," Owen said. "Terrible headache—hopefully not a concussion—but other than that, I'm stellar."

He dropped his hands from her arms, laced his fingers through hers, then took a step forward. He glanced around the yard beyond the barn. "But Ava—what even *happened*? One minute I was in here looking around, the next thing I know I'm waking up in the dark, covered in hay—and you're gone. Your phone..." He reached into his pocket, drew out her phone, and stared at it. "I thought whoever knocked me out must have taken you. Everything was silent, no sign of anyone anywhere. I had no clue what to do, Ava. I thought you were—"

"Shh," Ava whispered, touching a finger to Owen's mouth to signal him to stop. She knew what he'd thought. She'd thought the same about him. But none of it mattered now. They were safe.

Owen swallowed hard, ran a hand through his wild hair. A piece of straw stuck out, making him look like a scarecrow—a very handsome scarecrow.

"Police are on their way," Owen said. "I called them as soon as I found your phone. I didn't know if you'd been taken into the corn maze, to the farmhouse, to the nearby woods, or driven away. I wanted to stay near the barn in case you came back, then I thought about waking the McPhersons for help but—"

"It was Curtis," Ava blurted out. "All of it—it was Curtis McPherson."

Owen's mouth dropped open. He stared out across the yard to the McPherson farmhouse. His gaze moved to his gun, which Ava still held clutched in her hands, and he took it gently from her. His eyes lingered on the trigger a moment, and Ava sensed what he wanted to ask.

"He's still alive," she said, hastening to reassure him that she hadn't had to take desperate measures. "And still in the maze, as far as I know. I gave him about the same treatment as he gave you."

A cop car came coasting over the hill, blue and red lights flashing in the darkness, and slowed slightly as it turned onto the driveway. Ava felt her knees grow weak with relief at just the sight of help arriving, and she leaned heavily into Owen's side.

He wrapped an arm around her, gripping her shoulder. "How on earth did you manage to make it out?"

At this, Ava laughed. The answer was like something out of a storybook, absolutely preposterous, and she wondered if he'd even believe her. The cop car had pulled to a stop in front of the barn, lights still on, and Greathouse stepped out, looking every bit the hero silhouetted against the grayness of the sky.

Ava squeezed Owen's hand with her fingers, looked up at him, and smiled. "I'll tell you later. Let's go home."

30

Rose was the first one into Cafe Arcana the next morning. She came striding through the front door like a woman on a mission, her daughter perched on her hip, and strode toward the front counter without even removing her sunglasses. If Ava hadn't known the lecture she was about to get, she would've laughed, but she managed to keep her expression neutral.

"Good morning," Ava said, smiling as though a killer hadn't just chased her through a corn maze the night before.

"It *is* a good morning," Rose responded, whisking her sunglasses off with a flick of her wrist and shoving them back onto her blond curls. "And *you*, my friend, are *insanely* lucky you are here to enjoy it!"

Ava stifled a grin, which resulted in a smirk. "I know. Trust me, do I ever know."

"Ava, what the *hell*," Rose cried, pushing herself behind the counter and wrapping an arm around her friend so that Ellie was smushed between them. "I am so glad you're okay, but you are so—so—so *stupid*."

"I know that, too," Ava said, laughing now. She hugged her friend back, then gave Ellie a pinch on the cheek. "I'm fine, though. Promise."

Rose eyed her, biting back the lecture she wanted to let fly. She shifted Ellie to the other hip, though, and nodded her head toward the coffee urns. "Give me some of that dark roast. And details, Ava—I'm going to need details."

THE DAY WAS a blur of customers, curious townspeople who'd heard murmurs of a crazed murderer on the loose in a cornfield, and still others who had most of their information more or less correct, all stopping by Ava's cafe to see if they could glean any more juicy details. Ava took their questions in stride, answering honestly and agreeing whenever someone remarked that it might be wise to be more careful in the future. It amused her to know that, deep down, what they really wanted to say was, "You idiot!", but a small-town Nebraskan would never— not to an acquaintance, anyway.

Riley, who had begged Ava to let her stay home from school that morning, came all but running through the front door of the cafe twenty minutes earlier than she was due to arrive. When Ava had gotten home in the wee hours, she'd only briefly reassured Riley that she was okay, details pending.

Ava looked up at the clock, which read 3:38, then glanced at Riley's breathless, frantic face, and burst out laughing. "Girl, did you sprint all the way here?"

"I didn't sprint," Riley said, giving a flip of her short, blue hair. She was still trying to catch her breath. "But everyone has been asking me all day what happened, and I kept having to tell them, 'I don't know, she didn't tell me,' and I kid you not, pretty much everyone else knew all these details—"

"Whoa, whoa, whoa," Ava said, already grinding a shot of espresso for Riley. "Slow your roll, kid. Everything's fine. I promise, you'll have insider information soon enough."

Riley pushed her way behind the counter, flung an apron over her head, and leaned against the espresso machine, eyeing Ava like a hawk. She watched as silky espresso streamed down.

"You know," Ava remarked, casting a wry glance in Riley's direction. "I'm not sure you need more caffeine. You seem pretty antsy the way it is."

Riley opened her mouth to retort but the jangle of the front doorbell cut her off. As a herd of people traipsed through the door, Riley's eyes grew suddenly wide, and she turned to busy herself with the espresso machine's steamer wand.

Ava glanced to see who it was that Riley so clearly didn't want to make eye contact with. First through the door were Juanita and her Bible study friends, with Chief Greathouse lumbering on their heels. Bringing up the rear was a group of teenagers, and although Ava didn't recognize them, she suspected from the swishy athletic shorts the boys wore that this must be the crowd who'd pulled that awful trick on Riley at homecoming.

She turned to Riley, muttering under her breath. "Is that...?"

"Yeah," Riley hissed. "And don't even *think* about saying anything."

Ava sniffed. A tall order, to be sure. She would have enjoyed nothing more than to give those smug-looking kids the verbal dressing down of their young lives. Still, if Riley forbade it, she'd leave it. Chewing out a teenager wouldn't be a good look for her cafe, anyway, and one day without drama did hold an appeal.

"Ava!" Juanita gasped, reaching over the counter to throw her arms around Ava's neck. "Don't you *dare* scare us like that again—*me oyes*?! If I have to hear one more time about how you went and confronted a *killer*..."

Ava returned the hug, laughing. "I hear you, I hear you—but I'm never *trying* to confront a killer. And anyway, I brought Owen with me this time. We didn't think—"

"Didn't think he'd be so useless?" Chief Greathouse supplied from the back of the line. His mustache wagged as he obviously tried to keep a straight face.

Riley snorted, clapping a hand to her mouth. Ava had divulged enough before collapsing into bed the previous night for Riley to know that Owen hadn't exactly been able to help her fend off Curtis inside the maze.

"Oh, Matt," Marge Harding said, giving Greathouse a swat on the arm. "It's not his fault. It's just too bad—the whole ordeal."

"That it is," Juanita agreed. "But how did you and Owen even end up at the McPherson farm anyway, Ava?"

Ava glanced at Greathouse, unsure how much she should say. "Owen and I were at the farm for the fall festival yesterday evening. I wasn't getting good service on my phone, so I checked for a hotspot and—lo and behold—there was a hotspot called 'Mitch's iPhone'. When the hotspot signal got stronger the closer we walked to the barn, our radar went up. As far as we knew, the barn wasn't open to the public, so something fishy was going on."

"Really?" Juanita gasped, her eyes going wide. "And—was it really his? Was it really Mitch Fangman's iPhone?"

"I think so," Ava said. "Although I'm actually not sure. We never found it—we only found Curtis."

They all looked to Greathouse, who stood for a moment stroking his mustache before he sighed, giving in. "Oh, what the heck? It's all going to come out anyway, I suppose. According to Curtis, Mitch got out his phone during their altercation in the press box, started recording Curtis's tirade against him. After things escalated and the deed—shall we say—was done, Curtis knew he couldn't leave the phone because it contained evidence."

"Okay," Juanita said, brows knit as she tried to put the pieces together. "But why would he have turned the phone on then? Why not just get rid of it?"

"My guess is he wanted to *delete* the evidence," Ava said. "I know my photos and videos always go straight to the cloud, so getting rid of the phone wouldn't really help much. He'd need to delete the videos from the cloud, which means he'd also need to unlock the phone. And he hadn't figured out how to do that yet."

"Bingo." Chief Greathouse snapped his fingers and took the cup of dark roast Ava had poured for him over to a table and sat.

"And he didn't realize the hotspot was on," Riley snickered. "Typical."

"But wait—" This time it was Ava, jumping in with a question for Greathouse. "What about that golden pass? What was that doing on the press box stairs?"

Greathouse sipped his coffee. "Curtis hung onto his dad's golden pass after the old man died, figuring the middle schoolers taking tickets never check the passes very closely—which, I've got to hand it to him, turned out to be correct. He dropped it on the stairs."

"Cheapskate," Riley muttered. "No problem shelling out the big bucks for cologne, though."

"Which, speaking of—" Ava said, cutting in again. "How on earth did Curtis manage to handle wearing that cologne with all his allergies?"

"You know, I asked the same thing," Greathouse said, a small smile playing beneath his mustache. "I guess he bought it hoping to pick up a date or two, but only wore it once—to the game, as it turns out. When he realized he was going to sneeze himself into oblivion with it on, he decided to kill two birds with one stone: get rid of a cologne he couldn't wear and frame someone else for Mitch's murder."

"That someone being Jeremy," Ava said.

"Correct."

"Well, let's hope one good thing comes of all this," Marge ventured, sipping her coffee. "Let's hope Chase Wagner, Curtis's nephew, can pull it together on the field, now that he can... feel less berated during the games."

There was a hesitant round of chuckling, no one quite sure whether or not they should be laughing. It was, however, the unfortunate truth. And, Ava reasoned, it *would* be a blessing for the Wagner-McPherson family if Chase could snag his scholarship. Then again, how would the facts of his uncle's murder of a small town sports commentator settle with Chase or with prospective scouts? Only time would tell, but...

The image of the Fool card flashed through Ava's mind as a delightful realization clicked into place. She smiled. Although the new beginning the cards had pointed to may not have been meant for Jeremy, it *was* meant for someone else. The new beginning the Fool brought with him was meant for Chase Wagner.

The Bible study women put lids on the rest of their coffee in their to-go cups and moved to the door to head for their study group. Ava saw Flo Finkenbaum nudge Juanita and ask, "What *is* a hotspot, anyway?"

Juanita waved goodbye to Ava and Riley and laid a gentle hand on Flo's arm, whispering, "Don't ask."

Now it was only the group of teenagers who still stood in the shop, giggling and fidgeting as they scanned the menu and gave Ava their orders one by one. She'd given Riley a gentle shove toward the espresso machine, signaling that the girl didn't need to worry about having to interact with the gaggle of giggling girls. She could keep her head down, make the drinks, and the kids would soon be out of their hair.

As the group finished ordering and wandered to the front of the shop to wait for their drinks, one of them held back, drumming his palms on the counter and throwing glances Riley's way. His friends shot perplexed looks at him that he seemed to be pretending not to see. Was this Trevor Phillips? Ava had only seen him once and couldn't remember what he looked like.

"Uh..." Ava began, trying to gauge what was going on. "Can I help with anything else? Your drink will be ready in just a minute or two."

"Thanks, yeah," the boy said. "That's great. I'm just—ah—well, I just wanted to..." His eyes traveled to Riley's back. He cleared his throat. "Hey. Riley."

Okay, so it *was* Trevor.

There was no answer to his attempt at a greeting. Riley was humming to herself, acting as though she hadn't heard him as she slid the other kids' drinks across the counter to Ava. The kids came to collect their drinks and surveyed the scene unfolding before them in the unimpressed, yet still judgmental way that only teenagers can.

The boy tried again. "Riley—Riley *Novak*. Listen."

Riley spun around. "What?"

The boy's face turned red. He cleared his throat again, aware that all eyes in the shop were on him. "Well, I—uh. I wanted to ask if you'll go to the Halloween party with me next Friday."

One of the kids standing near the doorway chuckled, and that was all it took for the group to file out onto the sidewalk. Trevor ignored them, continuing his declaration. "I'd be pissed at me, too, if I were you. I really would. I have the crappiest friends, and some of 'em aren't my friends anymore after all this. But you gotta believe me, Riley—homecoming? Not a prank in the slightest. Summer was jealous I didn't ask her, so she told you it was a joke, and I was *so* pissed. She *ruined* it for us—not just for you, for me, too. Okay?"

Riley was watching Trevor suspiciously, as though she could read on his face whether he was telling the truth. "Really?"

"Really. I'm so sorry it happened like that, that I couldn't stop it."

Riley chewed her lip.

"So, will you go with me? To the party? I know it's not a dance, but it could still be fun..."

Riley looked at Ava, whose eyebrows raised, a hint of a smile tugging at the corners of her mouth, then back to Trevor.

"Alright," Riley said. She snapped a lid onto Trevor's latte and slid it across the counter to him. "Don't worry. I didn't spit in it."

Trevor stepped forward to take the drink and held his hand up for a high five. His face was still red, but he was grinning now as Riley returned the high five. "Unblock my number, yeah?"

"Fine," Riley called, rolling her eyes as Trevor made his way out the door. His classmates were long gone, but he didn't even seem to notice as he hopped on his bicycle and took off down the sidewalk. He flashed Ava and Riley one last grin through the window as he sped past them.

Ava was about to speak, but a familiar face in the bay window caught her by surprise. And—what on earth was *that?*

The bell atop the door jingled once more as Owen backed his way inside the shop. Riley and Ava exchanged glances as Owen held the door open with his foot and pulled a wheeled cart over the threshold and into the shop. The cart was loaded with wooden planks.

"Um," Ava said, raising an eyebrow as Owen let the door swing shut. He pushed the cart, clattering, across the floor. "Are you building a house in here?"

"Not too far off, actually," Owen said. He shook the hair out of his eyes and grinned at her. He folded his arms proudly across his chest. "It was going to be a surprise, but I've got a shipment in, and I need to get these out of my shop. You, Ava, are looking at what is soon to be your *sukkah.*"

Ava was stunned. *Sukkah?* Yom Kippur wasn't for another several days—there was still time before Sukkot, the Jewish holiday commemorating when the Israelites wandered the desert and slept in huts after leaving Egypt, began. She hadn't even *begun* to think about what she'd do for a *sukkah* hut this year. But, perhaps even more puzzling, was why on earth *Owen* was thinking about it.

"Wait—how do you even know what a *sukkah* is?" Ava blurted out.

Owen threw his head back, laughing. His green eyes sparkled as he grinned at her. He shrugged. "I've been doing some reading. I've been pretty eager to see what this 'dwelling in huts for eight days' thing is all about. My rabbi thought it'd be a good idea for me to build my own. You know, being handy and all. Said it'd really make things come alive—"

"Your *what*?" Ava shrieked, hardly hearing the rest of Owen's sentence.

"My rabbi," Owen said, his voice nonchalant, like it was the most natural thing in the world. He shot her a wink. "It's all pretty new to me—so don't get your panties in a bunch—but I've started sitting in on the Torah studies at Temple Or Hadash in Omaha. I met with the rabbi there, and he's willing to study with me, although I did have to call him a bunch of times. I guess that's a thing."

Ava stared at him. She was having a hard time processing the words coming out of his mouth. His *rabbi*?

"What do you mean 'study with you'?" Ava asked, gaping. Beside her, she could see the slow grin spreading across Riley's face.

"You know," Owen said, shrugging again. "For conversion. I'm not sure how long it'll take, but so far, so good. I'm excited to dive in."

Riley whistled, and Ava, still somewhat stunned, swatted at her. She turned back to Owen. "But—conversion... What for?"

Stepping out from behind the cart, Owen walked up to the counter, behind which Ava stood, looking helpless. Putting his hands on either side of her face, he smiled.

"Well, first and foremost, I want to make one thing clear,"

Owen said. He drew his thumb across her cheekbone. "It's for me. I haven't been a practicing Catholic in ages, and I started reading up on Judaism last summer when we met. It seemed like something that would hold a lot of meaning, and I was right. I feel really drawn to it, so there's that. But there's also you —and us."

Ava's knees felt weak, but she willed her expression not to change. She would keep her composure if it killed her. Instead, she whispered, "Are you sure?"

"Absolutely."

Owen dropped his hands from her face and held her gaze for a moment, a small smile still on his lips. It was only when Riley spoke up, that Ava even remembered where they were.

"Is Jeremy okay?" Riley asked.

Owen ran a hand through his hair. "Well, relatively speaking. Greathouse says he'll drop the drug charges on the condition Jer enrolls in some kind of live-in program—which honestly will be the best place for him. Both a place to live and one that helps him stay clean. So we're trying to get the ball rolling on that."

As Owen's gaze met hers, Ava's heart warmed. Jeremy's journey wasn't over yet, but he, too, was on his way to a new start.

"And your mom?" Ava asked, thinking back to the conversation she'd had with her own mom just a couple days before. She wondered if Owen had told his parents yet that he planned to convert, but was too shy to ask outright.

"She's just fine," Owen said. He fixed Ava with a look that said he'd understood her drift. "In fact, she'd like to have you for dinner one of these days—if that's okay with you."

Ava beamed. "I'd like nothing better."

When the doorbell jangled again, signaling incoming customers, Owen stepped back from the counter and placed his hands once more on the handle of his cart.

"I'm going to leave this lumber in the back room, alright? We'll find some branches for the *schach*, and we can set it up in your yard after Yom Kippur ends. See you soon." Owen winked, then turned to roll the cart toward the back of the shop.

As Ava turned her attention back to the shop—and to Riley, who was still grinning like a fool—she felt like she was floating. It was only after she'd given a few more regulars the details of her brush with death in the corn maze that it dawned on her, and she grinned to herself, not even caring if she looked like an absolute maniac. Owen's pronunciation of the Hebrew letter *chet* in the word *schach* had been as effortless as though he'd been raised in a synagogue.

He was a natural, and they were off to a beautiful start.

New beginnings for everyone.

LET'S KEEP IN TOUCH!

If you enjoyed *Shofar, So Good*, I'd love for you to let your friends know so they can follow Ava on her adventures, too! And if you leave a review for the book—whether that's on Amazon, Goodreads, or somewhere else—I'd love to read it. Email me the link at aliza@alizalevinebooks.com.

For exclusive updates and behind-the-scenes secrets, scan the QR code below to join my newsletter. You'll be the first to know about all things Cafe Arcana!

ABOUT THE AUTHOR

Aliza Levine is a writer, tarot reader, and homegrown Nebraskan who lives for that first sip of coffee each morning. When she isn't writing, she's reading tarot, sprinting after her toddler, or watching ungodly amounts of *Murder She Wrote*.